WHITE-MAA'S SAGA

Other novels published by Macdonald Publishers:
Juan in America
Magnus Merriman
Laxdale Hall
Position at Noon

WHITE-MAA'S SAGA

BY
ERIC LINKLATER

Publication subsidised by the Scottish Arts Council

Published by
Macdonald Publishers
Edgefield Road
Loanhead
Midlothian EH20 9SY

ISBN 0 86334 014 8

Printed in Scotland by
Macdonald Printers (Edinburgh) Ltd.,
Edgefield Road, Loanhead, Midlothian EH20 9SY

CONTENTS

To

LESLEY STORM

WHITE-MAA'S SAGA

I

THE Old Frigate is not more than two hundred yards from
the gates of New College. There are three public-houses
in the same narrow lane, and round the corner there is a
pawn-shop. Tall houses huddle shoulder to shoulder; houses
with historical associations and a sour smell; houses built for
claret and cognac, swords and velvet, and given over to thin
beer and second-hand clothes. The house where a duke lived
is a common lodging-house. He was a bad duke, but the
lodging-house is no more attractive. Slatternly girls carry
their babies, and women with enormous waists dispassionately
watch their elder children at play. The Old Frigate, the Earl's
Tower, the Apple Tree, the Hole in the Wall and all the
other public-houses are open for a few hours every day except
Sundays. They are not ashamed of a comparison with the
past, for their glasses are cleaner and their prices have
multiplied.

New College stands in this squalid neighbourhood like a
carved white island. It is immaculate, like a snow castle that
has defied corruption in the midst of a muddy thaw. It soars
into a hundred dazzling spires. It has the whiteness of a
bride-cake, and behind its darting ornaments and gilded
quills the massive solidity of a bride-cake. Through its
broad quadrangle and high arches cold winds perpetually
wander, for Scots learning has always put out its flowers in
discomfort and borne hard fruit in bleak composure. The
tower of New College, lofty and severe, looks out to sea or
boldly at the sky; it ignores the warren of lanes and courts
beneath it. But the distance from the gates of New College to
the Old Frigate is no more than two hundred yards.

WHITE-MAA'S SAGA

It was six o'clock or so of a Friday evening in March, 1921, and the Frigate was half-full. A few sailors sat in a corner, and a couple of coalmen leaned against the bar drinking draught beer and whisky alternately. The rest of the company were medical students.

Such a title normally gives the idea of youth crudely inflated with inaccurate knowledge of its own anatomy; of something callow but emboldened by a glimpse of the unobvious in dissection; of a cheerful pedantry too confidently certain of peritoneal geography to feel any doubt of the wider confines of life. But in 1921 things were different. The War was a lively memory, and most of the men who filled the Scots universities had seen death in stranger disguises than the frigid decency of the mortuary, and life painted more vividly than immaturity can paint it. And yet Peace, in 1921, had still something of a holiday spirit. It was still younger than the War. It was still possible to feel relief. And so men in some ways mature enough responded readily with all the exuberance of immaturity whenever an apt occasion suggested celebration, or a friend cried Rejoice! The two hundred yards between New College and the Old Frigate, then, was often covered in good time.

On this evening in March the results of the Second Professional examinations were being published; a notable obstacle in the medical curriculum, made of the two subjects Anatomy and Physiology. Physiology was like a bristly hedge, and Anatomy a broad water-jump beyond. Both took their heavy toll, so that however many might drink for joy of a happy landing, many also went to drink for consolation; and of neighbouring glasses on a table the one might fix more firmly the righteous satisfaction of a successful competitor, while the other became a solvent for the grief of a man who had failed.

PRELUDE: THE PUB CRAWL

In little groups more men left the College gates. Each carried with him the patent of two years' work, a printed card stating that he had satisfied—or failed to satisfy—the examiners in these two subjects. The envelopes in which the cards were issued were plain and unrevealing, but a single glance inside told their owners' fate; for the cards of the successful were printed in red, and the intimations of failure were done in solemn black. Rarely, a card bore one or two asterisks, the starry indication of outstanding merit. But red cards and black, constellated cards and plain cards, all went the common way, and most of them were swept up the following morning from tavern floors.

Evan Mackay sat with two other men at a table in the Frigate, staring thoughtfully at a glass in front of him.

'I had no real hope of getting through,' he said, 'and yet I wondered. Optimism, like a cancer, grows unnoticed out of an incalculable medium.'

Moncur and Gunn, who were with him, gave comfort and spoke reassuringly – for they had passed – of the chance for re-examination that would be offered in June.

'Work and summer are incompatible,' said Mackay, and drank in resignation to fate.

Newcomers entered noisily, banging the door back on its hinges, and replying to the immediate question, 'Through. We're all through.' And everyone asked everyone else, 'What are you going to have?'

'Does anybody know about Peter Flett?' asked Mackay.

'He was playing billiards in the Union with little Dickson when we left,' answered one of them, 'and beating him for the only time in his life. Dickson was nervous, wondering how many stars he was going to get.'

'These men with brains!' said Mackay. 'An asterisk after my name never meant anything but a profane silence.'

13

Again the door swung open, and a little reddish fellow was pushed in by a broad, light-haired man with a long, heavy jaw and a moustache so fair as to look nearly white against his brown face.

'Two stars for Dickson,' he announced, and the little man, embarrassed, tried to conceal his pleasure.

There was a generous noise of congratulation, and an empty bottle fell with a crash off the glass-crowded bar.

'And you?' asked Mackay.

'Ploughed,' replied Flett carelessly. 'Virgin soil like mine wants a lot of ploughing before its fit for anything. Is this my drink?'

'Virgin is as virgin does,' said little Dickson.

'Virgins don't,' Mackay reminded him.

'Look here, you fellows, these drinks are on me.'

Mackay turned to Flett.

'I'm sorry, Peter,' he said. 'I've failed too, if that's any consolation to you.'

Flett laughed shortly. 'What does it matter? Examinations are like Inner Circle trains. Though you miss one there's always another coming along behind it.'

Evan Mackay was a lean, dark man, with eyes that told of an almost childish good humour and a mouth twisted to keep it from laughing. He had alert, sharply cut features and long, restless hands. Peter Flett was taller and broader, a big man with square shoulders. He had a clear, weather-tanned skin and grey, brooding eyes. His mouth was big but the lips were curiously delicate. When he laughed he flushed, his eyes puckered, he showed his white, even teeth; his head went back and he laughed full-heartedly. When Mackay laughed his mouth was solemn but his eyes blazed with delight. They had this in common: that when they were resolved about anything they looked, each in his own way, capable of resolute

14

action; and when they were idle each in his own way looked like a dreamer.

There was not much light in the Frigate. A pair of dingy incandescent gas-mantles, shaded at the top, threw out descending cones of brightness which overlapped at the level of the tables and gleamed redly in tall beer tumblers, and with pallid radiance in the lesser whisky glasses. Somewhere in the shadows of the roof the dirty model of a frigate hung. Two barmen worked at the beer-handles like signalmen desperately intent on securing the smooth passage of a crowded express; or drew small measures of whisky from the polished oak barrels that stood in a row at the back of the bar. Talk swelled in eager groups and met in a general hubbub, growing afresh as more men came in, and now and then sinking so that a categorical imperative might dominate Babel with a demand for three large whiskies. Tobacco-smoke rose like a lifting mist about the lamps; laughter, now individual and again a chorus, broke like trumpets through the hubbub of talk; and a warmth of content, a contagious geniality, moved through the crowded tavern.

Unhappily one of the coalmen, insulated possibly by a layer of grime, was proof against the surrounding infection of goodwill and permitted himself to criticize the rather high-pitched laughter of little Dickson.

Dickson, the excitement of his academic success exaggerated by several drinks, turned on him indignantly.

'No, I'm not a bloody schoolgirl,' he said, 'and you can wash your face in that.'

There was only a little beer in his glass, but it splashed soundly on the coalman's cheeks. The coalman lost his temper and hit Dickson, hard but innacurately, on the forehead. Tumult gathered, loud and sudden, like the mob that collects round a street accident. There was some shouting, some contradiction, a chair or two upset, and an uncomfortable jam in the narrow doorway. When the noise subsided – it slowly thinned out in the cooler darkness of the street – Dickson and his assailant amicably shook hands. There were other pubs in the neighbourhood. Some men went to one, some to another.

Dickson was elated after his quarrel – he was unused to fighting – and immediately ordered more whisky.

'Two drinks, or three, invariably make me placid and speculative,' said Mackay thoughtfully. 'I have a low taste for pub-crawling at times, and for the bemused observation and irrelevant argument which accompany it, but I hate a riot.'

'Let's sing songs,' said Dickson suddenly, and rose to his feet. His exciting day, allied with a punch on the head and a rapid succession of drinks, was beginning to have a disastrous effect and his eyes were a little glassy. Someone pulled him down and he sat, contentedly enough, humming *Bheir-mi-o* under his breath.

'It's the twenty-first of March,' Flett remembered. 'Three years ago we were racing a German army to the coast.'

That fell aftermath of war, a telling of old tales and a fighting of dead battles, swept over them. The names which were for too long like bugles in the ears of men who had fought, and a deadly weariness in the ears of their womenfolk and the men who had omitted to fight, swung back and forth across the table; Dickebusch, Arras, the Somme, Passchendaele, and all the rest of them. Like bugles they awoke far echoes, anecdote, jest, and forgotten wounds; and like bugles they stirred the blood.

Dickson lay back in his chair, sleeping with slightly open mouth and a happy smile.

'We had better go across to Sandy's and have a grill,' said

Gunn. 'He'll be all right if he gets something to eat. That's the worst of these people with brains; they can't carry their drink.'

'It's his harmartia,' Mackay said. 'Harmartia; the essential, ineradicable, universal, individual weakness. Everybody's got one. Oedipus had one, Napoleon had one, and Dickson has one. Even I have one. And Peter has two or three.'

'A lust for fillet-steak is all I have at present,' said Flett, ignoring the challenge. 'Finish your drink and we'll go to Sandy's and eat.'

Sandy's was a chop-house with a tradition. It had a name – a dignified name – which only strangers used. The creative spirit of the original proprietor had survived his body and passed into his son's son. Father, son and grandson were Alexander Broun, mortal men. But Sandy Broun's their living and their monument did not die. Its grill-fire was like a vestal-hearth that never went cold, and a livelier than vestal atmosphere was warmed by it. The restaurant was a high room, black and gilded about the ceiling. The smoke of the richest, reddest steak in Scotland had darkened its mouldings, and ghostly vineyard perfumes haunted every corner, for Alexander Broun, the First and Second, had been men with a nose and a palate who bought up the remnants of famous cellars and did business with the great wine-shippers. Sandy's cellar would have beaten Aladdin's, and no thief would ever have remembered such a word as Sesame after an hour in it. It might be of little material moment that the riches of France, the Peninsula and the Rhineland lay under-foot when whisky was most often on the table, but yet there was a satisfaction in the knowledge. The wine-list was a liberal education, a commentary on history and a handbook to the aesthetics of drinking. In its way Sandy's was an annexe to the two colleges, Queen's and New, of the University of Inverdoon, and there the social third which the non-residential colleges of Scotland so sadly lack was generously nurtured.

But a difficulty in getting to it was found, for Dickson slept and refused to waken.

'A barrow. We must get a barrow,' said Flett. 'Wait here and I'll find one.'

He disappeared through the door before anyone could object. Not that anyone would have objected, for their normal inhibitions were dissolving rapidly and tides of irresponsibility flowed in everybody's veins.

'Now we're off,' exclaimed Mackay, as he and Gunn lifted Dickson to the door.

'Hearse ahoy!' he shouted, and Flett trundled a handcart out of a nearby lane.

'Lift him up tenderly,' he said, 'fashioned so slenderly, young and so fair – where did you find the barrow?'

'Up the lane,' said Flett briefly. His face was flushed and there was a glint in his eye as he pushed the handcart with its silent burden up the Kirkgate and down College Street. He was beginning to enjoy himself.

Gunn and Moncur walked at either side, and half-a-dozen other men joined the *cortège*, making a cheerful noise. Mackay marched ahead, reciting solemnly :

> 'Back and side go bare, go bare,
> And foot and hand go cold,
> But belly, God send thee good ale enough
> Whether it be new or old.'

'Eh, look at the students!' said shawled women standing on the pavements.

'Drunk again,' sneered a harsh voice.

And as the barrow came into a pool of light, 'Oh, Christ!' said one, marvelling.

'You flatter us,' replied Mackay. 'It's only Mr. Dickson.'

He held up the traffic in Queen Street – the main artery of Inverdoon – stretching out both hands and shouting : 'Gangway for the corpse of a naval officer!' They crossed the road and parked the barrow by the friendly kerb outside Sandy's.

Uncovering, Gunn and Moncur lifted the inanimate Dickson and carried him in past the grinning doorkeeper.

'Take off your hats, gentlemen,' said Flett to two passers-by who had stayed to watch. 'Have you no decent feelings?'

'God requite you,' added Mackay as the strangers foolishly obeyed.

They went inside and up a stairway where the long shallow steps were all worn in the middle, and where an ancient hospitable smell lingered warmly; down a corridor lined with framed cartoons from Vanity Fair, and into the Smoking Room. There a dozen men were listening to a stout, red-faced laughing man on the windy edge of intoxication; a man with a great crop of unruly hair that, like Cuchulainn's, had three colours in it – brown at the skin, red in the middle, and flaming gold at the tips. He had blue twinkling eyes and an old burnt pipe between his teeth. And he stood straddle-legged in front of the fire telling a story about a doctor, a farm-servant, and a bicycle.

This was Garry Duncan, the most genial man of his time in Inverdoon. He had been at the University before the War; in August, 1914, he had joined a Highland Territorial battalion, and gone to France as a private; he had been commissioned on the field, and returned in 1918, an acting major, to the University. He stopped his story as they went in with

Dickson and shouted gleefully, 'Lord, a corpse already! But put him in a chair and listen to this.'

Garry re-filled his pipe, his blue eyes twinkling. He spoke at will in a ripe Buchan accent that, because of the breadth of its vowels and the rolling significance of the consonants, cannot be bettered for telling a story that is inclined to be broad or, perhaps, goes deepishly into the native humour of vulgar humanity.

Dickson had wakened during Garry's story and, adding a hiccup to the laughter, said seriously : 'It's a good thing bicycles weren't known in Robbie Burns's day.'

'As a general rule,' said Mackay, 'I dislike lewd stories. But there's a sort of vital childishness in your nature, Garry, which enlists one's sympathy and disarms criticism. I might listen to another such tale.'

Flett took him by the arm and led him to the door. 'Grills first. Are you coming to eat with us, Garry?'

Food has a sobering effect, or at any rate provides the necessary foundation for a more permanent kind of intoxication, and when, an hour or so later, the six of them sat with empty coffee-cups and tall, slender-waisted glasses of whisky and soda before them, Dickson was the only one who was obviously and entirely drunk. In speech and the powers of physical co-ordination the others were not very far from normal. Their faces were flushed and their voices a little louder than usual. But the unseen changes were greater than that. Their mental discipline had fallen like the Bastille before the rebel shouting of their blood. The normal armour of civic righteousness had melted in the fire, and the breastplate of convention, the cuisses of urban respectability, had been loosened and laid aside.

'Come and play with the big world,' suggested Garry hopefully. 'Buy a bottle of whisky and see life.'

Mackay shuddered. 'That means interrupting an out-door Communist meeting, or some such thing, and I hate rows. I would rather you told us more stories of your dissolute youth and let me moralize quietly on my own beatitude.'

'Dickson's hearse is still outside,' said Peter Flett.

'Home, John,' said Dickson, rising at once and staggering to the door.

They found him outside, squatting cross-legged on his handcart and throwing pennies to a little circle of street-urchins who had gathered round.

Mackay took off his hat to an old woman with a shawl round her head and enquired courteously, ' Pardon me, madam, but could you tell me the nearest way to a cemetery? My friend there is about to decompose.'

'Awa' hame, ye drunken deevil,' she replied indignantly.

With difficulty they persuaded Dickson to leave his barrow and walk. But somehow or other they lost him. He slipped away from them. Irrational and unexpected activity awakened in him, and a stubborn memory, a dogged determination preserved like a museum specimen in alcohol, took him back to the handcart. The others, when they discovered that he was missing, began to look for him. But not till they happened to pass the dark alley that led to the Police Station did they strike his trail. There they met a man whose high spirits had forced a constable to arrest him, and whose wit had come at need, cold and sufficiently sober, to persuade the inspector on duty to accept bail.

'Dickson?' he said, and chuckled. 'He's in a cell. He was brought in five minutes after I got there. Walking in his sleep, arm-in-arm with a policeman. I couldn't bail him out because nobody could wake him.'

The thought of Dickson – hardworking, precisely-mannered, quiet in speech, prim little Dickson – in a police cell struck them as being exquisitely funny. They looked at each other and laughed, loudly, again and again. The story was repeated and their laughter brought out a suspicious policeman. Someone happily remembered the Communists.

At that time Communist and other agitators, bitter-minded men with a Glasgow accent, used regularly to hold open-air meetings under a statue of which Inverdoon was otherwise proud; a mighty granite statue of William Wallace, a towering image in stone mail, stretching to the north a colossal arm and holding in the other hand a ponderous sword. Beneath this rocky indifference men with grievances and hoarse voices would talk passionately of such things as Russia and the aristocracy and capital, and argue without reason on the fabric of society. And occasionally students went to their meetings, flown with wine or restlessness, to prick with jibes their windy propositions ; bear-baiting being an ancient sport.

A crowd, black figures in the dim light, was listening to a man who spoke of Karl Marx. He stood on the pedestal of the statue, a couple of feet higher than his audience, and talked bitterly about the Church. Then he quoted Lenin, and prophesied damnation and the red fires of hell – which was illogical in an atheist – for ship-owners, mill-owners, factory-owners, lords, and all who had served as officers in the army. Peter and Garry, Moncur and Gunn, pressed in towards the centre of the crowd.

'I've suffered for my opinions,' cried the speaker, ' but I'm not afraid. I've been in prison – '

'I have a friend there at present,' said Garry.

The agitator glared at him, and said again, 'I've been in prison, I say – '

'Perhaps you would like to hear about my friend, then. He's just been arrested.'

PRELUDE: THE PUB CRAWL

Someone in the crowd laughed and the agitator lost his temper.

'It's you and the likes of you that's the enemies of the working-man,' he shouted. 'You, the slaves and lick-spittles of the capitalists. I've stood at this statue before – '

'And I'm not here to make money, I'm here to advertise my firm. Every watch is guaranteed for five years and what I don't sell I'll give away.' Garry chanted this in the loud sing-song voice of a market cheap-jack, and some more of the feather-brained crowd laughed at the interruption. But a large, strongly-built navvy pushed a way towards him, and thrusting his angry face within a foot of Garry's shouted, ' Shut your bloody mouth! Who the hell asked you to come here and talk?'

'You have a smut on your cheek,' said Peter Flett politely.

The navvy spluttered and swore again.

'Leave them alone,' cried the agitator, who was in danger of losing his audience. 'I'm not frightened of them. There's no hireling of the capitalists can stop me talking.'

'No, I'll not leave them alone,' roared the navvy. 'Get out of this before you're kicked out,' he said to Garry.

'Gently, comrade,' Garry remonstrated; and the navvy promptly snatched off the soft tweed hat that Garry wore. At the same time Peter smacked the navvy's face.

A confused sound of excitement and delight drowned the voice of the agitator. Action was more popular than theory. A chorus of encouragement rose fiercely. The crowd faced inwards, wheeling and pushing, shouting advice. Occasionally words like ' Russia ' and ' slaves ' and ' free clinics ' came from the point on the periphery where the neglected speaker dauntlessly continued his address, but everybody's attention was fixed on the scrum in the centre. The navvy had his friends. The crowd was divided in its sympathies. Strangers told entire strangers to go to hell, and a friendly man with a raspberry nose advised Peter to 'hit the b— hard' as the navvy swung wildly at him. Arms and legs got entangled. Garry slipped and fell. 'Give him a chance!' shouted the nearer crowd. 'Hold back, there's a man on the ground!' 'Ah, to hell,' replied the circumference, 'Knock their bloody heads off!'

'Let Russia teach us a lesson of brotherhood,' shrieked the lone voice on the outskirts.

'That's the way to do it,' cheered the man with the raspberry nose as Peter hit the navvy on his right eye.

'Heads down and shove!' roared Gunn. He and Moncur broke through a weakness in the crowd and disappeared.

Then someone shouted loudly, 'Here's the police!' And as the crowd turned to the direction of the voice Garry said swiftly to Peter, 'It's time we were going.' And together, breaking through and running round the blind side of the crowd, they made for darkness and an evasive lane.

'I like the police,' said Peter, gasping, 'but I don't want to call on them to-night. Where shall we go?'

'The Howdie Digs,' said Garry breathlessly.

Howdie is a Scots adjective relative to the science of obstetrics; and the Howdie Digs were rooms where students engaged in acquiring practical knowledge of midwifery lived for the three weeks or so of their specialized course. The rooms were close to the Maternity Hospital, and as work proceeded irregularly during all hours of the twenty-four they made an open port of call for benighted wanderers.

When Flett and Garry Duncan arrived they found Mackay already there – they had lost him about the same time as Dickson – playing Vingt-et-Un with the two men in residence and four or five others who had dropped in during the evening.

'There's plenty of soda left,' said one of the hosts, 'but we're running short of whisky.'

'Here's some more,' said Garry, and pulled out two half-bottles from inside pockets.

'His favourite conjuring trick,' explained Mackay. 'What have you been doing?'

'Playing with the Communists. Give me a drink and I'll tell you all about it. Peter fell out with a navvy two stones heavier than himself.'

Peter yawned and stretched. 'I'm feeling better,' he said. 'I was oppressed before. Examinations always make me costive, but to-night's bit of fun has acted like five grains of mental calomel. I'm thirsty.'

'As a Communist myself,' protested Mackay, 'I must deprecate your hurting Communists to cure yourself. Healthy exercise is an admirable thing, but free speech is one of the corner-stones of the British Constitution – kindly note that I deliberately risked my reputation at that articulative Beecher's Brook – the British Constitution, as I remarked, is based on an unlicensed provision for free speech.'

'He's already given us monologues on popular religion, art, and dog-breeding,' someone commented. 'Now it's politics.'

'You will admit that a little disquisition on modern art was not unnecessary when I tell you that not one of these people – medical education is, of course, a misnomer; it is no more educational than plumbing – not one of these people had ever heard of Clive Bell.'

'Wasn't he the man who invented telephones?' asked Garry.

'And as to dog-breeding,' Mackay continued, 'that masterly little address arose, incidentally as it were, out of the fact that someone lost his temper and called the Queen of Spades a bitch, because she happened to spoil a winning sequence of five cards under twenty-one.'

'Well, what are we going to do now?' said Garry.

'Continue playing Vingt-et-Un,' answered Mackay promptly. 'Or if you prefer it, begin playing poker. I've made eight shillings and sixpence already, and with a larger field I hope proportionally to increase my winnings.'

'We're expecting a call in an hour or so,' said Grant, one of the men in residence, ' so you might as well stay and help to keep us awake.'

At a quarter-past three the telephone rang and Grant and his colleague sprang to their feet. One of them said, 'Make up the fire and stay where you are if you want to,' and slammed resonantly in the still night the heavy door behind him.

'Another insult to Marie Stopes,' Mackay said dreamily, and putting his head on the table littered with cards and money fell sound asleep. One man lay on a sofa, another in a big chair, snoring softly. Two others, hardy men, sat stolidly with flushed faces. Only Peter Flett and Garry Duncan were still lively, for the vitality of the latter was without limit – 'I've got blue eyes,' he said; 'blue as a baby's. And people with blue eyes are the only ones that drink can't kill' – and Peter's spirit, moody and uncertain, burned with an equal flame when warmed by excitement or the glow of Garry's company.

'Let's go and play with the world,' said Garry for the second time that night. His red face shone, and his blue eyes twinkled, and the light danced like gold in his hair. Vitality is king, and Mackay stirred in his sleep and opened a glazy eye.

'*In manus tuas,*' he muttered, and rose unsteadily to his feet.

'We'll stay and take these fellows home when they wake up,' said one of the other men. He got up carefully and opened a window. The clouds of tobacco-smoke eddied and swirled, drifted in long streamers, and poured through the open window like a blue funnel.

'Where are we going?' asked Peter at the door.

'The Fishmarket,' Garry answered. 'We'll have breakfast in a fish-porters' café and see the sun rise.'

He led them down steep deserted streets to the harbour, where lights threw long daffodil lanes across the black water, and out to the fish quays where trawlers were unloading. A salt breeze blew shrewdly from the sea and burly men in black oilskins, gleaming wet, unloaded a great harvest of silver fish from the gaping hulls of the trawlers. Fantastic shapes, stooping under burdens, moved about the quay; and hoarse voices called and answered. To the east an intermittent flash, a white pencil that fluttered and disappeared, showed where a lighthouse challenged the dawn. Already there was a greyness in the eastern sky, a harsh greyness out of which came the wind.

Mackay shivered and stammered 'Poor Tom's a-cold,' but Flett stood silent, listening to the noises of work and hearing beyond them the murmurous shrill duet of the wind and the outer sea.

'Breakfast!' said Garry suddenly. 'This way. Fried fish and coffee.'

There was a small, unclean eating-house on the quay, a bare place, open all night, with three deal tables and a fire at which a stoutly-built, rosy woman was frying fish. She looked suspiciously at the three who came in.

'Well?' she asked.

'Perfectly,' answered Mackay with the suspicion of a hiccup.

'Good morning,' said Garry affably. 'Pay no attention to him – '

'I'm not,' she snapped.

'But if you have three fresh, medium-sized soles; and if you can make coffee for us – '

'It's essence,' said the honest woman.

'We shall all be happy together.'

The woman shouted a name and her shabby, sleepy, thin, half-clad husband came in to cut bread-and-butter and garnish a table with uncouth knives and a battered display of salt-cellars and such.

The fish was fried and brought, odorous and enticing in the cold morning, and thick earthenware cups of coffee. Deftly, from an inside pocket, Garry drew another half-bottle of whisky and richly laced the coffee.

'Maskelyne cannot compare with him,' said Mackay, open-eyed with admiration. 'He is a walking pub, a peripatetic tavern, a pantechnicon of comely liquors, a mobile cellar, every drinker's complete *vade-mecum*, the perfect travelling companion. O Garry, I love you like Jonathan.'

'And now,' said Garry when they had finished, 'who's coming for a walk along the beach to see the sun rise?'

'Home,' pleaded Mackay as Peter considered the suggestion. 'Home,' he repeated, 'home for heaven's sake.'

They went out on to the quay. Half the sky was grey and a cold hard light was beginning to drown the lamps.

'Home,' again said Mackay. 'Home before it's light enough to see the bristle on our chins and the hollows under our eyes.'

'The rising sun,' said Garry, and walked away, whistling loudly, swinging his stick.

The birds were waking, twittering and chirping on roofs

28

and in street-side trees as Peter and Mackay reached the house where they had rooms together.

'I hate the end of anything,' Mackay said as he opened the door.

Peter Flett and Mackay were still in their dressing-gowns. They had wakened in time for lunch and now they sat on either side of the fire, smoking.

'I'm too old to take alcoholic remorse for the truth,' said Mackay thoughtfully, 'but I believe that it has its uses. You get sudden glimpses of comprehension when you're drunk that no dogmatically sober man ever has, and then on the morning after you can study those glimpses in the most unfavourable light possible. If they survive that scrutiny you can be pretty sure that they were glimpses of the truth. Damn it,' he said, as if in quick anger, 'we've got to get drunk. Our clay's too stiff. Women don't feel the same need because they're naturally more receptive and more responsive. But we're stiff. We have to wet the clay before it will take an impression. Last night I felt that life was a great thing, a magnificent, rolling, tuneful thing in time with the stars. You may think that I'm drunk still, but I tell you that I felt a better man last night; at least I was conscious of a gratitude for life, if that's being better.' He stopped abruptly, and rammed more tobacco into his pipe.

'Young love gives you the same feeling,' said Peter with a yawn.

Mackay gave a snort of laughter. 'And so does going on a roundabout. It's nonsense, of course, to claim vision as the specific accompaniment of drinking; but at least it shares merit with love and the roundabouts. And there's another thing. It's cathartic. It's mental calomel, as you said last night, and the best of us need calomel now and again.'

'I get drunk for two reasons, I think. The first is, quite frankly, that I enjoy drinking with people like you and Garry Duncan, and the second is that subconsciously, or half-subconsciously, I want to get rid of a vicious boredom. This life doesn't take enough out of us. France did. You lived on the edge of nothing there, and had all that you could stand. You had no superfluity left, no spare energy. But here we have, and we don't know what to do with it.'

'Most people use it to build up security; bank it; buy umbrellas with it. I'm going to buy an umbrella and settle down under it myself some day.'

'The devil take umbrellas.' Peter Flett scowled at the fire.

'I don't want to settle down,' he said. 'I've got a restless ancestry behind me. Their ghosts kick. Most of them died at sea or in foreign ports. I should have gone to sea too, only – '

'The curse of civilization stopped you,' said Mackay with enjoyment. 'The desire to improve your condition in the world made your parents educate you for what they thought was something better. Pure social vice and snobbery. You would have been far happier scrubbing decks, or brailing spankers, or whatever people do at sea.'

Peter laughed self-consciously. 'And now I've developed a taste for comfort and laziness, and sit by the fire like a cat dreaming of the jungle.'

'Or a gold-fish yearning for the Seven Seas, you inspissated Viking.'

The University of Inverdoon is fed by a wide area. Students go to it from all the northern part of Scotland. From manse and school-house in the Highlands, from lowland farms, and the prosperous small towns of the north-east; from the Western Isles, from Skye and the Lewis; from Ross and Cromarty and Caithness and from the islands still farther to the north, the wind-swept Orkneys and Shetlands, men go to it for the learning of Greece and Rome and for the arts of healing – souls, bodies, and soils. As twin beacons the two

colleges give out their lights of olden cultures and new knowledge, two shafts that sweep the northern sky and, like light-
houses, attract all manner of creatures: urban sparrows and
amiable tits and domestic pigeons, as well as gannets and
arctic gulls.

Mackay came of a long line of Highland ministers. 'Three
generations ago they learnt to speak English,' he would say.
'Before that they preached in Gaelic, and the Devil himself
was a regular communicant under my great-great-grand-
father. The Gaelic is a powerful tongue and improves any
gospel. But when my great-grandfather began to preach in
English the Devil went off in a huff and started a dissenting
chapel which became very popular. Times are hard in the
old manse now.'

Flett was an Orkneyman. Eight hundred years ago there
was a saint in Orkney ; a political kind of saint, for he was
Earl of Orkney before he became a nobleman in the hierarchy
of Heaven. And both because of his sanctity and his temporal
authority he had many enemies, so that one day he was
attacked on a small island and brutally done to death by half-
a-dozen ruffians in the pay of a rival to the earldom. One of
the ruffians was a certain Thorkel Flett, who was rewarded
for his share in such a notable murder by a grant of land.
And that land had pastured enough mutton to feed his line
for eight hundred summers, and grown enough corn to make
malt for their eight hundred winters of drinking; for little
work could be done in the dark stormy winters of the place.
And the sea which bordered Thorkel Flett's land gave generously too, of cod and haddock and lobsters and an occasional
wreck; and in its turn took the lives of perhaps two in three
of the men of the family. For one would farm and another
would sail; one plant cabbages and feed his beasts and another
go fishing in the Firth, or venture far to the north in whaling

ships. Peter's great-grandfather had commanded a whaler and had died within the Arctic Circle. His grandfather had commanded – in tall-hat and a tail-coat – a famous tea-clipper of his day, and he and all hands had gone down with her in a hurricane off Mauritius. Peter's father had stood on the bridge of a Western Ocean liner and, in the uniform of a Commander in the Royal Naval Reserve, had been killed in 1916 somewhere off the Skager Rak while shepherding a neutral convoy.

His mother had died nearly a year ago, and Thorkel Flett's land, grown little now because three generations of seafarers had given it small thought, was farmed by Peter's sister. Peter, eighteen years old and newly finished with school in 1914, went to France as a Second-Lieutenant in the Seaforth Highlanders in the spring of 1915. He was twice wounded, won a Military Cross and some time later a bar to it, at which he swore ungratefully for he had ambitiously expected a D.S.O. In the spring of 1919 he left the Army inconspicuously in the rush of demobilization. He did not know what to do.

He went to Orkney and told his sister that he meant to buy a fishing-boat with his gratuity and sail her round Britain while he considered plans for the future.

'Don't be such a fool,' she said shortly. 'Go in for medicine and get a degree of some kind before your brain ossifies. There are so many fools without degrees that a fool with one can always make his bread and butter out of the rest.'

'That's an idea,' said Peter, and took the next boat south to Inverdoon.

On the boat he met an Engineer-Commander – there were still ships in Scapa Flow, where the Grand Fleet had lain – who told him that there were good medical jobs in the different colonial services. 'I know a man,' he had said, 'somewhere out New Guinea way, who has an ocean district as big as the North Sea and spends most of his time going from station to station in an auxiliary schooner.'

That had decided Peter, and he had started the study of medicine with an enthusiasm which carried him through his first year. But in his second year enthusiasm began to get leg-weary and think of sitting on benches and unbuttoning after noon. For the scientific acquisition of knowledge is almost as tedious as a routine acquisition of wealth. The medical student's education is full of interest – it is even exciting – to the casual observer. But steadfastly for five years to commit to memory the minute details of even the most exciting facts requires a prodigious mental effort and almost inevitably connotes boredom. A well-dissected arm is a pretty sight, and the story of the endocrine glands is as absorbing as a mystery novel with the last chapter torn away; but when that arm has to be studied, the origin and attachments, blood-supply, nerve-supply, and contiguous relations of every muscle memorized; the whimsical reflexions of fasciae and the prolific sprouting of nerve and artery mapped, planned, and remembered; the shape, relations, structure, coverings, and fœtal growth of the underlying bones read until they become a familiar part of one's mind; when all this has to be learnt of every part of the body merely as a preliminary foundation for the practical arts of healing – medical, surgical and obstetrical – it is credible that a man with a restless imagination and a strain of indolence should grow weary of the task; and yet retain an interest in the ever-opening vistas of new knowledge that makes him unready to give it up.

This was Peter's case, and he found comfort in blaming heredity for his plight; and indeed it is written that the sins of the father live long enough to vex the children.

For some time he and Mackay sat without speaking, and then, 'The Orkney Vikings,' Peter said, 'used to make two cruises in the year, in spring and autumn. I suppose they did a bit of farming in between. And they spent the winters in their drinking-halls.'

'A dull life,' answered Mackay. 'Four months of piracy and getting hurt, three months of primitive agriculture, and five months of drinking without the comfort of tobacco, squabbling for the women they had stolen, and listening to dull stories of improbable adventure. The Vikings were the only great race that never produced anything more durable than illegitimate children and broken heads. Their imagination went to the table in the morning and to bed at night, and never took them farther.'

'It took them round the North Cape, and to Constantinople, and to America.'

'They were probably blown out of their courses and couldn't help themselves. At any rate, they died because they were essentially and shamelessly non-productive.'

'And why should we bother to be productive? Production is only a fetish; a vulgar fetish. Thank God there has been at least one race that died without building insanitary cities and evolving theories of economic wealth. Who the devil wants two blades of grass to grow where one grew before?'

'Cows,' said Mackay, yawning, and went to dress himself.

SUMMER WEATHER

I

IT was a May morning. Sunlight shone on the white granite walls of New College, and its tall tower soared into a blue sky over which drifted small clouds like unshorn fat sheep in a field of cornflowers. Light danced on windows, and the slender spires were immaculate conceptions of their Gothic architect. A clean sweet air, brisk with the cool northern sunlight, filled the quadrangle. There is no weather in the world so good as early summer in the North; for between the hills that are still capped with snow and the green sea that is always cold, summer comes alert and young, breathlessly gay, dancing on new grass, throwing great armfuls of golden broom on the moors, and setting the woods in an emerald blaze. Tawny burns flow deeply between rock and heather, and rivers run singing over white pebbles to the sea; and at the river's mouth terns and gulls wheel and swoop and dart, shining like silver disks thrown in the sun.

It is weather to make any man a gipsy.

But the policemen of civilization are hard on gipsies, and youth, grown astonishingly wise and lamentably cautious, has been brought up to honour and obey the police. And more than the police he honours economic laws, so wise and old has he grown. Youth will work even in a northern summer, under no more compulsion than the necessity, in some far future year, of earning his living. It is incredible and true. The thoughts of youth are so intent on to-morrow that he forgets to-day. He builds so earnestly his future home that he does not see how flowers are growing at his side and girls are passing, and music is making in the woods. There is bitter competition ahead of him, and summer must be left to dance by herself; for youth is working. Countless battalions storm the cities, fighting to throw themselves into factories and offices; countless battalions eagerly grow up to take their place; the world runs to work like a lover to his bride's bed; and the summer fields are empty.

Youth is wise in his generation; and it is a clownish jest that he should so often die when his house is built.

'Now I am too old to work in summer,' said Garry Duncan, where he sat on the steps under the tall white tower of New College. 'I can't afford to waste the time. Sitting here, when I might have been attending a lecture, I have already seen two pretty girls pass me; one stared at me boldly, and the other dropped her head – the nape of her neck had uncommonly good lines.'

'I have worked steadily, stolidly and unwillingly for fourteen days,' said Mackay. 'Peter has worked for sixteen, less steadily but more unwillingly. At present he is in the gymnasium punching a bag, or being punched by ex-Petty-officer Sims in preparation for a battle which he has ahead of him. And there are our brethren, our mates, our academic comrades, going forth to clinics, operations, ward-duties, and other sordid tasks. Shall I join them?'

A stream of men and women was beginning to leave the quadrangle in pairs and trios; here a lonely individual and there a group. They carried notebooks under their arms.

'I have no notebook,' said Mackay, 'and my fountain-pen – like my heart when I consider work – is dry. I shall not join them.'

And he felt in his pockets for a pipe.

'Is Peter really working?' asked Garry.

'He started in the vacation and he has kept going fairly well ever since. But he's trying to do too much. He attends surgical clinics and does ward-duties when he ought to be in the dissecting-room.'

'But so do you, don't you?'

'Well, the dissecting-room is unpleasant in summer and one can't spend the whole morning in it. The hospital isn't very attractive either. In another quarter of an hour those people will be standing, all jammed together, in the gallery of an operating-theatre to watch Tiger Tim explore abdomens, reseci ankle-joints, re-attach vagrant kidneys, and remove the prostrate glands of old gentlemen who have lived not wisely but indisputably well.'

'I did a post-mortem on a horse last year,' said Garry.

'It will be appallingly hot and the theatre will be full of chloroform and ether and disinfectant, and all they will see is a sheeted figure with a red gap in the middle of it, out of which Tiger Tim pulls shiny pieces of gut as if it were a lucky-bag. I was sick the first time I saw it. But Peter said that he once helped to butcher sheep – his sister has a farm – and a duodenal ulcer, I suppose, is nothing to that.'

'We used a carpenter's saw to get through the ribs of that old horse, and even then we couldn't find any reason for its death.'

'How the women stand it I don't know, but some of them are gluttons for blood.'

'They're gluttons for work too. They're so damned unimaginative that they can only think of one other thing to do, and as they're either too frightened or too respectable to do that they work instead. And they spoil the field for us.'

Peter Flett came round the corner from the steps which led down to the gymnasium. His face was redder than usual so that his fair moustache looked like a thin white streak across it, and his long jaw stood forward in a grin as he said,

'I knocked Sims against the rib-stalls ten minutes ago with a crash that shook the gym. He was enormously pleased about it, and said I ought to beat the Glasgow man easily next week.'

Mackay considered him with dispassionate eyes.

'You remember what Shaw says about the attraction of the Ring?' he asked Garry.

'I don't read Shaw,' answered Garry mildly.

'He says that the Ring has always had and always will have a fascination for weak-minded, romantic people. That's why it attracts Peter. He has a mawkish streak of romance in him, though you mightn't think so. He's too intelligent not to see the idiocy of boxing, of duelling without danger or provocation, and as he isn't a sadist he can't like getting hurt. But he enjoys boxing because his subconscious mind is full of Tom Sayers and Cribb and Mendoza; he reads Borrow.'

'That's nonsense,' said Peter. 'Boxing is more exciting than any other game. It stimulates you. It focuses all your energy and creates new energy. And when the fight's over you have a healthy, used-up, satisfied feeling.'

'And the clapping of hands is sweet music in your battered ears. Come for a walk and let me talk about life and its futility while the sun is shining to call me a liar.'

'I can't,' said Garry, getting to his feet. 'I'm going to play golf.'

Mackay turned to Peter. 'Let's walk to the Bridge End Inn and have lunch there,' he said.

'Clinics?' suggested Peter.

'Damn clinics. It's too fine to stay in town.'

The Bridge End Inn is seven riverside miles from Inverdoon, seven miles through woods and over patches of brown heath that lead to open grassland split by a little glen, down which a burn runs to join the river. And at the junction of river and stream the inn stands, grey and snug.

Half-a-mile away from it, where the road was still under trees, Mackay and Peter caught sight of two girls walking ahead of them.

'The outside one has shoulders which look familiar to me,' Mackay said. 'And her legs are not altogether strange. I've seen them going up to Ward Two ahead of me, if I'm not mistaken. I dislike the mingling of the sexes in hospitals and at lectures – co-education has no merit except cheapness – but she looks attractive enough here.'

'Who's the other one?' asked Peter.

'I've no idea.'

'She walks well.'

They were sitting at a table in the window of the small dining-room when Peter and Mackay went in. Both looked round and one smiled.

'Good-morning,' said Mackay. 'This is much pleasanter than removing stitches under carefully aseptic conditions, isn't it?'

'I finished those juvenile exploits years ago,' said the taller girl, smiling. 'Do you know my sister?'

Her name was Margaret Geddes; her complexion was better than her features, and she was in her fourth year of Medicine. Patricia, the younger sister, desultorily attended classes at Queen's College, where the Classics, Philosophy, and Modern Languages grew in a rich but untidy garden

They made a foursome for lunch and Mackay dominated the conversation. His egotism was inclusive, not exclusive, and though he liked to have the attention of others he always gave his own attention to them. He was gravely foolish in his treatment of Patricia, the youngest of the four; extravagantly derided Peter's pugilistic enthusiasm; talked about eating and drinking; and condemned, for Margaret's benefit, the place of women in the professions, and especially in Medicine, to a purgatory of insecure optimism and an ultimate Gehenna of defeat.

'Cook, Harlot, Seamstress, Doctor, or Politician,' he said, counting her prune-stones. 'And it comes round again to Cook. I think you swallowed a stone but that doesn't matter, for it was one of the two that you were destined to be, and you can't avoid it. *Naturam furca expellas, tamen usque recurret.*'

'But we're not expelling Nature,' said Margaret. 'We're allowing her to develop new types. We're teaching her to do new work instead of keeping her in a conventional prison.'

'Just as they send bad boys to Borstal, to show them new ways of disturbing society. You're trying to put Nature in an Industrial School to teach her useful handicrafts.'

'Then you admit that they are useful?'

'Things specifically designed for use are utterly abhorrent to me and entirely foreign to Nature. If Nature wants to transplant seeds from one place to another she creates humming-birds to carry them. Man evolves commercial travellers. My one ambition at present is to incubate humming-birds' eggs. Let's go and dabble our fingers in the burn.'

They lay on the grass where a square of firm dry turf was half-hidden by trees. The burn fell into a deep brown pool below them, making chuckling noises as it tumbled over a reedy fall. A faint breeze stirred the tree-tops, but the birds were silent in the stillness of afternoon and all that broke the quiet was the gurgling melody of the stream. Two or three cloudy galleons sailed on their landless blue sea.

The smoke of cigarettes rose in tiny spirals and stems that opened into vapoury petals and vanished. Peter, in training, chewed an empty pipe, and Patricia lay face downwards staring into the pool.

'Can you tickle trout?' she asked over her shoulder.

'I used to,' said Peter. 'There's an easier pool a little higher up. Let's try there.'

With long bare arms that the water distorted in its reflexion they poked and probed under an overhanging bank and round the roots of a tree growing half out of the stream; but their searching fingers never closed on a fish.

'Did you ever catch any like this – honestly?' Patricia asked.

'I like to think so,' Peter said.

Patricia leaned back against the curving trunk of the tree and tried to dry her wet fishing arm with an insufficient handkerchief.

'Let me,' said Peter. 'My handkerchief's as big as a towel.'

Her arms were smooth and round, finely shaped and very delicately tapering from shoulder to wrist. Wet, and in the sunlight, they had the sheen of ivory, and her fingers were still pink from the cool water. Peter, stretched full-length and propped on his elbows at her side, stared at her with a detached and yet absorbed scrutiny, seeing her profile against a vanishing background of leaves and branches, and her hair, light brown and untidy, in a warm shade. Her nose was faintly aquiline with small, very finely-cut nostrils, and her chin had a kind of childish imperiousness. Her mouth was sensitive, provocative, beautifully shaped; the central notch in the upper lip was curiously distinct. Her eyes were level and grey.

Disturbed by Peter's scrutiny she said aimlessly : 'What did Mackay mean by saying that you were a decadent Viking?'

'Mackay talks a lot of nonsense for his own amusement. I

was born in Orkney, where the Norsemen settled ages ago; that's all.'

'What do you do when you go there? Fish?'

'There's good fishing; trout lochs; and rough shooting. And sea-fishing's good fun. You go out to the West Sea – that's what the fishermen call it – and work along a great rocky coast; enormous cliffs that the wind comes off in black squalls. And you see the solan geese diving, white streaks going plump into the sea, raising little fountains as they disappear. Sometimes, if you're close in-shore, you find a seal fishing in front of you, sliding off a rock into a green smother of waves. And then you feel a tug on your line and you haul it in, ten fathoms perhaps, with a couple of haddocks or big codling on the hooks. Or perhaps it's only a dog-fish. You never know what's going to happen at sea; that's the fun of it.'

'I don't like Mackay,' said Patricia abruptly. 'I think it's he who is decadent.'

'Why?'

'He talks too much, and he sneers. And – well, there was no need to tell us that we had to be cooks or harlots.'

'But it's amusing to talk, and some people find it amusing to listen to Mackay when he's arguing on his favourite subject.'

'What is his favourite subject?'

'Anything that happens to crop up,' said Peter with a grin.

'I thought perhaps it was drinking,' said Patricia.

'Oh, that's too hard. Evan drinks no more than anyone else.'

'But he talks about it. He drinks ostentatiously, like – well, it's an upside down resemblance, but it reminds me of the Pharisees.'

'I must tell him that. He'll enjoy it. He says that women

43

distrust drink because they can't understand a generous rival.'

'I don't want to know what Mackay says. Tell me about fishing in the West Sea.'

'How old are you?' asked Peter.

'Nineteen. It's an intolerant age, isn't it?'

'Nobody minds intolerance at nineteen,' Peter said slowly. 'It's intolerance from old fools of sixty, crusted intolerance, that galls. And having a mild riot is sometimes no more than defiance against it.'

'But why don't you have sober riots?'

'It's a contradiction in terms. You can't do it.'

'I can,' said Patricia, looking demurely at a ladybird which had settled on her hand. 'In my last term at school, a year ago, I put a Belgian hare belonging to the gardener in the German mistress's bed; and her nightdress in the rabbit-hutch. It made a horrible scandal.'

Peter laughed uproariously so that a sleeping bird woke and rose noisily in the branches, and Patricia's mirth came like an echo of the tumbling stream.

'After that we all called the hare Gallant Little Belgium,' she said, and giggled helplessly. The disgusted ladybird flew away home.

A whistle sounded lower down the stream.

'Bother,' said Patricia, 'we'll have to go.'

Peter put out his hands to lift her up, and she came straight from the ground into his arms, still laughing, her mouth half-open. Peter, without forethought, put down his head to kiss her and for a moment their lips met.

Quickly, with a sudden thrust, she started back.

'Oh,' she said, 'that was unfair of you – to kiss me when I was laughing; when I couldn't help it. You've spoiled everything.'

'I'm sorry,' said Peter lamely.

What the devil made him meddle with a school-girl, he thought. They were all either prudes or vicious little sensualists.

Patricia looked at him with stony eyes.

'It was my fault **too**,' she said, 'but that doesn't absolve you of blame.'

Peter followed her down the glen, exasperated by a tuss about nothing, uncertain whether to be angry at himself or to laugh at Patricia, and tantalized by an irrational thought that he was letting her go when he ought to keep her.

II

THE gymnasium, dressed for tournament, was like a dark island in the centre of which lay a pool of light. In the pool two men, clad scantily from shoulder to mid-thigh in white, moved gravely hither and thither, hitting each other when opportunity offered, darting, feinting, mingling in a flurry of inward-swinging arms, and retreating to a pacing watchfulness. At intervals a bell rang, and from the island of darkness would come applause, a buzz and hubbub of conversation, a shout, a burst of laughter, a nervous medley of noise.

The University of Inverdoon was entertaining, as heartily as it might, the boxing team of Glasgow University, and to honour the feast patrons of the English art had gathered in large numbers. By a happy dispensation of Providence all arts have more patrons than exponents, and the surplus ratio increases in proportion to the violence of the art. Comparatively few people fight for their own amusement, but many find entertainment in the sight of others fighting. Aged men, professors even, substantiated their claim to an athletic youth or the title of sportsmen by occupying ring-side seats. Such professors as were present all belonged to the faculty of Medicine; for a medical training, by its familiarity with the robust compensations of Nature, inclines a man to heartiness, and association with the grosser manifestations of humanity tempers the fastidiousness of an academic spirit. The bulk of the audience, naturally, was young; an undergraduate audience, tutored in the discipline of silence while men were boxing, and keyed to enthusiasm in the intervals both by the spectacle of violence and by the fact that their own university, in the selected persons of the boxing team, was struggling for mastery over its favourite rival. A few women students were in the audience, some of them adventurous souls determined that no male activity should be beyond their ken, some merely inquisitive.

Mackay and Garry Duncan sat near a corner and watched the welter-weight contest won by Inverdoon.

'One up and two to go,' said Garry. 'How's Peter feeling?'

'Sulky and nervous. He always sulks before a fight and he's generally nervous. And a confounded girl has spoilt his training.'

'A good-looking youngster; fairish? I saw him dining with her a night or two ago.'

'Yes. A chit of a girl, and Peter has wasted a week of training in taking her to lunch, and taking her to tea, and taking her to the theatre; God knows where he hasn't taken her. He's done no work, but that's his own concern. What I'm grumbling at is the training he has lost. If he insists on boxing he might as well box properly.'

The Glasgow middle-weight was patently superior to his opponent and drove him pitilessly round the ring. The fight ended half-way through the second round.

'Level pegging,' said Mackay. 'Come and see Peter before he goes in.'

Peter was lacing his boots. His hands were a trifle unsteady and he looked worried. 'How are things going?' he asked.

'All square. Are you going to win?'

'How the hell do I know? There's a devil of a crowd, isn't there? Any women here?'

'A few. Are you looking for anyone in particular?'

'No. Where's my dressing-gown?'

The fight started slowly as fitted the dignity of heavy-weights. The Glasgow man was bigger and more broadly built than Peter, a stubborn imperturbable fellow, a little slow on his feet; a genial natural fighter who came from the long island of Lewis. His name was MacSween. Peter was clumsy and nervous. He missed badly with his leads and left himself open to shrewd punches at close quarters. Not till the last minute of the round did his nervousness disappear, and then his feet slid swiftly over the ground, his long arm shot out like a piston, like a long bird's beak peck, pecking at his opponent's head, and his right fist followed with a changing balance into the breach.

A roar of applause came out of the darkness on all sides. This was the last fight, the deciding factor, and the minute interval was full of clamour that swelled and shifted and died to a sudden quietness as the two men stepped again to the middle of the ring.

There is a beauty in boxing when men stand upright and step lightly. There is design in their movements, a significance as charged as that of the ballet. Counterpoise follows on poise, defence on attack, reaction on action with a balance, a trim symmetry that quickens as the blood heats and grows and swells into a pounding orchestration of thudding fists and shifting, sidling feet; eyes and heart and every muscle are tuned to it; for an instant there is repose, the sculptured austerity of two figures, motionless, poised like statues on the verge of life; and then their static energy is again released to mingle dynamically in a crescendo of action. The light of arc-lamps, a glowing funnel, is focussed on the struggle, and beyond the light is a deep belt of spectators, of alien minds concentrated on a dramatic spectacle with the perfect attention which casteth out sensibility.

Peter took the fight to whatever quarter of the ring he liked. His brain was clear, set on the solitary issue of defeating the man in front of him, and his body moved swiftly and harmoniously in obedience to the ceaseless orders of his mind. He leaned forward, imminent, like a gannet before it falls, and struck unerringly; his opponent's head went back with a jerk, and Peter's right fist that was held like an archer's hand plucking the taut string followed with the changing balance of his body and drove MacSween to the ropes. He stood to in-fighting and had his turn of rib-hammering. He took a swinging right on the head and jabbed shrewdly at the Glasgow man's jaw. He feinted and hit, side-stepped and hit, guarded and hit again. MacSween, though always losing, fought back indomitably and saved himself from the driving decisive punch that Peter had in his mind.

For two rounds it was like that, but in the forth round Peter was slower. He began to labour and his punches lacked sting. His opponent, bloody and distorted of feature, took heart of grace and fought more cheerfully. Peter was forced to the defensive and lost ground. In the next round, as if refreshed by his earlier visits to earth, MacSween came vigorously to the attack with a swinging right that sent Peter to the floor. They stood toe to toe and hit like blacksmiths, careless of defence. Each in turn drove the other to the ropes, and both were panting and bloody.

Peter's chest rose and fell tumultuously as he lay back in his corner waiting for the sixth round. Lack of training had told and he was nearly beaten. His speed, which should have won the fight, had gone and all he could hope for was a lucky knock-out punch in the opening seconds of the round. He tried desperately for it, and ran instead into a counter that felt like an iron bar thrust out. He fell with a thud and rose again with his head ringing. He tried to get into a clinch, but the Glasgow man uppercut him, and again he fell. He struggled to his knees, waited for the ninth second to be told, and with a final summons to strength rushed MacSween to his corner and hit him twice. But he staggered, being dazed and half-blind, and MacSween stepped sideways, measured his distance, and roundly hit Peter's jaw, a smashing punch that had the weight of his body poised behind it. Peter sprawled brokenly across the ropes, hung there for a moment, and slid beaten to the floor.

He returned unwillingly to semi-consciousness to hear the referee saying 'Eight – Nine – Out!' and became aware, somewhere beyond the roaring tides that had invaded his brain, of a muffled thunder of applause. They were cheering MacSween. A face and two hands came down towards him, and as he sleepily muttered, 'Splendid fellow; congratulations,' he was lifted up to see a dim audience and a vast hall surging like Atlantic waves about him. More cheers sounded maddeningly and someone shook his limp hands. Then a cold wet sponge was thrust into his face, water ran down his chest and down the runnel of his spine, and with a shiver he came to life.

There was a Club supper after the tournament. The broad silver loving-cup which Glasgow had won was passed round full of steaming-hot rum-punch. Peter touched the rim and handed it to MacSween, whose swollen lips drew back with equal haste from the heat of it.

'It was a good fight and it's a pity we can't drink to it more heartily,' he said. 'Man, you must come to the Lews and I'll give you white pot-still whisky that never paid duty to a soul.'

'Come to Orkney and I'll give you the same,' said Peter.

Neither drank much, for both their heads were ringing, but what they did drink excited them so that they began praising the islands of the North and the West, and telling old outrageous stories of battles and Viking raids, of Clontarf and Sweyn Asleifson's Broadcloth Cruise, of forgotten bickerings and bloody fights between the shore and the tide when Norse galleys went harrying their way down the West coast to loot the abbeys of Ireland.

'The Vikings took the best of your women then,' said Peter, his eyes alight.

'And by God, we took the lives of the best of you in exchange,' shouted MacSween in a roaring humour.

'And by God, it was a damned good bargain we both got,' said Peter.

'We'll sing *The Road to the Isles*,' said MacSween, 'for I'll be too drunk to sing if we wait longer. Who'll play for me?'

They crowded to the piano – there were thirty or so at supper – and MacSween started the ranting heather-song that they all knew. The chorus filled the room and echoed down distant corridors; midnight tolled through the second verse and again the chorus beat like a thunder of wings against the walls.

'Again,' someone shouted, and again the challenge rang :

> 'If it's thinking in your inner heart
> The braggart's in my step,
> You've never smelt the tangle of the Isles!'

III

SUMMER went her leisurely way in white and blue, in green and gold, sleeping lightly under the short nights that were scarcely dark before the cocks crew. And daily the disciples of sound commercial wisdom at Inverdoon performed their allotted tasks and kept pace with Time. Conscientiously they filled the unforgiving minute and calculated the probable interest on their investments. Doggedly, in summer weather, they armed themselves for the icy winds of winter; the majority, that is, for a minority of improvident fools slept in the sun.

Peter was too busy to remember winter. He woke on the morning after his fight in a state of physical content, though stiff about the shoulders and tender on his cheekbones. He stood stripped before a mirror. Red bruises mottled his chest and arms and his face was darker than usual, swollen round the mouth and blue under the eyes. But his mind was easy and a feeling of accomplishment filled his body. It was not until he was shaving that he remembered he had been beaten.

Mackay insisted that he should do some work and led him, unwilling, to the Dissecting Room. But Peter sat on his stool and contemplated on the slab in front of him the remains of a dismembered rate-payer without enthusiasm; no ambition urged his scalpel to explore that mine of information. Mackay, on the opposite side of the body, systematically correlated his own observation with the orthodox data supplied by unwieldy text-books. For two hours his versatile, lively brain picked, sorted, docketed and stored essential observation.

And Peter prodded aimlessly the partially displayed zygoma of the deceased citizen and thought: I hit MacSween twice just there in the second round. I'm hanged if I know how he stood up to it. A nice fellow, too. I'd like to see him again. His voice is nearly as rough as his fists – but it served its turn. A song at that stage is just as effective as another drink. He probably saved the Club a couple of bottles. I wonder if I could beat him. The trouble is I don't train properly. Or if I do I go stale and don't enjoy myself. I enjoyed it last night, after the first minute. I hate waiting for a fight. Mackay wouldn't mind, nor Garry. Damn it, he's going away for a week and I meant to borrow some money from him. Mackay's broke. And I must take Pat out some- where. To hell with those lawyers. Talk, talk, talk, and never getting any forrarder. There ought to be nearly a thousand, too, and I haven't a penny. I'll take Pat to lunch on Saturday. Lobster mayonnaise and a bottle of Sauterne; pity the last glass of Sauterne doesn't taste as good as the first. Then we'll go out somewhere. I wish I had a car. I might get one if the lawyers hurry up – a second-hand one. . . . I wonder if hair really grows after death. Either it does or this old fellow hadn't had a shave for a fortnight. I must do some work.

Unfortunately Peter's reluctant attention was no sooner fixed on the ramifications and immediate geography of the lingual artery than Mackay decided to stop working.

'The flower of my knowledge is blooming very prettily in this charnel-house,' he said, 'but it is too tender a growth to force. Come and give it fresh air.'

'Yes, I think we've done enough,' said Peter, aware that he had done nothing.

On the following day he sat and smiled at Patricia as blandly as his ill-treated features would permit. On the table between them lobster peeped pinkly between curling lettuce- leaves at adjacent tomatoes and hard-boiled egg, to blush the more for the scarlet vulgarity of one and shameless white nakedness of the other. A ladylike wine filled their glasses and sunlight crossed the table diagonally, so that one triangle

53

of it lay in the light, one wine-glass gleamed the more, and Patricia's hands were whitely lit.

'I hated it when you fell across the ropes and then slid down to the floor. That was horrible,' she said. 'But I liked the movement, the watching for a chance to hit. And I didn't mind very much when you knocked the Glasgow man down.'

'I don't know why you went. I scarcely ever watch other people fighting. I don't like it. It excites me, and doesn't give me a chance to get rid of the excitement.'

'I went to see you win.'

'And you were disappointed.'

'Yes, in a way. But not so much as Margaret. She thought you deserved to win and was fearfully angry at you for losing.'

'What does it matter who wins? It doesn't make any ultimate difference. I should hate to make a comic spectacle of myself – I'm always frightened of that – by failing absolutely in the first round. But if the fight lasts till I've had my fill of fighting I don't really care much who wins. Though of course so long as I'm in the ring I do all I can to knock the other fellow out.'

'I haven't got so far as that,' said Patricia. 'I don't think I ever shall. I like to win things.'

'You probably will. You're too beautiful to lose.'

Patricia looked at him doubtfully. And Peter was silent as he saw the double meaning of his words. She was beautiful enough to win success where beauty counted, or in events in which the judges might be influenced by beauty. And she was too beautiful for any man willingly to let go. Her look of April would pass, but all summer would come. The lines of her face were lines of beauty, and whatever the changing seasons wrote on them the beauty would remain. Her hands were exquisite, sensitive, mobile, full of strength in miniature; and her arms and shoulders were cast in so true a mould that strength had become delicate without ceasing to be strong. She was too beautiful to lose. And yet it was certain that he would lose her, for the only way to keep her, in a domestic civilization of social and economic sciences, was by marriage; and marriage was over the frontiers of possibility.

It was out of the question because neither had any intention of getting married. Patricia was obviously too young, and she had before her the prospect of too gay and varied years to give them up for any settled estate. She was young enough to prefer gambling to a bank account. She may fall in love with me, Peter thought – it was a warm, pleasant thought – but it will be summer love, not fireside love. He himself had no more wish to get married than to tie himself to a stake in the ground. He had never thought of marriage except as a kind of Sailors' Home to which one was eventually driven by the weakness of age. In any case, it was out of the question economically. Three years at least must elapse before he could graduate and become a potential householder. Meanwhile he was waiting for the residue of his mother's small estate, which would be just sufficient to keep him during that time. After his sister's share had been paid he hoped that there would be nearly a thousand pounds left for him, but he did not believe it. Eight hundred was likely to be a more accurate estimate, for he had already drawn several sums on the account of his expectations. The lawyers, confound them, had refused to give him any more till the final settlement.

In spite of all this Peter felt that he was perilously near to being in love with Patricia.

'In love with'; it was the devil of a phrase. It sounded like being-in-a-well-with. A deep well, out of which it was difficult if not impossible to escape. And yet merely to say 'I love her' had a paternal, almost impersonal ring about it, as if he stood at the top of the well and regarded with placid affection the Patricia who sat – it was a dry well, of course – in beauty at the foot of it; he would let pleasant foods down to her and warn off urchins who might be inclined to drop pebbles; but he would not lower himself on a rotten rope so as to be at the bottom alone with her.

He was *in* love, then. And it was summer love, and he would lose her. Perhaps it was the better for that; love for love's sake – like art – without a thought of the rewards of household comforts and dutifully responsive companionship in the dry years. . . .

'I was speaking as a critic, not as an investor,' Peter said. 'You are beautiful, astonishingly beautiful; but don't be disturbed because I who say so am paying for your lobster.'

'I adore lobster.'

'I'm not a bit jealous.'

'You needn't be. You wouldn't look pretty with lettuce round your neck.'

'And I should dislike being boiled even for your sake.'

'There's no gallantry left in men.'

'Nor generosity in women.'

'Nonsense. Women are more generous than ever.

Only with free samples for advertisement.'

'Aren't you coarse? I love being coarse myself, but I hate it in other people.'

'Like a princess exercising her prerogative. Can I be a faithful retainer? And kiss the princess's hands?'

'They're sticky.'

'The more reason for them to be kissed.'

And Time passed. Greybeard Time wearing a cap and bells, and carrying a pig's bladder instead of a scythe. Patricia was elusive. She would be grave with the gravity of youth and pass suddenly to April gaiety. She was intolerant, harsh in judgment, and stormy in denunciation of Peter's philosophy of life; or lack of philosophy. She did not like many of his friends. She had none of the bargain-hunting chaffering instincts of the coquette. She was young and without patience for bargaining. She had a boyish taste for adventure. She would listen to stories of the War, even ask for stories, and remember them; tales of raiding parties; and scarcely gentler stories of sea-adventures on the Orkney coast, when boats would run for shelter before a rising Atlantic gale; stories of poaching exploits. And had there been histories of antres vast and anthropophagi she might have listened to them too.

Once, when they had taken train to a village some miles from Inverdoon and supped at its shabby small hotel, she insisted on walking across a moor, over a hill, and down through the edge of a forest to a wayside station ten miles away. It was dark before they arrived – summer darkness – and it was by pure luck that they caught a north-bound train which had been delayed for an hour by some mishap farther down the line. They had a carriage to themselves and Peter sat in a corner with Patricia in his arms. Her shoes were dirty and her stockings torn; there was a rent in her skirt that a fence had made; she was tired and perfectly happy.

'I like being at college,' she said. 'There's ever so much more freedom than in living at home. Mother isn't fussy but she wants to know where I've been. And here nobody minds.'

There is almost unlimited freedom in the extra-collegiate life of the Scots universities. There are no residential colleges, no university discipline beyond the lecture-room. Students live in lodgings of their own selection. A quarter had grown up in Inverdoon almost wholly given over to such lodgings, and were it not for three things – the Puritan

inhibitions of the Scot, the respectability of landladies, and
the laws of the land, by which it is illegal to sell food and drink
during the more companionable hours – it might have become an approximately Latin Quarter. But confronted by
the three obstacles it remained unremarkable except in its
freedom from discipline. It was not constructive but it
enjoyed its liberty.

Margaret, the elder sister, was waiting for Patricia with a
certain anxiety. She felt her responsibility, and she regarded
Peter merely as a man; not as the particular man he was in his
relations with Patricia. Had she known him as that she would
have realized that her fears were groundless. In any case they
might have been groundless from her knowledge of Patricia.
But women, knowing themselves first, seldom have complete
faith in their sisters.

'Where have you been?' she asked coldly.

'Everywhere,' said Patricia, taking off her muddy shoes and
finding slippers behind the coal-scuttle. 'I dragged Peter
over rock and fen and moor and torrent till we tripped on a
station. If it hadn't been for a hot-box we should have been
out all night.'

'A what?' asked Margaret.

'A hot-box, wasn't it?' And she explained the arrival of
the fortunately delayed train.

'Well, it's late enough as it is,' said Margaret.

Peter got up out of the arm-chair where he had contentedly
been lying.

'You must have a drink before you go,' Patricia said
hurriedly.

'Do you drink milk?' asked Margaret inhospitably.

'Oh, Meg, you've got a bottle of port! You know you have!'

Margaret thawed. 'It's not very good port,' she said. 'I
was diffident about offering it to you.'

SUMMER WEATHER

'I don't know one kind from another,' said Peter with creditable mendacity; and drank indifferent port, watching Patricia, untidy, sleepy, but still excited, telling her adventures to Margaret; and thought how amazingly good it was to be alive in summer.

AND time passed. The work which he had not done mounted up in front of Peter like an ever-growing rubble-mound, and the date marked for examinations came steadily nearer.

'I dreamt that I was up against a wall I couldn't climb,' he said to Mackay one morning. 'Two or three times I scrambled half-way up, but I'm hanged if I could get to the top.'

'A well-known sex image,' said Mackay. 'Freud recognized it and it is perfectly obvious to me. Your subconscious mind is evidently as lewd as your conscious one.'

'But all the bricks in the wall were books. Gray's *Anatomy*, hundreds of them, and Halliburton, and Ellis, and that red one – what do you call it?'

'That was only because your dream-censor tried to drape the indecency of the image. They're very careful fellows, these dream censors. Mine has a keener eye for impropriety than a Park policeman.'

But the thought of examinations did not worry Peter so much as his increasing poverty. He found one day that he had no money at all. Mackay had none either. Peter asked him.

He replied sadly: 'I spent my last poor shillings at that book-sale the other day,' and looked affectionately at the *Memoirs of Casanova* in nine square volumes and an elaborately bound Greek Testament. He continued to read a novel by Edgar Wallace.

Except that his lodgings were paid for till the end of term and that he had sufficient clothes to wear Peter was in absolute poverty. His lawyers, adding the unnatural caution of their profession to the unreason of ordinary nature, declined to make any more advances; they had decided that a certain allowance was to be made until the estate was wound up and on two occasions they had supplemented the allowance, the second concession being to pay a term's lodgings in advance. Their bowels were now sealed.

Twice Peter had borrowed money from his sister who, with the aid of his father's pension and the farm on which she bred large white pigs and incubated hundreds of Buff Orpington chickens, lived in reasonable comfort. (Actually the farm was Peter's; his sister rented it from him at a nominal figure.) But it was unpleasant to ask a sister for help, and latterly he had collaborated with a pawnbroker in his attempts to solve the problem of living pleasantly.

It is a useful experience. Narrow stairs lead to a series of tiny chambers like confessionals and there an impassive Hebrew – lineal descendant, perhaps, of some Prince of the Captivity – gives in exchange for old clothes or trinkets a little money and teaches the wisdom that distinguishes between an Essential and an Accretion. He teaches humility, for he has power and his client has none. He demonstrates values and gives instruction in the art of impartial criticism. In exchange for a watch and a cigarette case, a microscope and a few gold studs, a bag of golf clubs, a pair of field glasses and some cuff-links, Peter learnt a great deal from the pawnbroker who had erected his confessionals at an easy distance from New College and the Old Frigate. But now he had nothing left with which to pay for more lessons.

He could have endured with equanimity the lack of further instruction but he could not stomach being cut off from Patricia. And to see her in circumstances of ease and comfort needed money.

The problem was difficult. Peter had a minimum of personal possessions. He lived in light marching order, which is convenient until one feels the need of reserve ammunition.

'I would like to help you waste more money if I could,' said Mackay. 'Too many people spend their money profitably and it's pleasant to encourage anyone (except myself) who feels inclined to combat that filthy spirit of commercialism. Is Rabelais no use to you?'

He quoted the Limousin scholar: ' "If by fortune there be rarity or penury of pecune in our marsupies, and that they be exhausted of ferruginean mettal, for the shot we dimit our codices, and oppugnerat our vestiments, whilst we prestolate the coming of the Tabellaries from the Penates and patriotick Lares." '

'I seem to have done all that.'

'Then stay in and work – which costs nothing – and thank God for virtuous poverty.'

Peter looked with sour distaste at a shelf full of ponderous text-books. Those who write on scientific subjects are laborious men who spare no detail and turn lustfully to footnotes, so that their books, even when sold by weight, are costly things. Peter, vainly searching for authors who treated their subject with reasonable felicity, had collected the works of several authorities. On the right of the shelf stood Gray's *Anatomy*, dark and forbidding; next to it a paunchy Cunningham; on its left twin volumes, sinister things in sombre bindings, by Ellis; three volumes of American origin that a publisher's canvasser had sold him; Halliburton's *Physiology*; Somebody Else's *Physiology*, in no material respect different except that it lacked the apostolic authority of Halliburton; Schäfer's *Histology;* and half-a-dozen more.

There was a world of erudition in these volumes. That, however, was not at the moment their primary appeal. They were also the instruments by which a way could be forced through the bolted portals of the Second Professional Examination – portals which had been slammed in Peter's face three months before. That was a sufficiently challenging aspect and yet it failed – at the moment – to engross Peter's attention. It had just occurred to him that this buckram world, these several quarto jemmies, had a market value. Thoughtfully he packed them in a suitcase and carried them to a second-hand book-shop.

'Four pound ten for the lot,' said an unshaven man in shirt-sleeves and spectacles.

'Most of them are as good as new,' said Peter with a certain pathos.

'Five pounds, then. Take it or leave it.'

Peter took it. And the following day he took Patricia to a coast village a dozen miles away where they lay all afternoon on the rocks and threw cherry-stones into green pools that the tide had left.

Time passed, a parti-coloured cap on his grey wind-blown hair, and banged his pig's bladder unnoticed on the face of the cliff.

They had dinner in the small hotel which lived on summer visitors and went back to the shore. The sun was going down behind the land and the sea was a deeper blue, graven with innumerable curving lines. They walked in the shadow of the cliffs over dry shelving rocks and stretches of shingle till they came to a crevice, a cup in the overhanging cliff, that blown sand had half-filled, and sat there watching the tide creep up in lazy waves that looked and hesitated before they fell.

Patricia had been in holiday humour all afternoon. They had made outrageous jokes about nothing, mimicked the familiar tricks of friends, laughed at themselves, played chess with words for queens and bishops, and ideas for common pawns. In the sunlight they had scarcely touched hands, and sentiment had flown from their laughter with the nervous wings of a frightened mallard. But evening fetched quietness.

The outermost strip of sea still glittered in the sun with a dying light. Patricia caught her breath in sudden response to it. The wondering sadness of childhood came to her like a quick pallor. The sadness of youth took her, the swift sadness of the beauty of youth. . . . Youth, that is a passing bloom; and growth is rubbing off the bloom, careless what lies beneath; sometimes it is ingrained, defying wind and weather, and sometimes it is the wearer's only grace. Youth, that is like a rainbow in the sky of Time, a rose, a moth that comes into the moonlight, the flame on Time's altar that lights for a minute the grey incense-smoke and dies. Youth that is a banner on the walls of a town that must be taken; the white topsail of a ship sailing to the weedy bed of lost galleons and forgotten triremes; the song that every man sings and the tune that no man remembers.

Peter saw it and could say nothing. This was summer love, living in the eye, and doubly precious for its frail habitation and certainty only of defeat. But he yearned for the beauty of her sadness as he had never yearned for her beauty laughing.

Patricia recognized it, the sadness of youth that cannot endure, and cried suddenly – the cry a dozen years younger than Time – 'Why can't we be like this always? To-day has been so lovely. If it hadn't been so lovely I wouldn't grumble at it going. Peter, can't you put a stick under the sun, even now, and keep it from going down?'

'I wouldn't, even if I could,' he answered roughly.

Puzzled by his voice, by roughness following a jest, she asked him why.

'Because I can't stand this any longer. Because I love you.

Because this is comedy – the best comedy in the world, too good to spoil – and it couldn't remain comedy much longer.'

'But I thought – oh, I don't know what I thought. I suppose I really didn't think at all. I was too happy to bother about thinking.'

'I'm hopeless, Pat. A landless man. But if this had been a few hundred years ago I should have picked you up and thrown you into a boat without worrying about that and – and followed the sun.'

'And I should have hated you.'

'I know.'

For a little they spoke nothing and then Patricia said, ill at ease, 'Peter, you understand, don't you? I love being with you but I don't want anyone to love me – like that – for years yet.'

'I know,' Peter said again, 'and I'm angry at myself for forgetting that I knew. Let's be happy again. Let me make hopeless love cheerfully – there's the new moon.'

Patricia laughed. The rebel was gay again, reckless of a losing battle.

'I don't believe you could make love properly,' she said.

'I could. Your eyebrows are twin crescents whose sharp horns pierce my heart. Your mouth is a pair of roses – '

'Oh!' she protested.

'A large bowl of roses now. Your eyes are gleaming quartz – '

'You're thinking about beer again.

'Quartz hewn from an unusually stony quarry, you mocker. Your hair is a wood at night in whose shades my lost heart wanders.'

'Tell it to look for the parting and find its way out.

'It won't listen to what I say.'

'Will it listen to me?'

'It's pricking up its ears already.'

'Then tell Peter, you silly heart, that I want him to stop talking nonsense and kiss me.'

It is likely that Time passed again – he circles the world with indecent haste for so old a traveller – but the fool's bells may have been muffled, for he passed unheard.

But on the following morning his pig's bladder hit Peter's bedroom door with a resounding bang, and Peter woke to a sudden realization that only ten days separated him from the hours of examination. He sat in a cold bath and soaped himself thoughtfully. I'll have to do a devil of a lot of work, he thought; and shivered slightly. The memory of an empty bookshelf embarrassed him, but he comforted himself by deciding that he and Mackay could work a double shift with the latter's books. I'll go to bed with Halliburton while he sits up with Gray, he thought, and dried himself more cheerfully.

There are those who study systematically throughout a term, and there are others who habitually leave an accumulation of work to be dealt with in a burst of fierce energy at its latter end. These incline to trust luck rather than system, and a scheme for abetting luck was long since elaborated.

An examination, it is clear, is a kind of race-meeting. On every subject it is possible to ask, one may say for convenience, a thousand questions. But to prepare in advance a thousand answers takes a long time, and those who have left for preparation only a few weeks – or worse, a few days – must pick and choose. They must back their fancy out of the huge field of possible starters. And as every professor has favourite topics – professors alone of mankind successfully defy Time and so their whims have a chance to become known – so there are certain favourites in the field. Some questions even attain a definite periodicity in their successive appearances. And while mathematically-minded students compile lists of probable starters, those with a flair for prophecy stake their chances of success on concentrated study of what they fancy to be certain winners.

Mackay had two such lists, one with a hundred possible questions in Anatomy, the other with a less number in Physiology, which is a more compact subject. Forty of the Anatomy questions and fifteen of those in Physiology were marked with crosses to signify that since the lists had been made up the odds on these had shortened. And Peter set to work, with borrowed books, to study answers to the forty and fifteen.

They were cloistral, uncoloured days that followed. All outside interests were banished. The hospital was neglected. Grimly Peter read from such books as Mackay was not using and certified the information gained on the white bones of a disarticulated skeleton. Mackay was generous in the distribution of his limited library and was as helpful as his slightly more ample knowledge permitted. He had wasted almost as much time on golf as Peter had on Patricia.

He only once questioned Peter about the girl.

'Is she interesting?' he asked one evening.

'Very,' Peter replied. 'How's the new mashie behaving?'

And Mackay, answering Peter's question as technically as the natural warmth engendered by a successful round permitted, had left the matter of Patricia there. Girls or golf, he thought philosophically; we must amuse ourselves somehow; our enthusiasms are all our own, perhaps the only things in the world we definitely possess. There was not a little similarity between girls and golf, he considered. The game – either of the games – is always in its essentials the same, but at every moment there are the doubts, the technical problems, the discussion as to how such and such a shot should be played, the competition, and the constantly arising unforeseen difficulties necessary to maintain the player's interest. You drove off from the tee. That was, as it were, meeting the girl. Some people, of course, carried the green in one; they were the cave men, the parish bull wooers. Others got into the rough immediately. They were the majority. Then there were men who specialized in a sound second shot; practical lovers who followed up an introduction with an invitation to dinner. And men who were useful with a niblick, men who got easily out of any kind of a lie; successful co-respondents, evaders of reputed paternity, free lances who never paid alimony or damages. And the good putters, the men who could send the ball pin-high from the edge of the green, were the devils on a stair, fellows who could land an heiress while the others were drinking thin claret-cup and wondering where the girl had hidden herself. Oh, both were good games if you knew the difference between a mid-iron and a brassie and could use either when the occasion arose; gentle flattery or a good sound smack.

Mackay was pleased with his analogy and made a mental note of it to tell Garry Duncan; who subsequently improved it in several particulars.

Sometimes Peter and Mackay would work together, questioning and cross-questioning each other. Occasionally, about bed-time, Garry would come in and drink a bottle of beer with them, and tell a bawdy story or two to mix with their savourless Anatomy. The thought of the rapidly approaching Long Vacation cheered them.

The Ides came, a day whose serene sky mocked blandly the idea of writing dull examination stuff. The broad stone stairway leading to the Examination Hall was crowded, full of anxious echoes and valiant protestations of unconcern.

Peter, moody and liverish, his head full of half-digested and ill-arranged knowledge, stood outside and grumbled.

'It's so damned childish,' he said. 'God Almighty, I'm twenty-four years old. Half the men here are the same. And we have to sit and write footling papers like schoolboys.'

'It's no more childish than going to somebody else's war because you were told to,' answered Mackay placidly.

'I wasn't told to, damn it. I went of my own accord. And so did you.'

'Then we were idiots, and idiocy's worse than childishness. Come on, and pray God you'll grow up to be a good sane man and an elder of the Kirk some day.'

Peter looked at his question paper with a blank feeling of despair. He read these questions:

(1) Describe the structure, fœtal growth, and contiguous relations of the œsophagus.
(2) Describe the prostate gland and the prostatic part of the urethra, including their minute structure.
(3) Describe the sterno-cleido-mastoid muscle, its attachments, relations, and actions.
(4) Describe the upper extremity of the tibia, including its ligamentous attachments and development.
(5) Describe the ciliary arteries and nerves, giving their origin, course, and distribution.

Number 2 was one of the select forty. Number 3 was in the hundred. With the others he had only a nodding acquaintance.

All around him men were setting to work, spreading their information in orderly and fair array. A few looked objectionably confident. Damn them for lousy windsuckers, Peter thought. Most of the examinees seemed impassive but competent. A few stretched legs beneath their tables, dug hands in pockets, and yawned dismally to the Gothic roof. Peter caught the eye of such a one and grinned in the sympathy of perfect comprehension. 'Christ,' he muttered, 'I must put up some sort of a show.' He started to answer question Number 2.

He wrote rapidly and well for thirty minutes, and for twenty minutes less rapidly and with diminishing authority on the third question. Then he considered the roof again, and turning in his chair dwelt on the huge multi-coloured arch of light that the great East Window made. The hall looked like a cross between a cathedral and a schoolroom. Lozenges of amber light, saints in blue mantles and knights in silver mail; a flush of gules; and the damned scratching of pens.

Peter's eyes went back to the roof and he repeated under his breath : 'Describe the structure, fœtal growth, and contiguous relations of the œsophagus.'

How the devil, he wondered, did œsophaguses grow? It ought to be something like the growth of asparagus, but I suppose it can't be. Saturday, Sunday, Monday. . . . I'll get the Friday boat to Orkney. Must write to-morrow and say I'm coming. I'm tired of Inverdoon. Pat's leaving to-morrow, anyway; going to stay with an uncle home on leave. She and her mother and her sister, and his wife and his two children. How many contiguous relations has my œsophagus got? There must be dozens. Relations are always a curse – they've made many a man slit his œsophagus before now. 'His throat was cut from ear to ear.' Damned good cut, too. What was that thing:

> 'Yesterday he gripped her tight
> And cut her throat – and serve her right!'

SUMMER WEATHER

Nora Criona. Woman who was always asking questions and trying to make her husband happy. There are people like that. Petticoat tyrants; altruistic tape-worms; women are possessive because they know they're so feeble alone. It's only when they're young that they're not frightened to stand by themselves. Like Pat. O God. And if it hadn't been for the War I should never have met her. I should have graduated and settled down to something before this. The War gave us an extra span of youth anyway. It had to give us something in return. And a taste for drink too, I suppose. The Rum War. What was Garry's story the other night about the woman who didn't drink? But it turned out to be something else that she didn't do. Good old Garry. Some people tell smutty stories for the smut, others for the laughter in them. And there's a lot of good fun in smut. Bodily functions. They're so ridiculous, looked at objectively. Like dogs, pathetic and straining. And yet people who strain at a gnat of bawdiness will swallow a whole camel-load of sex novels. Swallow them like oysters. They stick in my throat. God, how did my fœtal œsophagus grow? . . .

ORKNEY

I

MARTIN FLETT, Peter's sister, stood at the end of Kirkwall Pier watching the lights, white on top, red and green below, of the ship that had just turned out of the String and was labouring through the windy bay. It was past midnight, but in summer there is scarcely any darkness in Orkney. A shadow comes over the islands for an hour or two, and passes to leave a bare sky for dawn to paint.

The bay was greyish-white with breaking waves and the lights of the ship, dim in the half-dark, rose and fell. The wind played boisterous tricks with Martin's skirts, and the three Cocker spaniels at her feet crouched together for warmth.

A fat red man, Geordie Harcus the cattle dealer, came up the Pier leaning against the wind and holding a buttonless mackintosh about him.

'It's breezy,' he roared.

'Very,' shouted Martin.

'The boat'll no' be alongside for a quarter of an 'oor yet. We might as well bide in the shelter here till she comes. You'll be waiting for Peter, likely?'

'Yes. Are you meeting friends?'

'Na, na. It's a bull that I'm expecting. I doubt there'll be a few people sick aboard that ship, the way she's tossing. Has Peter gotten through all his examinations?'

'I don't think so. He said nothing about them in his last letter.'

'Ah weel. There's time enough for that. The warld's nae comin' to an end for a peerie[1] while yet.'

---

[1] peerie] little.

Geordie lit his pipe, cunningly sheltering the match in a huge hand, grunted, and blew a cloud of smoke that instantly vanished on the wind.

'Have ye any young pigs?' he asked.

'There are eight that will be ready next week. But they're good ones, out of the young sow I bought at the Highland Show last year, and I want more than you gave me for the last lot.'

'Weel, maybe you'll get what you're seeking if they're warth it. I'll be roond tae see them one of these days.'

Slowly the ship drew nearer, and as she came alongside unhappy, grey-faced passengers gathered on deck, eager to be ashore. Peter, a pipe in his mouth and a suitcase in either hand, came down the gangway.

'Hullo, White-maa,' Martin greeted him. 'Had a good crossing?'

'Splendid. How are you? And the dogs? And the pigs?'

'All flourishing. But come home before you start talking. I've been waiting here for hours.'

He put his suitcases and the three dogs into the dickey of Martin's small car and climbed in beside her. Ottergill, the farm, was six miles away on the north shore of Scapa Flow. During the War its familiar neighbours had been the ships of the Grand Fleet, when they came back to rest and refit at the gateway of the North Sea. Now it looked out at a few lonely masts, an upturned whale-like ship's side, a battle-cruiser's funnels, that stood sullenly in the midst of the waters – the grave-stones of the German Fleet that had sunk itself there.

Ottergill, the house, was a square, unpretentious, two-storeyed building that stood between a low cliff, brown with heather, and a burn that had cut its way deeply through a green meadow. A small boat-house stood at the end of the

garden dyke, from which a stone jetty ran into the sea. A
great living-room made the front half of the house. Two
projecting windows, wide and high, looked out on to the
Flow, and between them there was a double-arched door
opening into a porch, walled and squat. At either end of the
room there was a huge open hearth, in one of which a peat-
fire blazed redly. Leather arm-chairs, battered and comfortable, stood before it and at the other end of the room a
couple of high, straw-backed Orkney chairs. The floor was
black stone flags, half-covered with rough, brightly-coloured,
straw matting. Half-a-dozen pictures of ships hung high up
on the half-panelled walls. A black oak table stood in the
centre of the floor, and filling the middle third of the wall
behind it there was an open bookcase loosely packed with a
rich and shabby collection of quaintly varied literature.

Mariners' Guides and Tide Tables, Treatises on Naviga-
tions and the Laws of Cyclones jostled late Victorian poetry;
there was a surprising representation of the literary Nineties,
the monument to an enthusiasm of the late Mrs. Flett. On
one shelf there were volumes of Veterinary Science and on
another a brown leather Orkneyinga Saga, different editions of
the Iceland and Norway sagas, collections of Norse traditions
and superstitions, and records of the rentals of Orkney
parishes; a history of the Stewart earls in Orkney. Scott,
Smollett and Fielding made notable the curious absence of
Dickens, and Charles Lever lived jauntily in company with
Miss Austen. There was a mass of unclassifiable modern
fiction. John Buchan's *History of the War* came next to a
green *Encyclopaedia of British Birds*. There were complete
collections of Conrad and Kipling, Stevenson and Herman
Melville; an edition of Hakluyt's *Voyages*; *Tess of the d'Urber-
villes*, very lonely; the story of Scott's last expedition; heavy
histories of Arctic exploration rubbed cold shoulders with

accounts of adventure in Central Africa. Beside two black
Family Bibles stood in sound order, but all manner of editions,
the English dramatists from Marlowe to the Restoration.
These were of Martin's buying. She read them, but never
discussed them. Her other loves were detective stories and
works on animal hygiene. The only books on these catholic
shelves which looked new and untouched were half-a-
dozen Tolstoys and Turgenievs, the gratefully acknowledged
gift of a school-friend of Martin's.

It was not a gourmet's collection. There was nothing in it
more exotic than Dowson. But there was sound fare in
abundance, salted down with technical dogmas of the sea
and the soil, and inspired with a host of travellers' tales.

Peter and Martin sat in front of the fire, Peter nursing a
blue and white quart-mug of home-brewed ale.

'Did you get through your examinations, by the way?'
Martin asked.

'No,' he said, and looked up grinning, so that the white
line of his moustache came out of the shadow that the covered
lamp made.

'You're a fool, White-maa,' said Martin in a tone of placid
conviction.

A white-maa is a herring-gull, the fierce yellow-beaked
thief that steals eggs and chickens wherever it may, un-
frightened even by the farmyard cat. Peter had got the nick-
name when a small boy from old Tam of Eastabist, and it had
stuck to him closely enough in the parish where he was born.

He had been stealing new-made cheese one day, soft
creamy stuff just pressed into its mould. It had stood on a
table at the back-house door, unwatched, and Peter, being
eight or nine years old, had thieved greedily, like Gideon's
people before the Midianites thrusting his mouth into the
basin and eating what he might. Bending down, his out-

flung little stern had presented too good a mark for Peerie John, the herd laddie, to miss with the stone which he very expertly and promptly threw. Stung to the consciousness that an enemy was near Peter had sprung up and turned with a face well smeared in curds.

'Be God,' Tam of Eastabist said – he happened to be passing, as he was always passing if there was anything to see – 'Be God, he stood there, his mou' all white wi' cruds, just as like a white-maa as ye could think, and be God he lightit on Peerie John like a white-maa too, and catched him a clout on the e'e that laid him square on his backside. And Peerie John got up and shaft his naves at him, but be God, Peter cam' doon on him like a white-maa wance again, peck, peckin' awa', and doon Peerie John fell for the second time. And whan he got up that time he roared and he grat, and he took for hame as though the Deevil was after him. Ay, ye may call him Peter, but it's mair like a white-maa he was than the favourite apostle.'

So White-maa Peter had remained. And had Tam of Eastabist seen him fighting in a ring, more scientifically than of old, he might still have imagined something of the white-maa in his poise and stoop to hit, and perhaps in the clipped yellow moustache over his out-thrust jaw.

'You know you're a fool,' Martin repeated. 'But I suppose it can't be helped. What are you going to do to-morrow?'

'Fish, if the weather's decent,' replied Peter. 'Can I have the car?'

The next day, however, was all sun and wind. The half-gale of the night before had moderated to a hard sailing breeze. Thin rags of cloud flew over a sapphire sky and their torn shadows raced the leaping surface of the sea. The islands in the Flow were emerald green, and the vast bulk of Hoy, the barrier between Scapa Flow and the Pentland Firth stood proudly in green and chocolate, faced with shining grey cliffs, and flagged at the round summit of Ward Hill with a long pennant of cloud. The lighthouse on Graemsay was a spire of dazzling white.

Peter took a bannock of bread, a piece of cheese, and a bottle of home-brewed ale, and went sailing. He had a twelve-foot centre-board dinghy, yawl-shaped, decked in for two feet forward and aft, that sailed like a witch.

With double reefs in he crossed to the Hoy shore, turned south and east and sailed round the island of Cava, then north and east to beat up into Scapa Bay. All day he sailed alone, running before the wind with the seas curling faster and faster behind him, snarling softly; sailing with the wind squarely on his beam, while the tiller tugged at his arm like a two-year old stirk on the end of a rope, and the water came creaming over the lee gun'le and tore viciously past; beating to windward, smashing savagely through the short, steep waves that threw their white crests in his face. All day he sailed, and the wind that was full of sun and sea-salt beat on him and shouted in his ears and flung every thought out of his heart except vivid, sensuous recognition of stormy blues and greens, the buffeting of the ceaseless waves, the kicking tiller, the shaking leach of the sail, the greedy, joyous, pagan sea.

Somewhere, out of sight and farther still out of mind, there were men and cities. But the sea was greater than they. The sea was a turbulent, roaring mother-goddess who took your heart and hands and would take your life if she could. The sea was the mother and mistress of earth. Her breasts were mountainous, storm-driven oceans and her arms were vast Atlantics. The Pacific in a windless calm was her navel. Her hands had plucked up continents and thrown them into the sun to dry, so that the creatures she had spawned might grow and multiply and give their first fruits, their eldest sons and their tallest trees, back to her; back to the greedy mistress splendid in green and white, back to the omniscient mother, soft and benign in good-omen blue, of the world of men. And out of all the races of men that grew from her slime and pregnant ooze she had taken for her own, her sons and lovers, the Norsemen who in triumph harried for a season their comfortable brothers on land, and then went back to the brine-blood of her who had made them, leaving as their monuments the ribs of a buried ship and the promise that the men of their chosen islands, from Yell to the Scillies, should dare the wrath of their mother and the jealousy of their great mistress, while other breeds toiled on bare hillsides or slept in their fat valleys.

You do not ask for much more when the sea has given you herself for a day. You are at once – a strange enough state – full of new life and content. You have lain in love on the breast of the waters and battled fiercely and wantonly with them, and though old powers are exhausted you rise strong with a new might. And so when White-maa at last beached his boat and stepped out on to the shingle, he staggered, and yet felt full of a joyous strength.

For days he lived paganly under the sky. The sea was his and the islands, no part of which was beyond the sound of the sea, were his by birth. He walked for miles on their narrow roads and climbed their low heathery hills. He stood gravely by dark ploughlands and talked with the slow-spoken sure-thinking farmers, hearing of the wisdom of soil and season, the pest of rain and the benison of sun, the comely growth of animals. He laughed full-heartedly at ploughmen's jests and answered their women's jibes with tinker's wit. He fished in the two big lochs of the island, patiently and watch-fully throwing his flies on their shallow waters and taking

78

home at night perhaps a dozen trout that had fought gamely and adeptly their enemies of gut and line and springing rod. Body and soul he lived in the islands, paganly and fully.

And then a part of his interest – a small part, a wayward springing – began to find a narrower focus.

On the hill behind Ottergill stood the farm of Redland. The house, at first a mere butt-and-ben, had been pushed out at either end and on one side a second storey had been built, so that it had a lop-sided casual appearance. But the steadings behind it were large and well-constructed. The Sabistons of Redland were newcomers to those parts. The grandfather of the present farmer, John Sabiston, had bought the place, coming from an inland parish. And, as often happens with a sturdy growth that is transplanted to new ground, they had flourished exceedingly. The farm was prosperous and there was an air of riotous fertility about it.

Their crops grew high, and if there were weeds as well they were hidden by the surrounding riches. Their sheep invariably bore twin lambs at a birth, and sometimes three. There was an abundance of milking cattle, so that the midden in winter was as big as a cottage, and in summer the calves' park was full. The mares seemed always to have foals at their feet, and even the old sheep dog that was grey with years had just got their young brown bitch with pups. John Sabiston himself and Maria his wife had not been idle. They had nine children, or perhaps ten. It was difficult to tell, for neighbours' children constantly ran about the house, getting fed, scolded, and sometimes even put to bed along with the true progeny of the place. The eldest daughter was twenty and the youngest boy was two. The whole farm was prolific and everything on it full of sap. The milk bore deeper cream, the hens laid extravagantly large eggs, young turkeys stretched ungainly necks in every corner, and all the cats in the byre had kittens every third month.

John Sabiston was a tall, fair-skinned man with a short yellow beard. His wife had raven-black hair and eyes as dark, a handsome, good-humoured, laughing, lazy woman. It is said that there was a Spanish ship of the Great Armada wrecked somewhere in Orkney, and such men as were saved married into the islands. And it is true that here and there you find to-day men and women with a dark Spaniard's look and children like those Murillo painted. Maria Sabiston was such, and so was Norna, her eldest daughter.

Perhaps she should have been fair with that name, but she was called after a steel-masted barque on which an uncle had served his apprenticeship, so it did not matter much. She was a handsome, slim-built girl, quick-tempered, as dark as her mother, red-lipped and rather proud. She had gone to school in Kirkwall till she was seventeen and somehow had sloughed most of her Orkney accent. People said that she was 'maist aaful bigsy,' conceited, that is.

Peter had known the family all his life and was as much at home in Redland as he was in Ottergill. But he had never given much thought to the girls till one night he went home and found Norna sitting with his sister. They were laughing over something when he opened the door, and stopped suddenly as he went in. In a little while Norna stood up to go and Peter, in the habit of the country, walked home with her.

They spoke little at first.

Norna said, 'Don't you forget all your old friends, White-maa, when you're away so long?'

'No, not a bit,' Peter answered.

Norna said slowly, 'When I was at the Highland Show in Inverness last year with Martin, I thought that I would soon forget Orkney if I lived always among so many people.'

'Rot,' said Peter. 'I haven't been so happy as I am now for God knows how long.' And felt no liar's twinge in his conscience.

They came to the dyke running from the house of Redland and Norna leaned against it, looking at the half-moon that slid out of a black cloud to go behind a grey one.

'It's fine to come back here for a holiday,' she said, 'but would you like to live here always, and never go farther away than Kirkwall or Stromness?'

Peter laughed, 'You might do worse.'

'Martin took me up to your room to see the new wall-paper. But she didn't say anything about the new photograph you have on your mantelpiece.'

Peter, a little uncomfortably, said, ' Oh, that's a girl I know – a friend of mine – in Inverdoon.'

'She's pretty. Awfully pretty.' And Norna looked at Peter, and glanced at the cloudy moon, and stared at the ground.

'I must go in now,' she said.

Peter, with the thought of Patricia dragged suddenly into the forefront of his brain, said stupidly, ' Well, good-night, Norna. I'll see you to-morrow probably;' and went home.

The following morning a letter came to him from Patricia. He read, on the second page: 'I am not going back to Inverdoon. Mother and I are going to spend the winter with my uncle in Lahore. In a way I am sorry that I shan't be back – Peter, you know that, don't you? – but the thought of seeing India is wonderful. I am so excited–though we aren't sailing till October–that I can hardly write. I read nothing but guide-books. Mother is already bothering about clothes and things, but all I can think of is Delhi and Agra – the Taj Mahal by moonlight – and Benares. Palms and temples. And Sikhs and Gurkhas and Rajputs. . . .'

Peter put the letter in his pocket and coldly confronted a

sense of loss. It was like an amputation. But the operation
had been done under the anaesthetic of an environment
remote from that in which he had known Patricia, and the
pain of it was only dimly, half-consciously felt. Aimlessly
he walked up and down and stopped in front of the
book-case. There was a Tavernier's *Travels in India* somewhere. He pulled it out and it opened at a description of
jugglers.

Tavernier had seen the mango trick done, a tree growing
miraculously out of an empty pot. He turned the pages and
read a description of the Peacock Throne. Tavernier, the
little jeweller, had gone down on his knees and counted the
emeralds in it. Most of them had been flawed. Things
always were. And Patricia, for all her enthusiasm, would
likely spend most of her time dancing and riding and playing
tennis with senior subalterns and junior captains. Perhaps
it did not matter much, anyway.

Peter went fishing, and when his line screeched out after
a trout that ran here and there, leapt desperately out of the
water and sulked at the bottom, he forgot all about India,
and the thought of Patricia was savagely repressed.

That evening he walked over to Redland. There was a
stir of interest behind the house. A neighbour's cow had
been brought to the Redland bull, and the bull was unac-
countably coy. The cow slavered and the bull looked about
him with moody eyes.

'He's waiting for the parson to come,' Peter suggested.

In the byre two of the girls and the hired man were milking.
The jets of milk made an empty tin reverberate and splashed
rhythmically into half-full ones. There was a warm, comfortable smell in the place, though it was none too clean under-
foot. Peter looked in at the door and Jean, a fair, lazy, good-
tempered girl, greeted him cheerfully. Elsie, a younger sister,

a mischief-making chit of fifteen whose black hair grew down in a widow's peak, called to him, 'Have you seen Norna, White-maa?'

'No,' he said. 'Why?'

'She saw you coming and ran to put on her best clothes.'

'She's going to take a clucking hen up the hill to old Becky, and she's gone to dress herself,' Jean explained.

'She wouldn't put on yellow silk stockings for old Becky to see,' said Elsie sniggering. 'She thought maybe you'd be going with her, White-maa.'

'And why shouldn't I?' he asked.

'What would all your lasses in Inverdoon say if they saw you? How many girls have you?'

Country humour is limited in its application and ideas. Peter answered the chit good-naturedly, 'Six and a half. Will you make it up to seven?'

'Yes, if you'll take me to the market next week,' she answered promptly. 'There's Norna looking for you.'

'She's aa'ful flash aboot the legs,' said Tom, the hired man, in a sepulchral voice from behind a cow's tail.

Norna, with an indignant-looking hen tied up in a basket, said, 'I'm going up the hill to Becky Bews'.'

'I'll come with you,' Peter replied.

But as they turned to go there came a deep shout, 'Hey, White-maa, you that's a doctor. Come and see what you think o' this.' And John Sabiston led into the yard a foal badly cut across its chest.

'He's coming up to Becky's with me,' Norna said.

'Hoot, lass, you ken the way ower weel yourself,' John answered unsympathetically. 'Come and look at this, White-maa.'

Peter grinned and said, 'Wait a minute, Norna.'

But Norna replied coolly, 'It doesn't matter. I can go myself.'

'I'll come up later and walk back with you,' Peter said, and went to look at the foal which had got caught in barbed wire. His medical training, the precise nature of which was very dimly realized in the countryside, had given him a spurious reputation as a horse-leech which he thoroughly enjoyed. His name had been stabilized by successfully setting a dog's leg the previous Christmas.

The wounded foal was attended to and then Peter and John Sabiston leant against the peat-stack and talked of crops and cattle and of signs and wonders that occur in both. John told stories of prodigious injuries sustained by horses long dead, and detailed their treatment and miraculous cure. Peter, lying cheerfully, drew on his scant hospital experience to cap John's stories with anecdotes still more gory of human excursions to the edge of death that were spoilt by modern science.

Still talking – and now it was of leech craft in olden times – they went into the wide farm kitchen and sat one on each side of the open hearth.

Maria, John's wife, was cutting rhubarb for jam on a big deal table and scolding ineffectively first one child and then another. The kitchen seemed full of children. They appeared never to go to bed, and work of some kind always went on, cheerfully, unmethodically, in a perpetual muddle which disturbed no one. A small boy wound up a racketty gramophone that played a lugubrious hymn.

'Dareen on't,' cried Maria wrathfully, 'does thoo think it's the Sabbath? Stop that noise, I say!'

The small boy changed the record for a worse one out of which came a screeching strathspey.

The girls had come in from milking and Jean was hearing

a younger sister's lessons. In a dairy adjoining the kitchen Tom, the hired man, turned a milk-separator that hummed like a swarm of bees.

And through all the din John Sabiston's voice boomed undismayed and Peter, chuckling inwardly at the hubbub, answered as best he could. Elsie brought them mugs of ale and whispered to Peter that she thought he had meant to go up the hill for Norna.

Peter's memory awoke with an uncomfortable jerk. He hadn't given a thought to Norna. He was wondering whether it was too late to go even then, when the door opened and she came in.

She was bare-headed. In the soft light of the hanging lamp her complexion was like roses and ivory under the intense darkness of her hair. She was aloof, self-possessed, and moved with untroubled dignity through the disturbance of the kitchen loud with household noises, lit with yellow lamplight that faded before the crimson of the open hearth, and scented with peat-smoke.

Peter said, 'I was just going up to meet you, Norna.'

'Were you?' she said. 'What a pity you were late.'

It was impossible to attempt apologies or explanations in an atmosphere that stalked and chuckled past petty misunderstandings as a turkey-cock might pass a sparrow. There was an indefatigable vitality in the kitchen of Redland. It was so near the earth that the tireless vigour of the earth was in it, good-humoured unconscious vigour that never considered or doubted its qualities. And there was abundant beauty in its vitality. John Sabiston, fair-bearded, with grey eyes looking out from under jutting yellow eyebrows, and Maria his wife, dark and ivory, untidy, laughing like a Spanish gipsy; the children, half of them fair, with delicate sun-tanned complexions and clean-cut features, the others black

85

and ruddy like the boys Murillo painted; and Norna, slender and proud, flying southern colours of passion over a white tower of the north.

John Sabiston was telling a story of Mansie Harra who lived (this was in the time of his father) in the dirtiest house in the parish. His slattern of a wife could never sell her butter for more than fourpence a pound, while neighbour women were getting fivepence or even sixpence. She would go straight from washing a floor or working in a byre to thump the churn, and her clothes, contaminated by earlier labours, invariably spoiled the butter. Mansie lost all patience. 'Woman,' he said one day when she was going to make butter, 'Woman, thoo'll strip to thee skin afore thoo touches the kern.' And strip she did, and thumped the milk to butter in the old-fashioned churn, and turned it out into a shallow pan to wash it. She set the pan on a stool, and then the cat ran between her feet and tripped her.

'Doon she sat,' said John, 'her bare backside in the butter, and "God," says Mansie, "thoo've done it again, wife. That's fowerpenny butter still!"'

It was not the first time that Peter had heard the story, but he laughed robustly; and Maria, who must have heard it twenty times for every once that Peter had, laughed longer than he. The elder girls, for politeness has corrupted even the country places, pretended to hear little of such rude pleasantry. Norna shortly afterwards went to bed. And Peter went home.

II

S PREADING like a leaf across the sea a breeze blew out of the growing calmness of evening and filled, for a minute, the idle sail. With a little rushing noise the boat gathered way and moved through the sleepy water. The wind passed, the sail hung empty again, and the boom slid despondently inboard. Peter swore softly.

Norna, sitting on a rug in the bottom of the boat, looked out contentedly at the glassy surface of the bay, its green transparency, and inshore the shallows that mirrored cliffs and brown hills.

'The devil take this calm,' said Peter.

'Whistle for a wind,' answered Norna lightly. 'Stick a knife in the mast. Or say a Runic charm. It doesn't matter whether it works or not, does it?'

Peter grumbled again, glaring at the sinking sun which had swallowed all the wind in his descent. He had gone sailing and he wanted to continue sailing. Norna had gone sailing too, but wind was not essential to her enjoyment.

Peter had taken her partly because of a guilty feeling that he had disappointed her in the promised rendezvous at old Becky's, and partly out of a faint stirring of desire to talk to her, to see her again in circumstances remote from alien interference. A semi-conscious curiosity was moving in his blood, as at something newly seen that was familiar enough before; a tree in a wood suddenly made distinct from its fellows by last spring's growth. But his memory was still irritated by thoughts of Patricia and his curiosity in Norna was half-unwilling. While they were sailing, with the breeze coming fresh and strong, he had paid little attention to her, becoming more intent on the boat than the girl, and now with the wind gone he was ill-tempered.

Norna had accepted the invitation without enthusiasm, for Peter's offence still rankled, and during most of the afternoon she had been silent. But when the evening calm fell she threw a rug on to the bottom of the boat and sat there, close to Peter's feet.

'White-maa,' she said, 'do you remember, years and years ago, getting lost with me on the hills when the mist came down?'

'Not particularly,' Peter answered.

'You were bad-tempered and rude even then.'

'I'm sorry,' he said, laughing, and put his hand lightly on her shoulder. Confound it, he thought, I spend my whole time telling her I'm sorry about something.

Norna moved a little closer. 'Your hands are brown again,' she said, 'they were white when first you came.'

'Damn this boom,' said Peter as it swung idly inwards. He let go the sheet and pushed it far out over the side.

'What are you angry about? It's a beautiful evening.'

'You're quite happy, are you?'

'Almost. We're seldom quite happy, are we?'

The platitude passed unnoticed, for the open sky is tolerant of what beauty says or does.

'What do you need to complete your happiness then?'

'Why should I tell you?' Norna answered.

'Give me three guesses.'

'Well. Only three.'

'You're probably hungry,' Peter suggested.

'I'm not. And I'm not thirsty, so that saves you a guess.'

'Then you've got cramp in your legs through sitting like that.'

'Do you want me to move?'

'No, stay where you are. I like to look at your hair. It's lovely.'

88

She turned half-round and said gravely and a little wistfully, 'Do you think so, White-maa?'

'Yes,' he answered; and then, looking from the raven's wing lustre of her hair to the white sail, 'I wish a breeze of wind would come along.'

'Damn the wind,' said Norna inexplicably; and sitting up she turned round, knelt, and faced him.

'You have still one guess,' she said bravely.

She looked at him with wide-open unwavering eyes. Her mouth was a red bow and her cheeks had the warmth of the sun in them. Her skin was almost translucent in that light. Peter felt a pulse beating in his throat. And then the boom swung viciously in as a breeze from nowhere took the empty sail. He caught the boom in one hand, and shouted, 'Mind your head! Here's the wind! Haul that jib-sheet, Norna, it's going to blow properly this time.'

There was no conversation between them other than Peter's exclamatory heartiness until they landed, when Peter asked abruptly, ' Are you coming to the County Show with me to-morrow?'

'No,' said Norna shortly.

'You might as well. Martin isn't going, I think, and I'll have the car all to myself if you don't come.'

She thought for a moment or two and then said, 'All right, I'll come. I'm going home now.' And went off, leaving him to make snug the boat.

Peter sat for a long time outside the boat-house, smoking, and watching the sun set. He thought of Norna, kneeling before him, her breast almost touching his knees, and the curiosity he had felt became desire. He was excited by the thought of the next day. He had wasted the afternoon and, irritated by the thought of waste, desire grew stronger. A sudden, vivid recollection of her skin, warm on the cheeks

and creamy white at the neck, flushed him and heated his
brain.

In Orkney an old Norse habit of wooing survives. The
manner of it is unseemly to urban ideas, for in towns there is
more ample encouragement than in the country for the
inspissated amenities of courtship. There is only interrupted
darkness in the urban night, and light has elaborated a
hundred niceties of behaviour for which solid country darkness knows no reason. The politeness of towns has hidden
the sleep of virgins and the maiden bed, the vehicle of that
sleep, behind an unapproachable curtain. But in country
places the bed, which probably occupies a quarter of the
ben-room, is as discoverable an article of furniture as the
kitchen-table. Sleep has no mystery and the darkness of
night is still the proper cover for love-making.

Old custom took young men in the northern countries
naturally to the beds of young women to prosecute even the
preliminaries of courtship. In the daytime there was generally work to be done, and though there were no work there
was still no place in a farm-house both comfortable enough
and secluded enough for wooing. The maiden bedroom,
therefore, became, inevitably enough, the reception-room;
but a reception-room more partial to the individual than to
the crowd. And as nights are cold in the north, and a bed
is wasted in which a girl lies alone, the young men did their
wooing under the blankets. But still a certain propriety
reigned, even between the bolster and the bed-end. They did
not set a naked sword to keep them apart, but custom, or
inherent virtue, or a proper realization of cause and effect,
restricted their wooing to familiarities no closer than the
embrace of the modern ball-room. With every circumstance
of sin they did no sin, and amid all the evidence of utter
promiscuity a virgin might, and frequently did, remain a

virgin. This ancient courtship still persists among the hardy, weather-disciplined peoples of the North. In Sweden they call it *sova dolce*; in Orkney, less happily, 'running in the night.'

And Peter, with an unexpected hunger constricting him, thought uncomfortably of Norna's bedroom.

Only once had he gone 'running in the night,' when he was seventeen or so, and then the adventure, which had been undertaken with two other youngsters and was inspired more by mischief than a girl, had ended gloriously with an escape by ladder from the bedroom window, a wrathful father with a gun, a shot in the dark, and two lead pellets in Peter's rump, The snobbery of schooldays, however, had restricted his personal acquaintance with the custom to that solitary occasion. From the age of twelve he had been at school in Edinburgh, spending only vacations in Orkney, and after school the War had come. He was virtually a stranger to the custom.

Norna was also unconventional. The countryside called her proud, and that was partly because the young men always found her bedroom door locked (outside doors are rarely fastened in Orkney) and those, more enterprising or more ardent, who had set ladders to the wall and climbed to her window had encountered a girl flaming with wrath who very bitterly miscalled them and bade them swiftly be gone. One who had argued overlong saw the bed-clothes tossed back, two bare legs, quickly covered, swing to the floor, and a white-robed Norna reach for the wooden candlestick at her bedside. The next he knew was that he was sitting at the foot of the ladder with a cut head, his trousers torn by a nail, and his left wrist broken. After that Norna slept undisturbed.

Peter knew the story, and his mind dwelt on the picture of

her sitting up in her white nightdress, black hair and eyes, and angry mouth. . . . She would look magnificent, angry in bed.

He sucked at his pipe, and it was cold. The snob in him rose aloofly and shut the door on these pretty, lustful thoughts. Peter stood up and walked quickly homewards, regretting his mental aberration and convinced that virtue had conquered his wanton impulse. It was, however, only snobbery.

He found Martin setting out for another bedside. A young sow, a costly beast with an impressive pedigree, was in the way of farrowing, and Martin was going to spend a comfortless night watching it. Pigs, particularly expectant young mothers, are difficult creatures to manage, with a bent for unmeaning savagery. Having borne their young they not infrequently turn and rend them. Martin had decided not to trust her man with the potential mother of champions in her hour of trial. Peter suggested that he might take over these delicate duties.

Martin looked doubtful.

'As a medical man,' said Peter severely, 'as one who may, in time, usher scarlet Prime Ministers and toothless Admirals of the Fleet into an overcrowded world, surely I can be trusted to manage the birth of a few piglings, even though they are likely to be the finest piglings in all Britain.'

'All right,' Martin said, 'only for heaven's sake don't go to sleep, and call me if she gets difficult.'

So Peter, relishing the sour contrast to the sinful luxury of his earlier thoughts, spent the night with a pig in labour; sitting wrapped in a rug, in a corner of her stye, and every now and then stemming her endeavours to break through the door. Morning came without any youngsters having appeared, and Peter, after his white night with a pig, handed his charge over to Martin.

'I can't go to the Show, that's certain,' said Martin. 'She's bound to farrow to-day. I suppose you want the car?'

'I thought of taking Norna,' said Peter, yawning, and went down to the beach to swim.

III

THE County Show, to which the Kirkwall Market is pendant, is one of the outstanding events in the Orkney calendar. From all parts of the Mainland and from the outer isles men and beasts come in to the capital and cathedral city of the islands. Formerly they walked or drove in heavy farm-carts. Now only those leading horses or driving cattle go on foot; the others are carried by shabby, racketty motor-buses, or ride on bicycles – the roads teem with bicycles, and at night the police make enormous captures of those who carry no lamps – or drive in gigs.

All morning the white roads are full of traffic. Bearded farmers, heavy of hand and speech, dressed in ill-fitting Sunday clothes; women, cheerful and shrewd, whose garments smell vaguely of a box under the bed; red-cheeked girls, magnificently healthy, whose breasts strain at tight finery and whose strong shapely legs do honour to cheap stockings; noisy tinkers, full of drink and quarrels; young slouching men with clear eyes and ugly caps; children who suck sweets and stare in aweful silence at inexplicable novelties; ploughmen, broad-shouldered and lewd, and shopkeepers not so broad; wives and widows and orphans, grandsires and school-children, the parish bull and the village teacher; Established Church ministers and Free Church ministers and Plymouth Brethren; fat crofters and thin crofters; cheerful loud-swearing fellows and slinking quiet ones; brazen girls and sly girls; mothers with child and fathers as full of drink – all the country goes to market and enjoys itself as heartily as it may.

On a hill behind the town is the show-ring, where massive Clydesdale horses, heavily muscled, glossy of skin, white-feathered for pride, stalk magnificently past their judges, serene in their vast beauty and superbly contemptuous of the decision. Heavy straight-backed cattle with huge swaggling udders and mild eyes stand side by side, chewing the cud, thinking of sweet grass and feeling the weight of sweeter milk. Bulls, arrogant and compact, thick-necked, stare at the crowd with the insolent eyes of a Tarquin unashamed. Square white sheep crowd their pens. Dogs bark. The people laugh, talk, watch wisely and cunningly their neighbours and their neighbours' animals. There is a smell of trampled grass, and dung, and sweat, and rank tobacco; it is sifted by the breeze, swept round in eddies and then blown out to sea. Foals whinny, angrily nuzzling their placid mothers. A policeman, as blue and stupid as thunder, looks blindly about him. Bare white heads with protruding eyes thrust out of a pen, and a sheep's chorus plaintively fills the air. Men and animals divide the earth between them, for if one is master the other is wealth.

In the town, in the broad street before the Cathedral, there is a different world, a shabby, furtive by-world of tents and showmen. Mesdames This and That, palmists, profess to read the future and decipher character from the work-hardened hands of their clients; an easy enough matter in most cases, for character is naked in the country and destiny goes steadily through childbirth and work to the grave. A little, snarling man, his face a blotchy red and white, recites the titles, accomplishments and virtues of the Prince of the Ashanti, who for twopence may be seen dancing on spears; the prince, a tall grinning negro who never ruled anything more imposing than a dock-gate row in Liverpool, stands behind him, puffing his cheeks. A green and white tent holds the Armless Queen of the Amazon, an amorphous creature who manages tea-cups with her toes. Shrill-voiced tricksters persuade a gaping public to buy numbered cards for prizes;

and all the lottery ever yields is a packet of hair-pins or a farthing brooch. Gold watches are bartered mysteriously for ten shillings, and glittering chains are wrapped up with half-a-crown and sold for three shillings and sixpence. Rifles crack in the shooting galleries and slugs ping hard against spotty targets. A grand competition for the best shot in Orkney will be held at ten o'clock, with a handsome silver timepiece as the reward for level eyes and a steady wrist and a finger that wisely presses the trigger. Seven shots for sixpence, and a mighty chance for the silver clock. The Prince of the Ashanti is dancing on twelve blunt iron spear-heads, capering on a narrow platform, sweating prodigiously, and smelling vilely.

'Cross my hand with silver,' says Madame Valita, the society palmist. 'Beware of a dark man who seems to be your friend. You will have five children and some money left you when you are forty. You are going a short journey.'

With a screech that grows into a blare of brazen harmony the roundabout sets off on its dizzy voyage to nowhere, and country copulatives cling to their painted swans and wooden tigers, hold hot hands in gaudy chariots, or ride with seeming nonchalance on fearful griffons.

Jerking swings draw arcs through the lower sky.

'Sixpence a ticket and a prize for every ticket,' shouts a dirty man with a purple muffler.

The Queen of the Amazon lifts a tea-cup to her mouth with hooked toes and smiles wearily at the stolid sight-seers.

Ping! goes a rifle, and a clay-pipe shivers starrily into fragments. 'By God, Geordie,' says a lout in a cap, 'if thoo warked as weel as thoo shoot thoo'd be a grand man at the ploo.'

A bell clangs as a metal bolt shoots up a tall pole and hits the top. The man with the hammer, who has just shown his might, grins shyly and retires. 'Try your strength, try your strength!' bellows the showman. 'Great strength rings the bell!'

'Three cards,' says another, with a strip of oilcloth in front of him. 'Only three cards, and where's the Lady? Plank your money down. If you don't speculate you can't accumulate.' And looks warily round for fear of the police.

This is the world that the country goes to when it tires of the show-ring, when the champion horse and the champion heifer have been honoured and led away while the Highly Commended shake their heads in undisturbed and undisturbable pride. From cattle to the showmen's tents all the country streams, and voices get shriller when the day goes, and hoarse laughter shouts across the square as drink and excitement and the bustle of moving bodies heat the crowd. Naphtha flares take the place of daylight, and the Fair lives louder in their smoky brilliance. Life is warm. Wild promises are made. And all the time the vast body of the Cathedral towers behind the people and the tents of the showmen; the Cathedral of the Holy Earl who went pilgrim-wise to Jerusalem, the great edifice of God that grows like a rock in the Northern Sea, the old giant house that men built for heaven eight hundred years ago. It stands foursquare and awful by day, and looms like a shadow of the Keep of God by night.

The County Show and the Kirkwall Fair make a brave day and turbulent darkness.

Peter went up to Redland in the morning and found Elsie dressed in her best clothes, excited beneath an assumption of ease.

'You said you'd take me to the market,' she said, and got into the car without more ado.

Peter had no memory of such a promise, but the child looked so composed in her seat and then turned and laughed

at him with such frank delight that he answered, 'Of course, I
did. Isn't Norna ready yet?'

'She was dressed an hour ago,' said Elsie calmly. 'She's
just pretending to be grand by keeping us waiting.'

Norna came out in a few minutes.

'Hullo, White-maa,' she said. 'I didn't know you were
here.'

'Liar,' whispered Elsie.

'Elsie says you promised to take her too. She's probably
telling lies but you'll let her come, won't you?'

They drove slowly along the crowded roads till the town
came in sight. Elsie chattered like a magpie, gay and mali-
cious, dropping fiery comments on the gigs and cyclists they
passed, and once shrilling rudely at a larger car which dustily
overtook them. Norna tried to check her, but Peter laughed
and encouraged her. On the outskirts of Kirkwall they left
the car in a friendly farm and walked up the hill to the Show
Yard. For an hour or two they watched the succession of
horses led round the ring, or walked critically past fat rumi-
nant cows. Elsie was the most competent judge of the three.
Her impishness vanished behind a front of critical ap-
praising. A mare of Redland's, a chestnut satin colossus with
white-feathered legs, took first prize in its class. They were
delighted, and calmly accepted a score of congratulations.
A black polled heifer was given a third prize. They grew
irate. A pen of sheep came first. They were happy again.

Suddenly a voice boomed, 'White-maa, by God!' and a
hard, broad hand clapped down on Peter's shoulder.

A red-faced, square-shouldered, square-chinned, grey-
eyed man faced them as they turned.

'Billy Scarth!' said Peter happily. 'When did you get
here?'

'Yesterday,' said Captain Scarth, and putting an arm round

Elsie shook Norna's hand, saying, 'You're the prettiest picture I've seen for a twelvemonth.'

'And what pretty picture did you see then?' asked Peter.

'Norna, of course,' answered Scarth promptly. 'And I haven't seen anything as good till now. *And* I've been to Buenos Aires since then.'

He winked with hilarious sagacity and Norna said, 'You've washed the salt off your tongue pretty quickly.'

'I'm dry as stock-fish. Come and have lunch with me, all of you. White-maa, you're getting thin. Why don't you come to sea and rib up like I'm doing?'

Captain Scarth, D.S.C., commanded a six-thousand ton tramp steamer whose home was the Clyde and whose ports of call were any that freights made profitable. During the War he had been a penny admiral. His command was six trawlers and his flagship a hundred-and-twenty feet long, a slab-sided tin coffin with a high nose to punch through rearing seas and a twelve-pounder gun to comfort neutrals and fight the King's enemies. Scarth had come out of a North Sea fog one winter morning and found a German submarine, on the surface, firing into the brown of a fishing fleet. The submarine was straight ahead as it happened. Scarth took the wheel and rammed it very prettily. He picked up an odd survivor to corroborate the evidence of his broken bows and, by a miracle keeping his craft afloat, returned to the Tyne and in due course was given a Distinguished Service Cross. His next ship was torpedoed. Then he went to a Q-boat which was sunk by gunfire. When the War was over he went back with regret to the orthodoxy and comparative security of the Merchant Service and began to feel, at thirty-five, that he was growing old. He was a distant cousin, sixth or eighth, of Peter's.

The four of them had lunch in the Bay Hotel. It was a

long, noisy meal, for it started with Elsie choking over a mixture of soup and laughter, and having to be thumped on the back, and Billy Scarth, new-home from sea, was in a roaring humour. They drank Burgundy and Billy and Peter had more whisky and soda after it than discreeter people would have thought wise. Elsie was riotous and the men, backing her jokes with their laughter, prompted her to further wildness. Norna, comforted by a little Burgundy, grew happy and when she laughed her beauty was brilliant. Billy Scarth paid her compliments direct and unequivocal as the north wind and Peter, grape-warmed and malt-emboldened, followed suit.

'I've seen girls in Copenhagen and Stockholm, and girls in Marseilles who would make an ordinary beauty chorus look like straw bolsters or withered grandmothers,' said Billy seriously, 'but I've never seen one a quarter as pretty as you,. Norna.'

'Have you ever seen a mermaid, Billy?' asked Elsie.

'Dozens of them, with golden hair and silver tails, singing in their bath like Tetrazzini on the gramophone.'

'I saw Norna in her bath this morning,' said Elsie, 'but she wasn't singing. She was yelling like mad because – '

'Elsie, be quiet. I'll never forgive you.'

'Let the child alone,' said Peter. 'Why should she have all the luck and not tell us about it?'

'Because Jean had shouted to her that I was putting on her new shift,' Elsie continued triumphantly.

Norna was red as a rose and Billy shouted with laughter as he asked, 'And have you still got it on?'

'No. She pulled it off me. There it is!' And Elsie pointed to a white ribbon that showed on Norna's shoulder.

'Elsie's a pirate,' said Norna. 'I don't mind piracy so much, but pirates should keep quiet about what they steal.'

'She's publishing her reminiscences,' Peter said.

Billy went back to his catalogue of the world's beauty.

'I've seen girls in Valparaiso and Montevideo, and señoritas in Rio, and Yankee girls in Philadelphia who would make a crippled beggar get up and sing, but let me hang in chains for a buccaneer if I ever saw one like Norna. White-maa, where have you seen any good-looking girls?'

'Paris and Brussels,' Peter answered modestly.

'Have you ever seen one that did your eyes more good than Norna?'

'No, and I've given up expecting to.' Peter looked boldly at Norna, his eyes laughing.

She was embarrassed; but a girl will suffer more than embarrassment to be told that she is beautiful.

'I wish you wouldn't talk nonsense,' she said.

'Now why do you think it's nonsense?' asked Billy. 'If we told you unpleasant things you would immediately be frightened that they were sensible and true. But when we tell you pleasant things, which are true, you suspect us and call them nonsense. White-maa, am I a silky flatterer?'

'Never,' answered Peter. 'You're a plain, blunt, seafaring man, as honest as you're ugly.'

'Now there's a testimonial that any man should be proud of. We'll have another drink.'

It was nearly four o'clock before they left the hotel. Norna went to call on some friends in the town, and Elsie demanded to be taken to the Fair. They visited the shooting galleries and smashed an extravagant number of clay pipes; they shot celluloid balls that balanced tremulously on tiny fountains; Elsie deliberately fired at, and hit, the shining alarm-clock that was meant as a prize and escaped with Billy in the confusion, leaving Peter to recompense the furious proprietor. He found them on the roundabout, racing side by side on two swans that stretched ungainly necks after a red and yellow chariot drawn by stolid tigers. Then they visited the Prince of the Ashanti and the Queen of the Amazon.

A dozen yards from the Queen's tent there was an eccentric core of excitement in the crowd. A knot of people, like black bees, clustered round something, and as they neared it the knot broke and out of it came an old tinker, a wrinkled spae-wife called Nelly Macafie. Her dirty, grey hair blew in wisps about her face, a yellow, weather-aged face as lined as a puddle in the wind. Her black twinkling eyes were reddish at the rims, and she flung gnarled hands and curses at the people mocking her.

She came to Peter and Billy.

'I'm neether a witch nor a warlock,' she said, 'but I'll tell good fortunes to them that have one, and true things to all. Let old Nelly see your hands, and she'll tell you what to fear and what to hope for.'

Elsie held out her hand, giggling, but the tinker-wife would have nothing to do with her. 'There's nae fortune there,' she said, 'but flyting and stealing sugar. Give me your hand, you that look like a sailor.'

She took told of Billy's arm and drew him into a nook between two stalls.

'You are going great ways over the sea. Once you will go and come back, and twice you will go and come back. A third time you will go to the sea. And over that time there's the shadow of the finger of God, and past that finger I can't see. Give me a shilling, now. Perhaps it is happiness.'

'Come and take your medicine, White-maa,' said Billy. There were lines about his mouth that showed more clearly than a few minutes before.

Nelly Macafie looked at Peter's hand and stared into his

eyes. Her own eyes were black and beady and a great crow's foot was drawn in the yellow skin at their outer corners.

'There's death in your hand,' she said.

'God,' said Billy Scarth, 'let's get out of here and look for a drink.'

Nelly took no notice of him and said to Peter, 'You fought in the German War? But there's another death than the deaths there. Death and a fine white girl beside him, and the running sea and a dark sky. Give your old mother a shilling now. Don't be afraid.'

'I'm not afraid,' said Peter, and laughed to her.

'Give me another sixpence,' she whined greedily. 'Give me silver and I'll tell you better things. Maybe I was wrong. There's a tall white girl in your hand – '

'Come on,' said Billy and pulled him away. 'Damn these tinkers. I always listen to them and they always frighten me. By God, wasn't she an old witch?'

The crowd surged about them, hot and eager, like cattle stirred to excitement. The brown mass of the Cathedral stood solidly against a white sky and the strident voices of the showmen shouted over the murmur of the people. Music came harshly from the brazen womb of the merry-go-round, and the wind carried ploughmen's laughter in its hands.

'Come and have a drink,' said Billy, and over whisky and soda he condemned superstition to nethermost hell. Few men with the island blood in them escape superstitious fears. The northern winters are too long, and darkness breeds a consciousness of what daylight sense denies. Elsie looked at Peter with silent awe. Her high spirits had gone. But Peter laughed, and as he drank the last of his whisky said, 'If I ever become a doctor without knowing more about anatomy than I do now there's likely to be a devil of a lot of death connected with me. Don't be a fool, Billy. The old witch was probably drunk. You don't really believe in that sort of thing, do you?'

'Not now,' said Billy. 'But no one likes to hear that he's going to be drowned after another three voyages; and I don't suppose you cared overmuch for what she told you. The old hag will be run out of the town if she reads that kind of fortune in many hands.'

'Elsie made her angry by laughing, I expect, and she got rid of her spite on us. What's that song about the gipsy's warning? I'll have to be careful how I give anaesthetics next year.'

They went back to the tents and stalls. The last drink had gone to Peter's head and he made way for Elsie with unnecessary roughness. A wrist-watch of apparent gold caught the child's eye. It lay in white velvet on a little pedestal of its own. Beneath it was a gaudy array of dolls, brooches, red and yellow beads, little glass bottles, paper fancies, collar studs, trumpery mascots and such. A bull-necked hoarse man with a purple muffler was selling slips of paste-board.

'A number on every card and every number a prize! Sixpence a card, sixpence a card! Here you are, sir, sixpence each, and Number Ten wins the gold wristlet-watch.'

'Buy me one, White-maa,' said Elsie, 'maybe I'll get the watch.'

Peter and Billy paid their sixpences. Two girls and a gaping boy followed their example. The bull-necked man shuffled his little pack and dealt a three, a five, a two, a seven and a nine.

'A string of beads, a packet of hairpins, a doll, a shaving-brush, and a lucky mascot,' he shouted, and handed the prizes round.

Again they bought tickets; and again without more reward

than some collar-studs and a paper-windmill. No one secured the lucky Number Ten.

'There's no bloody Ten in the pack,' said a surly voice behind.

The same thought had already occurred to them both. The gold wristlet-watch was undoubtedly a permanency, a perpetual decoy-duck to lure sixpences from stupid and greedy pockets. And because the crowd at a Fair is always moving round, and because few people care to start a quarrel in cold blood, the deception had escaped punishment.

'I wish I could get that watch,' said Elsie longingly.

'I'll buy one more ticket,' Peter replied.

He drew a One. Quickly, as the bull-necked man dealt other cards, he pulled out a pencil and added to the one a bold nought.

'Now then,' said the bull-necked man, 'What's your numbers? Who's the lucky gent with Number Ten?'

'I am,' said Peter, and showed his card.

The bull-necked man's jaw dropped. 'You bloody liar,' he gasped.

'This is a ten, isn't it?' asked Peter, holding out his card.

A burst of passion took the showman and shook him like a rag. His face turned dark; he swore obscenely; and suddenly stooping he picked up a billet of wood and struck savagely at Peter's head. Peter ducked and as the man turned half-round, swung off his balance by the force of the blow, hit him very neatly on his right temple. The man dropped, and the crowd, which in a moment had become twice as thick, laughed appreciatively.

'Man, that was weel done,' said a tall countryman, and reaching forward he lifted the wristlet-watch off its pedestal. 'Here's your watch. Somebody should ha' taen it lang ere this.'

'Give it to the girl,' said Peter briefly.

The showman, spluttering, dribbling, cursing in stupid fragments, sat up and called loudly to a friend called Sam.

Sam came round the corner of the booth, a stocky fellow in a grey sweater.

'That bloody swine's got the watch. Knock his blasted head off,' said the showman, pointing to Peter.

Sam promptly attacked. Peter met him with outstretched arms and hands that gripped his dirty sweater. Then he heaved and swung, like a man throwing the hammer at a Highland Gathering. Sam went round in a circle, gaining unwilling velocity, and as the cycle was completed Peter let go and Sam shot, all legs and arms, into the stall where he disappeared in a subsidence of paper windmills, collar-studs, lucky mascots, farthing brooches and multi-coloured strings of beads.

There was a roar of laughter as the trumpery exhibition collapsed. Girls shrieked joyfully, the hobbledehoys guffawed, and men old enough to have known better shook with honest mirth at the ludicrous spectacle of the showmen sprawling like puppet Samsons in the ruins of their two-penny Gaza. It tickled their sides, this cardboard catastrophe. It would have tickled their sides even had the showmen been honest men, of course, and the added attraction of revenge for all their wasted sixpences made it irresistible.

Peter stood by the wreck as if reluctant to leave it, but Billy, with one arm round Elsie, took him by the elbow and forced him through the multiple, laughing, jeering, hallooing ring of spectators.

'You damned fool,' he said; and led them through darkening streets to the Pier and out to the end of the Pier, where the wind blew fresh and strong in front of the night.

'In God's name what made you start brawling? If you have

no character to lose, I have. And think of the child here, finding herself in the middle of that uproar.' Billy was very serious.

'It was the best part of the whole day,' said Elsie, 'specially when the man went swinging round like that – his boots near took my hat off. And I've got the watch,' she added.

'You'll take it back to him,' said Billy.

'Not I,' said Elsie.

'I lost my temper,' Peter admitted. 'The fellow was so confoundedly secure in his idea that he could swindle all these country lads that I suddenly hated him. I felt that I wanted to hit somebody, in any case, and when he picked up the club everything became beautifully simple. So I hit him.'

'Do you think there's any chance of your going berserk again to-night? If not we'll go and meet Norna, and then you had better come out to Stromness with me and have supper.'

'I'm all right,' Peter said. He yawned widely, facing the wind, and walked up the Pier.

Stromness rises steeply out of the sea on one half of an egg-shaped bay. The water-side houses have stone jetties instead of gardens, motor-boats instead of motor-cars, tide-waste and gulls beneath their windows instead of flowers and blackbirds. Behind them other houses precipitously climb the hill, and from their doorways the inhabitants look out across the island-studded expanse of Scapa Flow and over to the twin round hills of Hoy. Scarth lived with his mother in a little square house high up on the slope.

They called for Norna. She saw that something unpleasant had happened and was troubled to find it out. Elsie rushed in with an explanation, proudly showing her watch. Without comment Norna got into the car. Billy and Elsie climbed into the dickey and they started for Stromness.

'I suppose you think I was drunk,' Peter said in a little,

' but I wasn't. I admit that I went out to look for trouble. I felt oppressed for some reason or other. I think the crowd annoyed me. I had to get rid of it – the oppression, or depression, or whatever it was. And then I lost my temper over that silly swindle.'

Norna laughed softly, 'And you knocked one man down and threw the other into the middle of his stall! Oh, White-maa, you are a ruffian.'

'His heels went in the air and the whole thing collapsed round him.'

'It was a dreadful thing to do. But I wish I had seen you doing it.'

Peter stopped the car abruptly. 'I'll go back and knock someone else down if you like.' He turned round and kissed her, deliberately and calmly, on the mouth.

There was a shout from the dickey, 'What the devil are you playing at?'

'A damned good game,' answered Peter, and drove on.

Billy Scarth's mother was like a Roman Emperor whose eyes had seen all the sadness of the world, and who had lived proudly on. Her white hair rose from a broad brow; her nose and chin were like eager marble; she was tall and straight as a grenadier, and as gracious as the gracious mother of a convent; her eyes were sadder than another woman's tears. Two of her sons had been killed in France. Three, and their father, had been lost at sea. One, the wastrel, had disappeared. She had borne no daughters.

After supper she put on the table old-fashioned decanters of port and whisky; nuts and foreign fruit that Billy had taken home. She brought out crystal goblets, bright and rough to the hand, and silver knives with yellow carved ivory handles. She loved such things, and the coloured fruits, because they were beautiful; Norna she loved for the same reason, in a queer, impersonal, almost inhuman way. Of her feeling for Billy it is not safe to speak, for she had disciplined herself to loss and knew that she would survive him. Two things she hated with all her soul: cowardice and the sea.

There was a quietness in the room, a remote and ordered peace, that made the roar and bustle of the day seem like a fretful puppet-show. Here was a disciplined acceptance of life in the midst of unmeaning tumult; peace in the heart of straggling lust; an island made by hands in a purposeless sea. Here was a household which had said, 'The Lord gave and the Lord hath taken away. That is the way of the Lord, who is a jealous God. Let us be strong and abide His jealousy.' And if the old lady had confounded God with His sea there is little wonder in that, for the sea was His present instrument and His ineluctable manifestation.

But she was gracious. She laughed, softly and easily, at Elsie, and Norna she petted as a queen might pet. She looked at Billy and Peter, and warmed to their strength. She talked whimsically of bygone Fairs, and in her memory old brawls and noisy country-dances became delicate things, silly lavender keepsakes or quaint engravings. Billy told of Corpus Christi processions and bull-fights that he had seen in Spanish America. They had ceased to be actors and were spectators, detached and sensitive, of a rude and picturesque world. The spectator's seemed the better part.

They were silent as they drove home. The three of them sat together, Norna close to Peter. The quietness and order of the house was on their minds. The mind is a gentle thing, delicate to receive impressions, loth to destroy them; but bodies are more robust, more forgetful, and hotly responsive. Norna was very close to Peter. Her shoulder was pressed hard against his and their legs touched. And though the calmness, the gentle aloofness, of the old lady lingered in Peter's brain the old lady's whisky played hunt-the-slipper with all the tumbling imps in his blood. The mind may be drilled with the culture and wisdom and art of the centuries, and touched impersonally with beauty, so that it is willing and even eager to dismiss its primal origin, but no body forgets the life of the forest till it is ready to share the decay of the forest.

They reached Redland. Elsie, tired and sleepy, got out at once. Norna hesitated. And Peter took her into his arms.

She gave back his kisses. His hands went under her coat, that he might hold her more closely, and felt her shoulders move beneath their thin covering. For a moment her body yielded, and then she pressed back, with her hands hard against his chest.

'No, Peter, no!' she said. She was frightened. And Peter let her go.

He took the car down to Ottergill and walked straight back to Redland. He gave himself no time to think. His brain was cold and out of touch with his body, and his body was full of reaction against the excitement of a restless day. Dimly in his memory there was that old Norse habit of wooing. He was suddenly lonely, with the primal loneliness of Adam. The day had emptied him, as a pitcher is emptied, and into the void might come the loveliness and comfort which Norna could give. The contagious hubbub of the Fair, the silly shock which the tinker-wife had given him, his anger and the struggle with the showman; all these had tired him and weakened his independence, his normal ability to be alone. He had drunk heavily and the fire of the malt had burnt out. That house in Stromness with its strange and barren beauty had tired him; it had touched, and exhausted, some barely definable emotion. He went to Norna for strength in his weakness and comfort in his loneliness.

The light in her window went out as he neared the house. Darkness had invaded her room like a sea. Like a sudden tide, flowing from nowhere, it had drowned the things that light made so familiar. A wave had fallen from unseen heights on the puny candle. Somewhere, in the depths of the sea, Norna lay breathing.

He found a ladder and lifted it against her window.

Dark clouds, bringing rain from the west, covered half the stars. There was no sound in the night except the crumbling noise of the sea. The house stood dark and silent, its inmates, lonely and unknowing, lost in the uncharted wilderness of sleep.

The top-half of Norna's window was open and Peter, quiet and cautious and unaware of his caution, climbed over the sash on to the inner sill.

He stood motionless in the bedroom and felt his heart beating like a trip-hammer. The room was blacker than the night outside. Gross darkness held it. It might be illimitable, a pit of utter darkness far over the edge of the world, and the greyish square of window was a trap-door opening on to a roof immeasurably remote. Somewhere in the darkness was Norna.

A soft tumultuous movement broke the black silence and there was the crackle of a striking match. A candle-flame leapt up like a spear and Norna's voice, sharp and unafraid, said, 'Who's there?'

The light spread, forcing back the darkness, rearing gigantic shadows, and she saw Peter.

'Norna,' he said, 'Norna.' And stood beside her.

'What do you want?' she said. 'How dare you? Oh, White-maa, go away, go away!'

One hand opened and closed convulsively on the sheet.

Peter took it and drew it, unwilling, to his lips. 'Let me stay,' he said hoarsely. His face was white in the candle-light, drawn and haggard. It was unfamiliar, like a mask, and the thought went into Norna's head that he was drunk. Fear and hatred and outraged pride flamed in her. She snatched away her hand.

'Get out of my room!' she said. 'White-maa, do you hear me? Get out of my room.'

'I want you.' Peter's voice was sullen and dogged.

Throwing back the blankets Norna sprang to the floor and faced him.

'You beast! Get out of here. Get to hell out of here! Damn you, I say, get out of my room!' Her eyes blazed with temper and her voice was a rough, passionate whisper; a muted scream, scarcely under control.

Peter looked at her, standing in front of him, and felt his own anger mounting, an ember of wrath glowing in a banked fire. He saw her breasts, rising and falling under her thin nightdress. He could take her in his arms and her pride would crumple. She would struggle and hit, fight like a wild-cat, and then softly yield. Anger heightened her beauty. Perhaps her anger was only a peacock's tail, flung out as a gaudy lure.

Norna waited, white and fierce.

'What do you think I am?' she said. 'A country trull, to be taken by any drunken ploughman who can climb through a window? Would you treat your Inverdoon friends as you treat me? Oh, how dare you think that I would welcome you like this!'

There was an inner door in the bedroom leading to a room where Elsie and Jean slept. Neither of them heard the faint creak when it opened, and Elsie's voice suddenly startled them.

They heard a titter of laughter and then, 'Ho, ho, White-maa! Running in the night?'

The door closed again, hard and suggestively.

'Will you go now?' Norna asked quietly.

He seized her and kissed her roughly, once.

'Yes, I'll go now,' he said. 'I may be a beast, but you're a coward and a niggard and a respectable hypocrite. So there's not much to choose between us.'

He climbed out of the window, clumsily this time, and down the ladder.

As he stood at the foot of it he heard another window open, and Elsie's voice, struggling with laughter, mocked him.

'Mind you put the ladder back where you found it, White-maa,' she shouted.

IV

SLASHES of rain drove across the grey waste of morning.
Clouds, full of rain, rolled heavily off the lower slopes of
Hoy, and white streaks of foam cut into the grey, cold sea.
The wind was whining under the clouds, driving them like a
lean dog driving enormous, shapeless flocks.

A hand lifted above a wave breaking on the shore, a head
reared up out of its crest, and Peter staggered to his feet, fell
on the slippery shingle, picked himself up, and hurried to
the towel and old coat that a stone held from the thieving
wind. He was red and gasping with cold as he ran up to the
house.

He had wakened an hour before dawn to a savage vision
of himself stripped like a fool for the scorn of all the universe.
He saw himself, naked and ashamed, under a charging sky,
and hated the sight of his shame. It was still half-dark and
the twilight before dawn is pitiless. There is neither darkness to hide nor light to comfort. He looked at himself and
bitterly saw a failure and a fool. He had failed, once and
again, at a paltry schoolboy's task in Inverdoon; he had
even failed when he set out to rape a girl who was probably
half-willing, under a chary hide, to be raped – by him, at
any rate. She wanted a more respectable approach, that was
all; the pretty pomps of courtship to minister to her pride,
chocolates and a ring and the twaddle of congratulatory
gossip.

He was a weakling. He had wanted her and he hadn't
taken her. A double weakness. But she had been right.
Her pride was a lovely thing, and he had touched it and spoilt
its whiteness. Oh, God, why was all beauty meant to be
broken by men? But if he had taken her, loving her, and she
had loved too, then no beauty would have been lost except

114

for profit of more beauty. But the risk was too great for her, and what she had to give was too fine to be given easily.

He got up and went to the window and looked out at a leaden stretch of sea and cloud. A spurt of rain blew in on to his face. It would be good to go through the world with a front of iron, mailed in contempt, greedy and without fear. Like the north wind in a fat English valley. Regret was an arrow in the soul and the more you pulled the faster it stuck and the sharper the pain. Damn regret. He had played badly and the crowd would jeer. Let them jeer. They couldn't play themselves, they could only watch others, so what did they matter? Damn all cheering, jeering crowds who laughed without heart and clapped to warm their cold hands.

The thought of Norna standing before him, defying him, took shape in his brain, and his hands went out to it; and gripped the wet edge of the window. The whine of the wind changed to a snarl and the sea looked colder as the light grew. It was difficult to believe that it was the same sea as he had cursed for calmness when he and Norna had gone sailing. With curious insistency a memory of that evening came back to him and he realized with a bitter, vivid apprehension how he had rebuffed her then. He had held her off with a blanket of unresponsive stupidity and now she had beaten him off with a broomstick of reaction and mortified pride. Again a slatter of rain beat coldly on his chest, and Peter went back to bed shivering.

He buried his face in the pillow and through the blackness ran mockingly, like a flickering sky-sign:

> 'The man that will nocht quhen he may
> Sall haif nocht quhen he wald.'

And Norna was in a like case. It was a mad world. If two triangles, ABC and XYZ, are equal in all respects they shall not coincide. *Reductio ad absurdum*. He might as well go to sleep again. Though it was *Seductio ad absurdum* that he had been playing at. . . .

The morning was half-gone when Peter woke for the second time and went down to swim in the unfriendly sea. He had nearly finished his breakfast when Martin came into the room with a white, stony look on her face.

'What happened to the car last night?' she asked.

'Why? Is there anything wrong?'

'One of the wings is broken.'

Peter looked at her in surprise; and then, remembering, said: 'I'm awfully sorry, Martin. I remember now. I just touched the door going into the shed. It's nothing serious, is it?'

'You were drunk, I suppose.' Martin's voice was deliberately hard.

'I'm damned if I was,' said Peter.

Martin flushed an angry red and her voice rose. 'Then if you were sober why did you break into Redland last night like a drunken ploughman? What were you doing in Norna's room if you were sober?'

'And what has that got to do with you?'

'It has this to do with me: that the whole countryside will be laughing and sneering and making beastly jokes about you by to-morrow, and I have to share in your disgrace. People know about it already. Elsie saw you there and told Mary, and Mary told Betsy. I heard them sniggering and talking about it in the kitchen an hour ago.'

'Damn Mary and Betsy. Do you think I care two whistles in hell for them? Or for the whole damned country? What business is it of theirs, the poking swine, what I do?'

Peter had risen to his feet. Martin stood opposite to him, across the table. Her face was white again by this time, and tears were coming up on the heels of her anger.

'You care for the country's opinion as much as I do. You wouldn't lose your temper if you didn't care. And you know that you've made a fool and a beast of yourself.'

'Well, what if I have? That's my look-out, isn't it?'

'And what about Norna? She's my friend – almost the only friend I have here – and you're my brother.'

'Oh, hell! For God's sake keep off sentiment.'

'Then for God's sake stop swearing. Peter, I won't be sworn at. I can't stand it.' Martin turned to the window, sobbing, sniffing, fighting her tears.

The story she had heard from her kitchen-girl that morning had been like a clumsy finger on a raw wound. She lived a lonely life; lonelier than girls in town, at any rate. There were few men of her own mental or social stature in the place, and cut off from their lesser familiarities, trifling at dances and the like, Martin had become at once severe and sensitive in her attitude to life. Her mind was robust enough; she had not read Elizabethan drama without toughening her mental fibres. But, like most women's, her brain was a fifth wheel when she rode her emotions.

Peter damned time and space again and said: 'I wasn't cursing you. I was swearing at your sentimentality, at the world, at myself, at everything. Oh, damn it, stop crying!'

'There you are again. You are swearing at me.'

'Martin, I'm sorry. For heaven's sake don't make such a fuss about nothing – '

'Do you call that nothing?'

'It was less than nothing. But even if it had been everything I don't see why you should mind.'

Martin looked at him, drying her eyes, and said very

quietly; 'You're my brother. And you're all I have to love.'

She went out, leaving Peter cursing himself anew. He admired Martin whole-heartedly, her resource, her energy, her independence. Physically she was good to look at, tall and trimly built, brown-faced, with regular features and smooth eyebrows arching into a broad, level brow. And he supposed that he loved her. One didn't give much thought to that sort of thing. Family sentiment was such uncomfortable slipped-poultice stuff. But it was damnable to have hurt her so. He felt like a clumsy fellow running for a train who turns round and sees that he has knocked over a cripple.

Miserably he stared at the drying sky. The wind had gone down and the rain was off. The hill would be soaking wet underfoot, but squelching through a bog was better than counting his sins indoors. He took down a gun and filled his pockets with cartridges. One of Martin's spaniels, a well-bred, nicely mannered little bitch, was lying at the fire. He whistled to it and went out.

There was a good road as far as the farm of Overbigging and from there a rough cart-track, brown mud with high grassy strips inside the cart ruts and puddles every few yards, led past two hillside crofts into the moor. At Overbigging two dogs ran out, barking; a big, dark, harsh-coated collie and a lighter-built youngster, the same colour. They sniffed excitedly at the spaniel, snapped at each other, and followed at her tail. The spaniel, seeming to ignore them but tossing her head, kept close to Peter's heels. He turned and spoke roughly to the farm-dogs and they drew off a little, but still followed with suppressed eagerness.

Peter tramped on through the mud. Skirting a turnip-field, coming fast but cautiously, he saw a lean, red dog, a half-bred setter from Redland. With a deep *woof*! it sprang forward as they passed, planting its forefeet stiffly in the mud, and looking at the spaniel with kindling brown eyes. The other dogs growled at it but the spaniel, though still demure, seemed inclined to coquet, and Peter drove the setter away with a threatened kick. The three suitors followed at a safe distance till they reached the lower croft.

A square-set grey collie scattered them there with a sudden rush. It was a fighting brute with light yellow eyes. It sniffed ardently at the spaniel, who very properly ignored it, so that it went back to a brief teeth-and-shoulder fight with the old black dog. There was a snarling, biting, barking flurry in the ditch for a minute or two, but when Peter looked round he saw the four dogs following in a motley-coloured bunch; and slinking behind them there was a dirty terrier, a tinker's dog that had come from nowhere. He beat them off with his gun, half-losing his temper but finding it again in a gust of laughter.

The amorous procession followed him, faith and hope in their doggy eyes and envy in their hearts. The spaniel was lagging and Peter had to speak severely before she would keep to his heels. There was reproach in her pathetic eyes as he spoke to her, so that again he felt a female thing had put him in the wrong. But he hardened his heart and cuffed her when she tried to stray again, for there was a rakish brown dog at the upper croft, a dog with a sweeping tail that curled over onto its spine and the air of a conqueror. It was waiting for them, as Peter had feared, and immediately challenged the spaniel's heart. It took a smack on the head with equanimity and a kick under its tail with a snarl, and joined the cortège.

Peter stopped and looked desperately at the pack he had collected; the old harsh-coated black collie and the lean young one; the mongrel setter and the dirty terrier; the stocky grey collie and the proud, high-tailed brown one. They looked back, boldly or furtively as their nature was, stood still or sidled uneasily, some with a half-bark of defiance, some growling softly. The spaniel lay down and bit daintily at the mud lodged between her toes.

Abruptly there came a shrill, high-pitched yap-yapping beside him, and a dishevelled half-Pomeranian appeared on the dyke, a skinny excited little dog with a piece of grubby red ribbon round its neck. Still yapping frenziedly it leapt down and approached the spaniel in a series of frog-like jumps. It lay on its belly, ingratiating, and snuffed at the spaniel's nose. The rest of the court drew nearer, growling dangerously. Peter looked at them, and then down at the latest wooer, the ridiculous eager little Pomeranian, and laughed tumultuously. The unhappy court came nearer as his laughter echoed over the wet moor and the Pom drew back, frightened.

It was indecently ridiculous, this wholesale response to a smooth spaniel's lure, and it had to be discouraged, for he could not expect any shooting with a procession following him. He slipped a cartridge into his gun and fired low over the heads of the pack. They scattered immediately and an old woman, startled by the shot, came out of the cottage.

'It's all right, Becky,' Peter said to her. 'I had all the dogs in the country following me – the spaniel's in heat – and I had to get rid of them somehow, so I put a shot over their heads.'

Becky called to the Pomeranian – it was whimpering under the dyke – and nodded with perfect understanding.

'Ay, ay,' she said, 'they'll follow a bitch from far and wide. It's just their nature, and a dog's no' shamed to show it. Come awa', Nigger. A peerie cratur like thoo has no business wi' great muckle hounds. Come awa', ye villain.'

V

A PLATE fell off the table and broke with a crash on the stone floor.

'Dareen on't,'[1] cried Maria Sabiston, 'that's the third to-day.'

She turned to her guests with an apologetic smile; they were not embarrassed.

'Where there's bairns there'll aye be broken plates,' said one of them, and raised to his ready mouth an enormous piece of plum-pudding snugly balanced on the broad blade of a knife.

All evening they had been cutting bog hay at Redland. The natural meadow grasses keep sweetly for the winter, and the cattle turn eagerly to them when turnips are dry in the mouth. And as bog hay has to be cut with the scythe – for it grows in broken ground, by the side of a burn and in reedy patches harsh with meadowsweet – they wait for a moonlit night and then, as soon as the dew falls, a man and all his neighbours will set to work. The scythes swing in a steady rhythm and the grass falls over them. Step by step the men move on; the calm night is full of the susurrus of steel and grass, the swish of the blades in rhyme, and behind them the rougher sound of a whetstone grinding a scythe to new keen-ness. The meadow is thick with wild bees' nests and the smell of honey rises as they work. Girls bring ale in buckets, and huge china mugs, lipped with foam, pass down the line of workers. It is thirsty work and sweet work. And when it is over supper is ready. Half-a-dozen chickens have been boiled (or three or four old hens if the housewife be thrifty) and a plum-pudding cooked in the calves' pot – the only pot big enough to hold a pudding of proper size.

[1] Dareen on't] a harmless imprecation.

Redland's bog hay was cut and Redland and his neighbours, and some half-dozen of his family, sat at meat in the
stone-paved kitchen. The ale had been good and a glass of
whisky had met every man as he came in, so their voices were
loud and their laughter rang deeper than the clatter of plates
and knives; deeper than the voices of the children (only the
very youngest had consented to go to bed) and Maria's voice
as vainly she scolded them. A smell of ale and of cooking
mingled with the sweet-smelling lumps of wild honey the
men had brought in, and the lamps shone in a steamy heat.
They talked of the Kirkwall Fair and Mansie Bews, a crofter,
said loudly, 'Where's White-maa? Man, he was fair enjoying
himsel' at the Market.'

'I thought he was coming,' John Sabiston answered.
'Have thoo no' seen him, Norna?'

Norna shook her head and Elsie, farther down the table,
giggled loudly.

'God!' said Mansie Bews, sucking his moustache, 'he took
that cheap-jack wha'd been swindling folk aal day and flang
him fair in the middle o' his toys and bruck[1]. He just
grippit him under the oxters and whirled him roond. Man,
it was the best piece o' wark in the hale Market.'

'I heard no word o' this,' said Redland. 'Were thoo with
him, Norna?'

'No,' said Norna shortly.

'I was,' said Elsie, and told the tale again.

John Sabiston considered it in silence. He talked little –
unless he was in the mood for telling old stories – and sometimes he heard little of what went on about him. He knew
nothing of Peter's midnight visit.

'Wild wark,' he said, 'but the men o' his family were all
alike. His grandfather was a gey man for the women.

[1] bruck] rubbish.

Thoo've heard tell of Auld John Corrigall wha bade in the upper hoose o' Dykeside? Weel, John had the twa bonniest daughters in the parish, but his wife was half blin' and John was as deaf as a stone. So he was aye fearing that some swack lad would be bedding wi' the lasses. Twice or maybe three times on a Saturday night he'd look into their room to speir if there was anybody there. And one night White-maa's grandfather took a notion to see the lasses o' Dykeside, so awa' he gaed. And first he got a man ca'd Daft Rob who wasna so daft as folk thought, and syne he banged on the door o' Dykeside.

' "Wha's that?" said Auld John, pitting his head through a window.

' "There's a lass o' thine lyin' wi' a man that looks like a sailor in the Hillside barn," said White-maa's grandfather.

'The Hillside barn was an auld hoose that stood maybe half-a-mile from there. And Auld John on wi' his breeks and his boots, never looking to see if baith his daughters were at hame or no', and awa' to the Hillside as hard as he could pin. And White-maa's grandfather gaed too. And when they came to the barn Auld John was into't like a rabbit gaun into its hole, and as soon as he was in White-maa's grandfather shut the door and jammed the sneck wi' a piece of wood that he had ready. And back he gaed to Dykeside and found Daft Rob waiting for him.

' "Go thoo in and lie wi' the goodwife," he says, "and if she speirs what was wrong say never a word, but grunt as though it were nothing at all. For she'd ken thee voice though she's owre blin' to see thee face."

'So in gaed Daft Rob to the goodwife, and in gaed White-maa's grandfather to the lasses, and there he lay all night between them. And they were the bonniest lasses in Orkney at that time.'

Half the table listened to John Sabiston's story attentively and heard its conclusion with approving laughter. The lower half was busy with its own affairs, and Maria interrupted both by constantly supplying the plates that were never allowed to lie empty and the ale-mugs that must be kept abrim.

'But White-maa's no' the man for the women that his grandfather was,' said Mansie Bews.

Elsie whispered something to Alec of Hunda, a wild-looking boy whose hair hung in a russet fell over his brow, sitting at her side.

Alec grinned and said to Mansie, 'He's a grand hand at climbing ladders though.'

'Wha's grand at climbing ladders?' asked Maria from the far end of the table.

'White-maa,' said Elsie.

'Whatna ladders has he been climbing?' Maria demanded, eager for good gossip.

Jean, who had been quiet all evening, said, 'Our ladder.'

'And what was he wanting with our ladder?'

'He came to see me,' said Norna in a clear voice.

There was something as near to silence as was possible in Redland kitchen.

'Goodsakes, lass, thoo're no' blate[1],' said her mother.

'Why should I be? I asked him to come and he came.' Norna was flushed and her eyes were shining but her voice sounded cool and assured. She had taken the wind out of Jean's sails and Elsie's mischief. She looked steadily at her mother, and Maria, who loved a joke as much as anything in the world, put her hands on her hips and laughed happily.

'Best[2] forgie us,' she cried, 'would he no' come till thoo asked him?'

[1] blate] shy.
[2] Best] God.

124

A solemn-looking man with a long moustache said to her: 'Did thoo have to ask John here to come and see thee when he was courting?'

'Not I, faith,' said Maria, laughing again. 'He broke the sneck o' the door one night when I'd fastened it.'

John Sabiston looked gravely at his eldest daughter and said nothing.

VI

Billy Scarth started the engine of his motor-boat. Dick Heddle, a tall red-haired boy, a Stromness doctor's son, cast off her moorings from the bow, and Peter, at the tiller, swung her round and steered neatly through the crowded harbour towards Hoy Sound and the West Sea.

He had left Ottergill a day or two before to have a week's sea-fishing with Billy Scarth. The change was welcome. Martin had heard of his brawl with the showman in Kirkwall, and there had been another scene of recrimination, lost tempers, tears and apology. Wanting nothing but complete oblivion for his exploits Peter had been compelled to hear their double rehearsal and twice to see Martin in tears. He had pleaded with her to believe that there was really nothing in either matter to grieve her, and when all his arguments had failed he had humbled himself, sworn truthfully that the last thing he wished to do was to hurt her, begged forgiveness, and promised to walk more circumspectly in future. He had left Martin reconciled and almost happy; but there was a bitter taste in his own mouth and he wanted sea-salt to cleanse it.

There was a strong tide running in Hoy Sound, throwing the water into swirling hollows and frothy ridges. Miniature whirlpools, calm in the centre and ringed with petty turbulence, made a dizzy pattern on the sea, and the engine throbbed sulkily as the tide wrenched and tore at the propeller. Beyond the tide-rip was broken water, and the torn crests of little steep-pointed waves flung over the bows. The sea was lead-coloured in the early morning, but the sun was rising over a cloud and the sky was already breaking, like curds, into brighter patches that promised clear weather.

Billy Scarth and Heddle were busy over tangled fishing-lines. An iron half-hoop, lead weighted, fitted with yard-long droppers and massive hooks; a wooden frame of stout line; and a bucket full of a soft writhing collection of limpets, ready shelled, and black sand-worms were each man's equipment.

The waves roared into whiteness over a reef a quarter of a mile ahead of them, and now and again a foamy line of broken water would run between the reef and the shore.

'We'll have to go round the outside of Braga,' said Peter, looking with narrowed eyes at the reef and the long wave that smashed, as he watched, into a white thunder between it and the shore.

To go to the outside of the reef meant an extra mile or two, but to be caught by a breaking wave inside it meant going to the bottom.

Billy watched and considered. 'It's only the ninth wave that's breaking,' he said. 'We'll risk it. Keep midway between Braga and the shore.'

Peter shrugged his shoulders and did as he was ordered. Billy knew more about the sea than he did. Heddle grinned and said nothing. He never spoke very much. He was an Edinburgh University Rugger Blue and incidentally a medical student whose knowledge of his presumptive trade was about equal to Peter's. But he was an excellent inside three-quarter who found his own openings in attack, and in defence would go headlong for the knees of a thirteen-stone Border forward with the zest of a spring salmon leaping a fall.

Billy slowed down his engine as they drew near to the dangerous channel. On the one side there was a continuous roar as waves broke splendidly on the reef of Braga, and inshore the tide growled along the beach. A wave bigger than its fellows – the Ninth Wave, the Mother-wave of the sea – was coming.

'Now for it,' said Billy, and opened the throttle.

The wave rose, huge and white-capped, snarling from reef to shore and smashed itself in a wild surge of foam on the hidden shoal in front of them. It gathered itself again, and the boat rose to it; slid down its green back; and went hard into the creamy smother behind it. The water was nearly calm in the rear of the giant wave, but there was a long way to run to safety. Slowly they passed the danger zone. Slowly they left the reef on their quarter. They crossed the debatable land. And scarcely were they out of harm's way before another wave heaved past, reared, seething in a yeasty flurry of rage, and fell in smoking thunder behind them.

'We've saved more than a mile by coming through there,' said Billy, and went back to his fishing-lines.

The shore rose steeply into black cliffs as they left the Sound and turned northwards. The west coast of Orkney is a ragged barrier of rock, splintered by storms, pierced with echoing caves, populous with gulls and gannets, puffins and shags and eider-geese; here a little bay strikes through the cliff, shelving over a rolling beach to soft grasslands; there a lonely pinnacle, split from the solid rock, stands blackly on a white carpet of foam. This is the Atlantic wall.

They anchored in twenty fathoms of water and began to fish, baiting each hook with a juicy cluster of limpets and black worms. They shifted their ground, went farther north, and anchored closer in-shore. Fish began to bite. They pulled haddock and codling to the surface, gaffed them and heaved them into the boat. To pull a ten-pound codling through fifteen fathoms of water is good work. The long wet lines rubbed their fingers raw and the salt water smarted to the bone. But the haddock still came. They saw a seal fishing faster than they. It lay on a shelf of rock over which the sea broke in a curtain of foam, and plunged into the smother beneath, strongly, gracefully, like a lithe black bolt. To seaward of them solan geese were diving for mackerel, dropping through the air like white arrows. The sun shone in a clear sky, and the green shore-sea ran sharply into deep-sea blue.

Suddenly Billy said: 'Give me the gully, White-maa.'

An ugly, black, eel-like fish hung writhing from a hook, its shark's mouth gaping, its tail beating the sea. Peter gave Billy his sheath-knife, and Billy drew the dog-fish over the gun'le. He held it there with a piece of wood and cut off the villainous sharp spines which grew on its back. Then he tore out the hook and threw the creature back into the sea.

All the fishermen use dog-fish like that, unless they want them for bait. Their spines are dangerous. They cut to the bone and, it is said, leave poison in the wounds. And they frighten away the haddock.

'There's no use fishing any longer here if the dog-fish are coming,' said Billy, and started his engine.

North and south they fished, till the bottom of the boat was covered with a silver mail of cod and haddock and the sun had crossed overhead and begun his descent to the west. Then they turned homewards, throbbing through calm seas.

They talked of the inland lochs. Trout had been shy for the last week or two, and neither Peter nor Heddle had caught any.

'You want to go down to Pegal Burn with a net,' said Billy. 'What's the use of playing with a fly at the end of a string, fishing all day for half-a-dozen, when you can get three score in a net?'

'What do you say, Dick? Would you like to try a little poaching?'

Heddle grinned. 'I'm keen. Isaac Skea's watching Pegal Burn, though.'

'Damn Isaac Skea. I'm not frightened of him.'

'He doesn't love you, White-maa. I heard he was in Stromness the other night, drunk, and swearing that he'd have your life yet.'

'Because I got him six months in gaol. He's a bad hat. He was in my platoon, Dick, after I came home wounded in '17. I checked him twice for insolence, and then one day at musketry I wasn't satisfied that the sergeant had examined the men's magazines – it's a regulation – and I told Skea to pull back his bolt. It was early afternoon and he'd been in the canteen. He told me to go to hell and then tried to hit me. Well, he had time to repent it.'

'He's done worse than that,' said Billy slowly. 'You know he was in a mine-sweeper early-on in the War, along with Tommy Bruce and Harcus and some more of the town lads. And Tommy was lost overboard. Well, it was Skea that knocked him over, as sure as I'm here. No one saw him do it, but they were both keen on the same girl and Tommy was the favoured one. They were on watch together, and it was a calm enough night when Tommy disappeared. Harcus is positive that Skea murdered him, and so are the other lads. And then he got the girl into trouble and went off into the army. He's a damned bad hat, White-maa.'

'You're a gloomy couple,' said Heddle. 'Are we going to net Pegal Burn or aren't we?'

'We'll net it if you want to,' said Peter.

Pegal Burn is a stream on the island of Hoy. It empties into Scapa Flow and its tiny estuary is a famous place for seatrout. Skea was a game warden. Nobody who knew him would have employed him, but a manufacturer from Glasgow had bought the island, and finding it impossible to persuade anybody else to live in so lonely a place as that part of Hoy, he had taken Skea. The man was a surly ruffian, black-bearded, tall and strong, foul-mouthed and vindictive. He lived alone in a one-roomed cottage about a mile south of the burn and kept perfunctory watch over it and the surrounding moors – the lonely black slopes of heather, inhabited only by birds, of the gloomiest island in Orkney.

Two nights later the motor-boat left its moorings and with a dinghy in tow throbbed steadily out of the harbour and into the Flow. The sun had set behind a bank of brown clouds and dusk, like the shadow of a giant, was slowly covering the sky. To the south-east, clouds were piling themselves into a growing mountain. A single star glittered in a patch of smoky blue. The sea was calm, and in the shadow of Hoy the cease-less tide murmured of invisible things to the shingle and the hidden rocks.

Billy Scarth stood with his hands in his pockets, staring at the southern sky.

'There's going to be wind before the night's over,' he said. 'A devil of a lot of wind, unless I'm far mistaken. I don't like the look of that sky. A south-east wind makes a nasty sea in the Flow.'

'He's frightened of being sick,' said Peter. His eyes shone in the glow of a match as he lighted his pipe, and Heddle grinned back.

'If we hadn't gone to all the trouble of getting the nets ready I'm hanged if I'd have started.'

Three round baskets stood in the boat, each holding a long net, carefully coiled, weighted at the bottom, and strung as if with giant beads with cork floats along the top. They had been smuggled aboard under oilskin wraps; passed as in-conspicuously as possible from Heddle's pier to the dinghy and from the dinghy to the motor-boat; poacher's gear makes any man modest. Scarth picked up a sack which he had stowed carefully away, untied the string which fastened it, and pulled out a double-barrelled gun.

'What are you going to do with that?' Peter asked.

'You sometimes find a seal in the burn,' said Billy, 'and we don't want a seal tangled up with the nets.'

He spoke in the manner of one offering an excuse rather than giving a reason, and Peter looked at him in some perplexity as he put the gun in a locker.

'You don't mean to shoot Skea, do you?' suggested Heddle.

Billy stood silent for a moment, frowning. 'No,' he said. Then, 'Look at that damned sky. There's going to be wind, I tell you.'

He sat down and said: 'Do you know little Willy Hossack? I saw him this morning. He and his brother went down to Pegal Burn last week and set a net. Not for fun, I fancy. His father's crippled with rheumatism, and God knows what they live on. Well, they were hauling the net in when Willy got hit in the face with a stone. Friend Skea had been watching them, and this was his way of letting them know it. Willy's left eye is still out of sight. Then Skea shouts that he has a gun, and they're to let go the net or they'll have lead instead of rocks about their ears. Willy and his brother are only youngsters. They were frightened and threw the net over – they had the sense to keep a few fish, though – and Skea hauled it ashore, with probably a good number of trout in it. Now if Skea happens to come along to-night and tries to bluff me out of my nets, he's going to get a shock.'

'You've got Skea on your nerves,' said Peter.

The sea was growing darker and the huge bulk of Hoy was black, a vast barrier of sombre hill and cliff. Little gusts of wind blew off it, coldly ruffling the water. A seagull shrieked. They passed a sunken German battleship, looking like Sin-

bad's moving island where she lay side-up. A bluff headland
thrust out in front of them. They rounded it and came into
the silence of a small estuary.

Billy stopped the engine. An anchor was thrown out and
the dinghy hauled alongside. They lifted the nets into it.
Quietly they rowed inshore, into the deeper shadows of the
land. They could not see the beach; only a grosser darkness
showed where the shore was. An oar, dipped deeply, touched
bottom. The noise of the sea had become a distant murmur,
and the burn made a little chuckling song of its own that was
like a freshet of sound flowing in a desert of silence – like
water pouring out of a narrow-necked bottle in a silent,
dark cathedral.

Speaking only in whispers they set one net in front of the
burn-mouth, and the other two in line thirty yards farther
out, where the estuary broadened. Then they went ashore,
pulled up the dinghy as quietly as they could, and found a
sandy hollow under a high bank whose crest leaned out,
ragged with heather, over their heads.

The stream babbled quietly in the darkness, and the sea
snored on the beach. Here and there stars shone at the edge
of a cloud and were swallowed in its soft, rolling advance. A
gust of wind, coming from nowhere, brought a new note,
a fretful, whirling, high-pitched note, to the lazy nocturne; it
seemed to hush the stream and frighten the tide and leave
behind it utter silence.

'I told you so,' muttered Billy.

The burn came to life again, and suddenly a loud splashing
broke the musical monotony of its song. They sat up, listening hard. It sounded as though something were leaping and
playing in a rock pool.

'It's a seal,' said Heddle.

They stood up hurriedly and went to the water's edge.

The noise came from upstream and seemed to grow less as cautiously they approached it. In a little it died away; and then the silence was broken by a harsh cry, and a grey shape, dimly seen and looking huge in the darkness, rose in front of them with a heavy beating of wings.

'A heron. But a heron wouldn't make that noise, would it?'

Billy shook his head. 'I don't think so. There may have been a seal. But listen to that. That's more important than seals.'

Another gust of wind shrilled fiercely over them, a wilder, longer gust than before. It passed, and following it there came a sullen, confused murmur. In the south-east black clouds had mounted high and the wind was massing in their skirts.

They went back to their sandy hollow. It was quieter there, and when Billy said: 'We'll have to get the nets up and go,' the others were unwilling.

Their plan was to wait till the tide was low and then walk down the burn – their sea-boots reached to the thigh – and frighten the trout seaward into the nets. Billy waited undecidedly for ten minutes. The wind blew louder. It no longer came in gusts but in a steady drive. As they listened its burden rose to a savage howl that echoed off the cliffs.

'Get a move on,' said Billy sharply. 'That settles it.'

They pushed the dinghy down the beach and climbed in. The first net was hauled without any fish in it. Hauling the outer two, which were joined together, was a longer business, and as they worked they could hear the wind shouting outside, whining to the sea, bellowing at the cliffs.

They were twenty yards from the shore when a figure rose at the water's edge and a voice shouted: 'Let go that net or I'll put a shot in your guts.'

Billy, who was standing in the bow of the dinghy, felt a pull at the net, and nearly fell overboard.

'Who are you?' he called.

'Mind your own bloody business. Are you going to let go that net?'

'Keep hold of it, Dick,' Billy whispered, and boldly shouted 'No!'

'Then take that,' said the man on the beach, and threw a heavy stone which hit Billy on the shoulder. 'Now drop the net, or by God I'll shoot you, you bloody thief.'

Billy stooped, picked up his gun, and fired over the man's head. The sound of the explosion seemed deafening, a metallic violence that splintered into staccato echoes up and down the burn-mouth and woke to shrieking life a hundred sea-birds, gulls and shrill terns and whistling redshanks.

'Two can play at your game,' said Billy, and as the man dropped his end of the net he called: 'Stand still there, or I'll put the next one into you.'

He turned to Peter and Heddle.

'Row on, White-maa, and get the net in as quickly as you can, Dick.'

They were almost aground before the end of it came in, and Skea stood on the beach cursing and miscalling them with the overwrought obscenity of barrack-room and fo'c'sle.

'I know you, all three of you,' he roared, 'and by God I'll see you in clink for this, you bastards!'

'Stand still, or it's the porter of hell you'll see in a minute,' answered Billy. He turned and knelt in the stern as they pushed off, covering Skea.

'Now row as hard as you can, boys, for he's got a gun somewhere and he'll shoot as soon as he thinks I can't see him. I'll put another shot over his head in a minute, to frighten him, and then row like blazes.'

Billy fired again, high in the air, and almost immediately two shots answered from the dark shore, the double crack mingling with the echoes of his. They saw the twin flashes as Skea fired and heard the whine of pellets striking the water. A few hit the side of the boat and one flipped on Peter's sleeve. But in a minute they were out of range.

'So that's Mr. Skea,' said Peter. 'It's a good thing you brought your gun, Billy.'

'Do you think he recognized us?' asked Heddle a little anxiously.

'No,' answered Billy. 'That was bluff. White-maa is the only one of us whose voice he knows, and White-maa kept dumb, luckily. It was too dark to make out anybody's features. I couldn't recognize him really, so I'm perfectly certain he couldn't recognize me.'

'There's the motor-boat,' said Peter looking over his shoulder.

It was fairly calm where the motor-boat lay, though she jerked anxiously at her moorings in the fringes of the gale which was blowing outside. They climbed aboard and made fast the dinghy. The motor roared and settled to a steady beat as they headed out into the Flow. Great black clouds swung sullenly overhead, showing for an instant narrow rifts of lighter sky between them in which stars flickered windily and went out again in driving darkness. The wind shouted, and as they came into open waters it beat deafeningly on their ears; the boat lurched over a wave and staggered in the trough.

They turned northwards, running before the waves which lifted them high, passed under them, and left them in vague hollows over which other waves reared threateningly. The dinghy, towing behind, rose on the lip of such a one, raced higher and faster than the motor-boat, and fell with a crash on its stern. Falling back it slewed half-round, shipped the crest of another wave, and answering the tug of the tow-rope bore down on them again. Again it reared, and as it threatened to fall Heddle tried to fend it off and nearly broke his wrist. The nets were in it, wet and heavy, and it was shipping water.

'Get the dinghy alongside and take the nets out of her,' Billy shouted. 'Look alive, or she'll fill and sink.'

Twice they tried to hold her, but both boats were in the grip of the fast, following sea, and it was more than their strength could do to tame the wildly charging dinghy.

'Cast her loose, then,' said Billy, 'and we'll go about head to wind and try to manage it that way.'

Freed of the dinghy the motor-boat raced ahead, turned and hung drunkenly on the side of a wave, turned again, and they felt the wind in their teeth, beating tears from their eyes, deafening them, forcing itself like a black wave into their lungs. Slowly and with infinite care they approached the dinghy, Billy at the tiller, Peter and Heddle waiting with ready hands. They caught and held her, fought and struggled with her. The broken crests of waves whipped over the bows and lashed them soundly, but they lightened the dinghy of her load of nets, made her fast again, and turned homewards.

The Great Bear shone clear for a minute and the lighthouse on Graemsay showed like a great yellow star. The dinghy rode more easily now, and they plunged tumultuously on.

They shouted to each other, excited by the black waves which roared at their heels.

'When are you coming poaching again, Dick?'

'To-morrow, Billy. Wish my girl could see me now. She think's I'm a poor fish because I can't dance.'

'She's never seen you beating off game-keepers with a gun, eh?'

'I'll bet Skea's cursing like hell. He's got to walk home against this wind.'

'It'll do the swine good. Hasn't he got a pretty flow of language?'

'What would you have done, Billy, if he had had his gun beside him?'

'Lord knows. Look out, there's the dinghy coming again.'

'The sea's getting worse, isn't it?'

'We're all right so long as the engine keeps going. And you can swim, can't you, White-maa?'

Slowly they neared the harbour, and as they passed from the wildness of the sea into its landlocked calm the noise of the motor seemed like heavy gun-fire. It was three o'clock, and the town was utterly quiet, sleeping between the sea and the hill. They felt suddenly tired, and worked wearily to unload the boat.

VII

ISAAC SKEA stood at a corner in the narrow street of Stromness. He had been drinking. His eyes were red and he swayed a little on his heels. Nobody would tell him what boats had been out on the night of the storm, for no man in that country gives information lightly; food and drink are yours for the asking and the begging tinkers prosper; but news is a valuable thing, and no one was likely to give news away to Isaac Skea.

He had just seen Peter Flett and Billy Scarth go into a tobacconist's shop, and unreasoning suspicion had wakened in his drinker's brain. He knew little about Billy but he hated Peter as the author of his six months' imprisonment. . . . He saw himself on parade again, in 1917, sulkily listening to a sergeant talking about rifles and muscle-exercises: 'On the word Two, drop your left hand and take the first pressure!' And then a damned white-faced officer, newly out of hospital, saying: 'Have you examined arms and pouches, Sergeant?' There had been a scare two days before over a live round being found among dummies. And the officer—who had already checked him for dirtiness—had come up to him and said: 'Pull back your bolt, Skea, and let me see your magazine.' And he, with three or four pints of canteen beer in his belly, had said: 'Pull the bloody thing back yourself,' and knocked—oh, quite casually—knocked him on the elbow with his butt. The next thing was: 'Fall in, two men. Take away his rifle and march him to the guard-room.' Six months in gaol for that little joke. He had a bad character, of course. But God! how he hated that bastard Flett. And Scarth was a friend of Flett's. He had heard of them shooting grouse on moors that did not belong to them, and it was quite likely that they had taken

139

a notion to poach Pegal Burn. If he could only make sure. . . .

Billy and Peter came up the street. Skea watched them as they passed, muttering to himself, and then lurched after them.

'Here!' he shouted.

They stopped and turned round.

Skea licked his lips. 'Was that you setting nets down at Pegal Burn two nights ago?' he said hoarsely.

'What do you mean?' asked Peter.

'Mean? You know bloody well what I mean. Was it you that tried to murder me, eh?'

'You're drunk, Skea,' said Peter, and turned on his heel.

Skea sprang after him, raging, and gripped him by the the shoulder. Billy clapped a hand on Skea's wrist, wrenched his grasp free, and said in a quarter-deck manner: 'Now look here, Skea. I don't want any confounded nonsense from you. You're obviously drunk, and if you don't go away quietly and sleep it off you'll land in trouble. Do you understand that?'

Skea glared down at him – he was a head taller than Billy – for a moment, his eyes bloodshot and his teeth showing in a snarl. But he said nothing and presently walked away, a little unsteady on his feet.

Billy was going to sea again in a few days' time, and his mother grew more proud and tender with every hour. She had sat by the fire waiting for them on the night of their expedition to Pegal Burn, listening to the wind that roared its chorus of rage and drowning, and seeing in the red glow of the fire and the white peat-ash old pictures of ships and the men who sailed them; of the sons who left her, almost as soon as they could walk, to sail crazy boats in the harbour, and left her more decisively for deeper, wilder seas before the first hair was on their chins; of the husband who had come home from sea and taken her, and gone back to sea, and returned like a bridegroom from his voyages perhaps a dozen times – a dozen months of marriage, each under a white moon of rapture and fear that seemed in memory no longer than a summer night. Perhaps it was more than many wives could remember.

But she had toddy waiting for them when they came in, and said only: 'It was too rough for pleasure, wasn't it?'

'As rough as we wanted it,' Billy answered.

Peter made some story of Billy's seamanship in saving the dinghy.

'It was a nasty job,' he said, 'to get alongside with that sea running, but Billy nursed his boat like a mother.'

'It's all he has learnt to nurse,' said his mother.

While he was in Stromness Peter heard from his lawyers that they had finally settled Mrs. Flett's estate, and he discovered that after all his debts were paid he would have £873 exactly to furnish his remaining years of apprenticeship. It was as much as he had expected, but it brought him face to face with work, neglected and new, which would meet him in Inverdoon.

'You're going to struggle on with medicine?' Billy asked him.

'What else can I do? Go to Rhodesia or Kenya and start farming? I hate farming – or I would if I had to make a living out of it. I'm too old to go to sea, and I couldn't go back to the Army even if I wanted to. I can't think of anything else.'

'Come for a voyage with me – I'll sign you on as purser – and see what you think of the other side of the world.'

'Wait till I've finished at Inverdoon and then I'll come.'

'But how long will it be before you have finished?' asked Billy, grinning.

'I can still do it in three years if I work like the devil. And I'm going to, Billy.'

'Well, if you get tired of it – I'm hanged if I could sit on my bottom with a book in front of me for three years – let me know, and there'll be a berth ready for you when you come. Don't waste your money even though you waste your time. Time doesn't matter much. You've fifty years ahead of you probably, and that's a lot more to draw on than eight hundred pounds.'

Billy went off to sea and Peter returned to Ottergill for another two or three weeks before going back to Inverdoon. He had not seen Norna since the night of his unfortunate adventure, and he felt embarrassed at the prospect of meeting her.

He was relieved to find that there was a visitor at Redland, a brother of John Sabiston who had made a comfortable fortune, as fortunes are counted by humbler people, in British Columbia, and who was revisiting with overflowing pleasure the familiar places of his boyhood, seeing in them beauties and delights which he had never recognized before, and praising from the driving-seat of an expensive car the roads which he had cursed as a footsore boy leading horses to the smithy or cattle to market. Uncle James kept their minds occupied at Redland, so that they thought less often of Peter, and he generally had Norna with him in the car which was the symbol of his prosperity. He was a cheerful man, and on his first visit to Ottergill – he came alone – invited both Peter and Martin to spend the following summer with him in Vancouver.

'Norna's coming, I hope, and one of the others too, probably. I want John to come but he won't leave Redland.

His roots are too firmly set by now. But you haven't got any roots yet. Leave your pigs for three months and come to Vancouver. I'll show you what a lumber-camp looks like and give Peter here better fishing than he has ever had in his life.'

A hearty man was Uncle James. He drank a quart mug of ale and emptied his cigar-case on the table.

'Put away that pipe and smoke these,' he said to Peter. 'They smell nicer than a pipe, don't they, Miss Flett? But I can't get John to smoke them. He just chews one till it's a wet, brown blob, looks at it and shakes his head, and throws it into the back of the fire. Well, I must be going. You haven't been up to Redland for some time have you, Peter? John was asking about you the other night.'

'I've been in Stromness for a couple of weeks,' said Peter.

'Oh, yes. Somebody said so. Well, good-bye, Miss Flett. We'll talk about Vancouver again.'

Martin laughed softly as he went out.

'He's such a dear,' she said. 'He buys the most ridiculous things for them. The house is full of toys, and the children are sick every day trying to cope with Uncle James's sweets. He bought three hats and a fur coat for Maria, and she spends the whole day in front of a glass, trying them on. But Norna says she'll never dare go outside with any of them.'

Martin was very well pleased with life, for she had had a most successful summer with her pig-farm, and the previous week a flattering description of it, illustrated by artistic photographs of young pigs and their owner, had appeared in *Scottish Country Life*. She had entirely forgiven Peter and laughed at the rueful plans for work and overwork in Inverdoon which he sketched for her. He said nothing about the unsuccessful poaching of Pegal Burn.

But it was driven into his memory again before he left

Orkney. Dick Heddle and he had been shooting on a distant hill and were returning to Stromness in Martin's car when a stone, thrown from behind a dyke, smashed the windscreen. It was early evening, but the nights were drawing in and dusk had already fallen. They stopped at once and saw a man running hard across a field and up a little hill. They followed, but he had had a good start and at the top of the hill there was nothing of him to be seen.

Heddle looked worried and said, 'I'll swear that was Skea. There's no one else would do a thing like that.'

Peter nodded. 'The fellow looked about his size, whoever he was, and I don't know of anyone else who has a grudge against me.'

They drove on, wondering, but said nothing to anybody about their suspicions.

And then, a few days later, Peter saw Norna. He walked to Redland unhappily, screwing his courage for the moment when he would meet her face to face. And after all it was her back that he saw first.

She was leaning over the garden dyke. Her shoulders shook in a strange manner and a little incomprehensible cry escaped her as Peter approached. He felt worried and embarrassed, for it seemed that she was weeping. She heard him coming and turned, and her face was indeed red and there were tears in her eyes.

'Oh, White-maa,' she gasped, 'come and see this,' and laughed helplessly.

Peter looked over the dyke and saw a score of white Aylesbury ducks that were behaving in a manner utterly foreign to the normal character of a duck. Two of them, waddling side by side, suddenly collapsed and lay with outstretched necks and vaguely questing beaks. A third was on its back, feet paddling frantically in the air, and its feeble earth-bound wings flapping. Rhubarb, giant overgrown rhubarb, grew in the garden and a duck, essaying ambitiously to fly, landed with a crash in the middle of a too-luxuriant plant and disappeared into its green depths. A white wing-tip protruded and a plaintive quack! rose above the general squabble.

'Whatever's the matter with them?' Peter asked. 'They look as if they are drunk.'

'So they are,' said Norna, weak with laughter. 'That's what they've been eating' – she pointed to a damp, brown, cereal-looking heap under the dyke – 'and they're all drunk. Even the ducks. Oh, White-maa, isn't this a dreadful country?'

The brown heap was draff. They had been brewing ale at Redland and the sodden grain, thrown carelessly away, had attracted the unhappy ducks.

There was an air of ridiculous geniality about them, a vague and contented inconsequence in their uncontrollable antics; an imbecile attempt to maintain gravity; and now and then a rollicking adventure in flight over the rhubarb. With a curious appearance of ponderous age a duck waddled up the heap of draff and quacking loudly seemed to address his fellows. There was a responsive chorus of quacks. Even the ducks sleeping with their heads untidily tucked beneath their wings woke and quacked gratefully to the speaker. He – it was probably a drake – was encouraged and spoke loudly. Then, with the gesture of a cabinet minister opening his heart to a friendly audience, he tried to flap his wings. But the effort was too much and he rolled helplessly down the little hill. None of his late audience paid him any attention. They were busy about an ineffectual fight.

Norna, still laughing, put her hand on Peter's arm and said:

'Isn't it ridiculous? Poor ducks. I wonder if they'll all have headaches to-morrow?'

'Probably,' he answered. 'And they may transmit the taint to their eggs. You'll have to be careful with the next lot you hatch.'

The squabbling of the ducks grew quieter. They were falling asleep.

Peter said: 'Norna, I don't know what to say to you. An apology is such a useless, weakly thing.'

'Don't say anything,' she answered. 'I hated you for a little but I've forgotten all about it now. Don't talk about it, please. I don't want you to. You must come in. Father has been asking where you were.'

Uncle James's latest purchase was a gramophone, and after the habitual tumult of tea was over he wound it up, inserted a loud needle, selected a record, released the catch and simultaneously the deafening volume of *Land of Hope and Glory* sung by an impressive choir. Half-way through the performance a thin, rattling noise, a screech, and a jerky melody interrupted and began to race the stately thunder of the choir. One of the small boys was playing, on the older gramophone, a record of Harry Lauder's. Nobody, however, was annoyed; not even Uncle James.

He and John told stories against each other and the children broke their toys. Maria showed Peter her new hats and her fur-coat, and laughed with the utmost good-humour when Elsie, recklessly pinching and pulling them, tried them all on after her. It was the usual kind of Redland evening with the new factor of Uncle James adding to its geniality.

Peter stood up to go. John had taken his boots off, for comfort, and begged Peter to forgive his omission of the mannerly rite of accompanying a visitor half-way home. Norna went out with him instead.

146

'White-maa,' she said, 'I told you that I never wanted to hear you talk about that night again. I told you that I had forgotten it. But there's one thing I can't forget. You called me a niggard. Oh, can't you understand? You don't really think that, do you?'

'Of course I don't,' he answered. 'I was mad and you were sane; that's all.'

'Sanity isn't always attractive, is it?'

'No, but it pays.'

'You're making things worse. I may have been sane, but I wasn't calculating and sane. It was impulse – or instinct, I don't know – that made me angry. I had so much to lose, White-maa.'

He looked at her. She was probably right. In any case there was nothing to gain by arguing. Some women liked to show their motives, others their legs.

'You're right enough, Norna,' he said, laughing. 'And I'm going to be sane – calculating and sane – after this. I'm going to work like the devil when I get back to Inverdoon. And now you had better go in and get to bed. Good-night.'

She held up her face. He kissed her lightly and walked home, humming the Harry Lauder chorus which had so rudely disturbed *Land of Hope and Glory*.

THE WINTER OF DISCONTENT

I

A CLUSTER cf lights, struggling through the darkness, showed where Inverdoon lay between its two rivers. Seaward of them all, more proud and brilliant, was the conscious gleam of a lighthouse. From the North Foreland to Duncansby Head the East Coast stretches like an irregular pavement marked with these tall white lamp-posts to warn the traffic of the dangerous broad street that ebbs and flows, laughs and roars and whines greedily at their rocky bases. The ship moved slowly on, throbbing to her engines like a tired runner. It was cold on deck and Peter shivered as he looked down at the black water, streaked momentarily with white, gleaming for an instant in the passing reflexion of a light. It was almost incredibly black between those flitting, broken gleams; a swirling blackness so dead and heavy that you could think a bucket let down would bring up not water but Indian ink.

A smell of oil and a smell of cattle hung coldly about the ship. Sheep, draggled and miserable with spray, crouched wretchedly in pens on both sides of the deck; huddled together, all wet wool and ammoniacal stench. Below there were pigs and cattle, more sheep, and passengers; the latter crowded aft in an atmosphere of stale cooking and seasickness. A general perfume of nausea and unhappy half-sleeping humanity – the crossing had been rough – filled the saloon; a fitful, piercing odour of pickles blew through it when a door opened. Women and children, too ill to undress themselves, lay in the stuffy cabins and commercial travellers slept stertorously on settees.

Peter had spent the night on deck thinking of his winter's

work, framing resolutions and considering ingenious plans
for economizing in time. Errant memories and vagrant
suggestions obtruded themselves; he thought of Evan Mackay
and Garry Duncan and a dozen other good fellows; of nights
in Sandy's in front of the great fire there, with a waitress
bringing eight or ten glasses on a tray, and the tremendous
turbulent argument, philosophies, jests, that followed each
other pell-mell and filled the room with noise and content;
he thought of Patricia Geddes – she might be on her way to
India by this time, dancing, possibly at this moment, on the
deck of a P. and O. liner; he thought of Norna, but he could
not get the two thoughts to stand side by side; he could not
compare them. And then, walking up and down, he staggered as the ship plunged, steadied his feet and his mind,
and considered work again.

He would have to sit the examinations in Anatomy and
Physiology in March again, and to avoid wasting six months
he meant to attend Third Year classes and do as much
hospital work as he could fit into his complicated programme.
The Third Year classes were Surgery, Materia Medica, and
Pathology. At the hospital there were clinics to attend and
ward dressings to do. It was a fairly heavy year without the
dragging burden of Anatomy. Still, there were encouraging
old stories afloat of men who had spent six or seven years at
the University without doing any successful work, and then
bestirring themselves had mopped up all the confusion of the
past in a few vigorous months. Perhaps he could do the like.

A bell rang, the engines slowed, they crossed the bar,
and slid slowly into harbour. White-faced, weary passengers
gathered on deck. Two sheep bleated tremulously on
different notes. A fine rain was falling.

Inverdoon is an old town, prosaic enough as most towns
are, though strong and clean to look at. But every year a tide

of new strength only partly its own flows into it from the country districts, and the two colleges, like two pulses that have been quiet all summer, fill with life and enrich the dull stream of municipal activity with their robust presence. Peter, who arrived a few days before term opened, watched the incoming tide : youngsters from country grammar schools, sturdy, thickset, solid and unimaginative for the most part; healthy fellows able to work hard, fit to be the backbone if not the inspired brain of enterprise.

He saw the men of his own time, harder and quicker for their years in France or Mesopotamia or the North Sea; men who knew their own strength and were dangerous and careless by turns; former subalterns who had mothered discontented platoons, inspected their unsightly feet, damned them on parade and jollied them under fire; sometime pilots in the Air Force, reckless fighters who had seen the War as a rugby field, themselves as wing three-quarters, and brought back to civilian life a technical vocabulary and an extravagant thirst; late surgeon-probationers, with manners learnt in a destroyer's ward-room and a taste for gin; farmers' sons, retaining through the attrition of their foreign years all the broad, blunt habits of speech and behaviour that the Buchan farmlands breed; Highlanders, men from the Western Isles, melancholy and wildly hilarious in turn, men who drank their whisky neat and loved the saddest of songs. From the North and the West they came, eager to work, hot to succeed, and girls of the same breed with them.

Mackay was late in arriving. It was the first Saturday evening in term before Peter saw him. Peter, Garry Duncan, and three or four other men were sitting in front of the fire in the smoking-room at Sandy Broun's when the door was flung open and Mackay came in.

'I knew I would find you here,' he said, 'and I ordered

half-a-dozen drinks on my way in. How are you, Peter? And Garry? And Moncur? All these dear remembered faces! Garry, I've had the most delightful journey. I came down from Inverness with two girls, a girl called MacRae, Joyce MacRae, and a Miss Innes. Note that I say *Miss*. She's worthy of all respect. But I'm going to introduce Peter to the other one. You have far too high an opinion of women in general, Peter, and it must be dissipated. Miss MacRae will dissipate it – not by her own example, of course, but by persuasive theory. She doesn't like women. She says that they were meant for nothing more than child-bearing, and now that they won't bear children she really sees little excuse for their continued existence. I'm going to introduce you to her because I like Miss Innes better. She listened to what I said – my occasional remarks, you know – with the utmost attention and believes in a Primitive Matriarchate, but Miss MacRae continually interrupted me. But don't let me monopolize the conversation. Garry, you're getting fat. And Peter, how are you after your months of eupeptic paganism in the extreme North?'

'Peter has just been telling us how hard he means to work this term,' said Garry, 'and his eighty-four hour week doesn't leave any time for Miss MacRae.'

'That's nonsense,' Mackay replied immediately. 'Man cannot live with work alone. This matter of work is like making a plum-pudding. You shovel in your flour and bread-crumbs and raisins and sultanas and spice and so on, but a time comes when you've got to stir it. Now if Peter's going to load his basin with Anatomy and Pathology and things like that all week, obviously his mental pudding will need to be stirred up from time to time. And what better stirrer than the slender forefinger of Miss MacRae? My dear Peter, I've already invited her – on your behalf – to dance next week.

You, I, Miss MacRae and the charming Miss Innes are going to make a pleasant foursome.'

'You'll have to find someone else,' said Peter. 'I'm going to work this term, not dance.'

'How detestab y melodramatic. Garry, what can we do to save this young soul from the sin of bourgeois pride and accomplishment?'

'Ply him with liquor,' said Garry, pressing the bell.

Behind them other little groups of men talked and argued; snatches of sporting gossip were heard, laughter, confidential wisdom whose hoarseness betrayed its secrecy, personalities, conversational driftwood. Before them the fire gleamed, black and red, yellow spurts of flame and white ash. A waitress, expert of memory, brought trays of drinks. Peter felt a vast geniality spread over him, obliterating the grim coastlines of determination that he had drawn, and filling his mind with lively contentment.

Garry told a story about an Irishwoman applying to a magistrate for advice on the procedure of divorce. Infidelity was the ground of the discontent; an Irish evasion of responsibility the point of the story.

'A striking criticism of humanity in general,' said Mackay. 'There you have the slipshod inaccuracy which essentially typifies our national thought; the mental obliquity which makes politics such a game; the inability to distinguish between cause and effect; and, of course, a re-writing of the old wisdom, *Tous nos malheurs viennent de ne pouvoir être seuls.* Though now it is more accurate to say that all our adventures spring from inability to stand a solitude *à deux.* Garry, you have the bawdy mind of a true philosopher. You are probably a reincarnation of Socrates. I was talking to my father about him a few weeks ago. I asked him why clergymen didn't quote Socrates as often as they quote Isaiah, since they were both heathen and both wise old men. My father had just preached an optimistic sermon on "The bricks are fallen down, but we will build with hewn stones" – which is in Isaiah – and I looked through the chapter afterwards and told him there was a better text for these times in an earlier verse: "Thou hast multiplied the nation and not increased the joy." '

'What did he say?' asked Moncur.

'That "not" was probably a mis-translation,' replied Mackay gloomily.

Moncur put down his glass with a bang. He was a natural enemy of all established religions and their priests. His grandfather had been one of the rebels of '43 and the domestic atmosphere of dissenting piety had bred in him a general iconoclasm. His almost habitual silence was broken.

'That's typical of the Church and its servants to-day,' he said. 'You ask a question and they quibble. They know the text of the Bible is hopelessly corrupt and full of ridiculous errors, and they use those errors to screen themselves. They daren't come out into the open. They still haggle and shrug their shoulders over the Virgin Birth, in an age when every educated man except themselves has at least an elementary appreciation of biology. They know it isn't true, and they haven't the guts to throw the idea away, or confess that it's only a metaphor. What use is talk about Virgin Birth to-day?'

'You mean,' said Garry gravely, 'that what the people want to-day is not discussion about Immaculate Conception but advice on immaculate contraception?'

'I don't agree with you,' said Mackay, ignoring Garry. 'The Virgin Birth is the Church's one foundation, and it has never been easier to believe in than it is to-day. "*Credo quia impossibile*" was the best effort at believing it in previous centuries; but what is impossible to-day, in biological or any other science? Nothing. If you can fertilize frog-spawn with the touch of a needle – and you can – well, damn it all, you must surely credit God with a little more ability than that of a Carnegie Fellowship researcher.'

Moncur was sulky. 'You're making a joke of it,' he said.

'I'm not. Take it another way if you like. If you want to deceive people you tell them a careful lie, a likely sort of a lie, a lie that won't shock their sense of probability and make them suspicious at the very sound of it. But if you're telling the truth you don't mind what it sounds like. The very innocence, the childish *naïveté*, of the Virgin story is its best recommendation. Don't you agree that something very much out of the ordinary must have happened before a lot of Jews were simultaneously *naïve*?'

A sound of brazen music and the blatant rhythm of a popular hymn rose powerfully from the street outside. It was the Salvation Army.

'Go down and join them,' said Garry, grinning. 'You're in good voice to-night.'

Peter looked from one to the other lazily. He was willing to believe in Socrates and Isaiah, Plato and Buddha and Christ and Baldur and all the biologists who had ever looked through a microscope and shouted Eureka! They seemed like members of one magnificent orchestra playing in praise of life. Dimly he remembered something about Logic Absolute and the two-and-seventy jarring sects.

'I had something of an adventure a few weeks ago,' he said inconsequently, and told them the story of poaching Pegal Burn, the storm, and the encounter with Isaac Skea.

He told it well, so that they saw the darkness of the beach under the great black hill, heard the storm growing wildly outside, and felt the shock of the keeper's sudden appearance at the waterside and the excitement of being shot at over a slowly widening strip of water.

Garry asked the question which had troubled Peter himself.

'What would your friend Scarth have done if the other man – Skea, was it? – had had his gun beside him?'

'But he hadn't, and that's the sort of accident that keeps us all from homicide,' Mackay suggested. 'Most of us come pretty near to murder or being murdered once or twice in our lives, but modern conditions tend to make one of the parties always unfit, or unable, or unwilling to fight, and so nothing happens. Primitive passions still exist, but they no longer synchronize as they used to do.'

'Are there any policemen in Orkney?' asked Garry.

'Queer things happen that no policeman ever hears of,' said Gunn. Gunn, who came from Sutherland, was a man almost as silent as his friend Moncur. He was sitting with his legs stretched out to the fire, his chin on his breast, and a pipe in the corner of his mouth. His words came between puffs of smoke.

'I was out early one morning this summer,' he said. 'It was a little before sunrise. It doesn't matter what I was out for.'

'Deer stealing,' said Garry thoughtfully.

'The last of the old moon was in the sky, low down, like a left-handed sickle. I was lying on the edge of a little cliff, and there was a bit of a beach below me. Two women came round a corner on to the beach. They were both stark naked. One was old and the other young. I could see them plainly enough, and it was getting lighter all the time. They talked together for a minute, and then they started to walk round in a circle on the sand. They walked widdershins – against the sun, you know. The old one went first, and she limped a little as she walked. The young one was always looking over her shoulder as though she was frightened of being seen. But the old one kept her eyes on the sand. They walked round and round for a long time. Then the sun came up, over some mist, and they went away.'

'But what were they doing?' Mackay asked.

'Cursing somebody, I suppose,' said Gunn slowly. 'The girl's lover, perhaps, or the man who refused to be her lover.'

The waitress brought more drinks and threw a shovelful of coal on the fire. Outside, the Townhouse clock tolled heavily and melodiously.

'Civilization,' someone said, as if on the verge of platitude; but Mackay interrupted.

'That word is one of the most vulgar pieces of self-flattery in which we indulge. We have changed our habit of life in some respects, and so we dismiss all other fashions as barbarous. We give "civilization" a meaning of unique superiority and apply it to our own state of society; which is both illiberal and unscientific. Civilization connotes change, certainly, but not necessarily superiority. It means factories instead of pasture land, tram-cars instead of walking, complicated interdependence instead of independence. Civilization means that we invent cures for diseases which naturally tend to disappear, and evolve new diseases for which there is no remedy. Personally, I always spell it "syphilization." '

The challenge to modern medicine awoke its champions. The air grew thick with Lister and asepsis and anaesthesia and War surgery and endocrinology. Mackay parried a thrust here with the scornful word 'Palliative!' and evaded another by a reference to epidemiology. The argument grew louder and fiercer and attracted neighbouring groups of men by its vigour. Mackay's generalizations were pierced by the sharp points of specific instance. Garry tried to tell a story about a bull, and nobody would listen to him. The

fervour of the Scot, roused to defend its own, filled them, and
Mackay stood hemmed in by the spears.

The anxious voice of the waitress calling, 'Time, gentlemen, please!' finally brought him relief.

'And now,' he said to Peter as they walked homewards,
'they will all forget my excellent *mot* in the excitement of
their own worthless contributions to the discussion. Conversation should be more one-sided, don't you think?'

II

THE first few weeks of term were uneventful. Peter and Mackay attended lectures and stood submissively at crowded clinics in the hospital. From bed to bed they walked, in the dutiful flock that followed the white-clad shepherding surgeon. In bed after bed patients displayed their fractures and dislocations, their congenital malformations and their acquired disabilities. Some were sulky; it is excusable for a man whose tongue has been attacked by cancer to be sulky. Most of them were prone to be flattered by so much attention and exhibited deformities or the grievous scathe of street accidents with the pride of those whose powers of attracting interest are beyond the average. The women were loquacious and loved a surgeon who would joke with them.

Only the children were shy. It troubled Peter that they should be sensitive where their elders were callous. Why should children be ashamed of their hurts, and cry when they were asked to show them, when older people who might reasonably be thought to have a proper appreciation of their import were complacent or even proud of an unusually developed tumour? Did the consciousness of abnormality hurt the mind of a child because of a subconscious realization that what was normal was right – a realization not yet dimmed by adaptation and blurred by expedient? Or had children a fiercer though inarticulate desire for the freedom of perfect health, and a bitterer grief at its infringement?

He could look at men and women, mis-shapen and immobile in their splints and plaster, with detachment, as if they were museum pieces. But about a child in a hospital bed there was an almost unendurable pathos. There was no accumulation or memory of satisfying experience to balance the misery.

THE WINTER OF DISCONTENT

It was misery at the outset, pain at the threshold, punishment – the Presbyterian heritage of Scotland prompted that thought – punishment before enjoyment. The men and women had presumably lived and loved in their own fashion. They had won something, however ephemeral, out of life. A crippled child had nothing but crippledom.

Mackay confessed to a similar feeling but pleaded a different reason. Peter found him one day telling stories to a child, swathed in cotton wool, whose life, almost ended under a kettle of boiling water, had been preserved to suffer existence in the disguise of one red embracing scar. They were outrageous travesties of fairy tale morality that Mackay was inventing – the good little girl invariably went hungry to bed while the bad boy supped extravagantly with his wicked uncle – and he defended them by saying that there was little use in equipping a child, hideously scarred for life, with the conventional assurance that the good and the beautiful always prosper.

'Do you feel uncomfortable when you look at these children in hospital?' Peter asked him.

'Horribly, I want to cry,' he answered.

'But why? Why should they affect us more than grown-up people do?'

Mackay considered awhile. 'There's a number of sentimental reasons,' he said, 'but I think the real one is that the older people are generally ugly, and the children are pretty. There's something essentially pretty in most children, however plain their features are. It mayn't be much, but little as it may be their elders have lost it. And so they don't attract us emotionally as the youngsters do. Our sympathies aren't so ready to feel their griefs. If I were Freud, now, I could carry the argument further.'

'Damn Freud,' said Peter shortly.

'Did you notice that red-haired girl, a student, in the operating theatre to-day when Tiger Tim was opening up a rate-payer to look at his kidneys? – There's wasn't anything wrong with them of course; there never is. Nephrectomy is only a convention, like calling spades when your partner's in mourning. That girl's a sadist, I'm sure. She was gloating over the horrid sight. A lot of women are unnaturally cruel to-day, purely in reaction to their grandmothers' habit of fainting. A honeymoon with a sadist would be more fun than a honeymoon with a fainter, of course; but the latter might be more comfortable for the long winter evenings of maturity.'

They attended lectures with exemplary regularity. Both had been summoned to interview the Dean of the Faculty, and the seriousness of their failure, on two occasions, to pass the Second Professional Examination was pointed out to them.

'It is not usual,' said the Dean, 'to permit a student who has failed in this examination to attend any Third Year classes. Rules, however, may be relaxed. We recognize our debt – we gladly recognize our debt – to men who intermitted their studies with service in His Majesty's forces overseas. If, then, you feel able to do the work – neither of you has shown much capacity for intellectual effort hitherto – you may attend the classes of Surgery and Materia Medica. Pathology? That is inadvisable. Nor, of course, must you do any hospital work."

There was no argument. They accepted the refusal of Pathology, because the Dean happened to be the Professor of Pathology, and quietly ignored the prohibition of hospital work.

Peter tried to discipline himself to a machine-like acceptance of information; to a regular programme of mental digestion; to a methodical division of attention between

Anatomy and Surgery, Physiology and Materia Medica and the hospital. There was little time left for exercise or amusement. He boxed occasionally but gave up Rugby; he was an undistinguished unit in a superfluity of forwards, so this mattered nothing to anybody but himself. For two or three weeks he thought smoothly and worked doggedly through his time-table. But doggedness began to turn to a sullen distaste for methodical effort, and smoothness gave way to stretches of fierce endeavour broken by patches of irritable inertia.

There was too little freedom in his programme. A wasted hour dislocated a whole day, and a lost day upset the week. Peter had a natural distaste for routine and an unnatural regard for its merits – the regard of a man in whose nature laziness and spasmodic vigour alternate, and who sees, without being able to acquire it, the benefit of a level unhurried pace. Mackay, who was also lazy, denied the merits of routine and saw no reason to lament his failure to adapt himself to it. But Peter rebelled against nature and circumstance.

Work became a penal labour. He had no time to dally over what interested him, to play with fascinating scraps of knowledge. The uninteresting things were the most important. He began to dislike the contented, methodically-minded people who worked on either side of him.

They would go through life like that, he thought. Doing the job in front of them, gratified by arm's-length successes, and not worrying about farther things. By-and-by they would look up for a moment, see a girl and marry her; then head down again, and more work; happy work, probably, with suitable holiday intervals at the sea-side or on the links; children growing up, educated a little more expensively than their fathers had been – as the paramoecium gets a wider education than the simple amoeba its parent – and taught to look straight ahead and do the job that lay in front of them. That was how life went on. You must be productive and unimaginative, and evolution will look after itself. Monocellular, multicellular, out of the slime, on to dry land, creeping instead of oozing along; lying on the rocks and sucking in virtue from the sun; climbing the trees now, testing your strength; conscious perhaps of hunger and a definitely recurring rut; down to the ground again, with ideas about property, and after property, propriety; and then compulsory education; things had been speeded up in the last few thousand years. Perhaps evolution was entering another chapter. Perhaps you might see the meaning of it – or the beginning of the meaning – if you could keep alive for 100,000 years or so; and still the sons and parents of evolution would be doing the job in front of them. It was interesting to think about it, and it would be more interesting to stand aside and look at it. But there was no time to stand aside if you were going to be a good, honest link in the chain.

The girl Joyce MacRae, to whom Mackay had introduced Peter, was also rebellious; an amused, academic rebel, perhaps, but certainly one who would refuse to take the oath of allegiance to Common Sense. She was working for Honours in Zoology and combined a social dissatisfaction with a kind of biological fatalism. She had said nothing socially disintegraitng at the dance to which Mackay had taken them; nothing wilfully striking about the functional incapacities of modern women or the possibility of a laboratory substitute for child-bed, as Mackay had hinted.

She had said: 'Dancing is one of the few things worth living for,' – a statement which is generally idle but may be the expression of a definite conviction – and, answering Peter's raised eyebrows, added briefly, 'Rhythm.'

Peter met her occasionally and took her to tea. She was

pretty, with an oval face, eyes almost almond-shaped, a flawless complexion, and short, fair hair. Her legs were particularly beautiful, and she admired them frankly.

She said once: 'I'm one of the very few girls whose legs, above the knee, look nice from behind.'

'I suppose women do owe more to their dressmakers than men to their tailors,' Peter said.

'Of course they do. Women were made for use, not beauty, and it's a German idea that beauty's inherent in use. It's only a man who can afford to look beautiful – I'm not talking about faces, you know; they're adventitious – when women spend half their time being pregnant.'

'But they don't.'

'They were meant to.'

'I don't think that male beauty is superior to female beauty at its best, though.'

'Of course you don't. No man dare, in case people say he's a pervert.'

'It's better to be a common Philistine than a suspected paederast,' Peter reflected.

Joyce MacRae leaned back and carefully crossed her legs.

'I'm sure that they're more beautiful than any man's,' Peter said.

'Mine are exceptional. That's why I drew your attention to them.'

'It never strays, except from the left to the right.'

'That's sweet of you. Isn't it nice to hear pleasant things about one's-self? – even though one knows that they're either hopelessly silly or utterly false. You're enormously strong, aren't you?'

'Is that silly or false?' asked Peter, laughing.

'Neither. But you would have enjoyed hearing it even if it

had been false, wouldn't you? I hate my family, because they never say nice things to me. They brought me on to the earth purely for their own amusement, and now they've lost interest in me. My father is possibly the only man in the world on whom my legs would have no effect.'

She recrossed them, sighing.

'Stay and have dinner,' said Peter. They were sitting in a hotel lounge.

'That's really intelligent of you. If you can choose a dinner as well as you can respond to a suggestion, I'm going to enjoy myself. But please remember that I'm virtuous. Mentally I'm free-thinking, promiscuous, free-loving; but physically I'm a Victorian.'

'I thought as much.'

'But how?' Joyce looked distressed; her eyes were long and reproachful.

'Instinct. Men have a much sounder instinct than women. But don't worry; I'm quite pleased that you're virtuous.'

'You speak as though you were getting used to it. Little provincial towns must be horrible for men. There's something pleasant about the thought of a virtuous girl, but a male virgin, unless he's very young, doesn't seem so attractive.'

'Have a cocktail,' said Peter tactfully.

'It's all right; I'm not going to ask you about your past. But – yes, I'll have a cocktail.'

Joyce was quiet for a minute or two, and her voice, when she spoke again, had lost something of its lightness.

'I was dying to talk to someone, and there are so few people that one can talk, oh, anyhow, to. I don't like girls, and men are so excitable.'

'Your legs, of course, are a barrier between you and your own sex and intoxication to mine.'

'Now I'm in a good temper again. And you?'

'I am a hermit in a strait waistcoat and an asbestos shirt. Only my eyes are appreciative.'

'And your tongue knows its manners. We're going to have a lovely dinner.'

An hour later, looking at the shiny brown body of a wild duck and an orange salad, she said: 'I believe in predestination. All good birds go into the stomachs of good men who love what they eat, and bad birds are consumed by women who don't appreciate them. Probably every little grouse and pheasant is taught to think of women as acid hells. But I'm greedy, and so my gastric juices are mild and beneficent. Isn't it lovely to think of oranges from Seville and a mallard from the Moray Firth meeting on a plate, for the first time, and going to heaven together in me?'

'Heralded by an oyster or two and blessed by the grapes of Burgundy,' added Peter. 'Our minds may be insular but our innards are cosmopolitan.'

He had played a secondary, responsive part all evening. Joyce's energy had spent itself on talking nonsense flecked with occasional seriousness, the kind of nonsense that covers like running water a darker bed of thought. And Peter, without quite knowing why, had encouraged her to talk, had listened, answered her or been silent, and was vaguely conscious of giving her relief.

Later she said abruptly: 'I was miserable this morning. I felt greedy and impotent. Everything was lovely, and damnable because it was impossible. I wanted to look at everything, and taste everything, and know about everything, and go everywhere. And life was stationary and meant chewing instead of tasting; and falling in love and poetry and pictures and music were only trimmings to reproduction, and shouldn't have more attention than trimmings deserve. I know what this outburst means; don't tell me. But isn't it unfair that we should be slaves to our – '

'Our chromosomes,' Peter suggested.

'They're dreadful things, aren't they? Fancy all the sins of our fathers and mothers, in equal parts, strung like beads on a bit of chromatin, being transmitted endlessly through time. We're not individuals, we're only carriers. And if we happen to carry anything more interesting than usual Nature says, "That's not an economic mutation!" and disinherits it.'

'You can stand aside and watch other people carrying their chromosomes to eternity.'

'It's difficult to get far enough aside to see them properly. And if you succeed in that you'll be lonely, and miss all the fun of the caravan.'

Peter took her home. They walked through city streets, some splashed with light and quick with the indeterminate traffic of night, some dark and silent like passages through an artificial rock that was pierced with innumerable caves – caves warm and peopled with semi-conscious, mysteriously impelled, heredity-driven, stupidly striving and senselessly contented human beings. Joyce had rid herself of discontent. She had talked it out. And all her devils, puff-bellied like question-marks, had lodged in Peter's brain.

His work suffered. The monotony of it irked him, and increasingly often he asked himself: What's the use of it? The obvious answer that its use was to provide him with bread and butter did not satisfy him. He felt that his desires were like Joyce's, to taste and to see and to know; not to earn and chew. He tried to find refuge in cynicism, and to believe that he could serve time with one hand and himself with the other; but neatly to dovetail pleasure and profit was beyond his powers. He needed something to which he could put both his hands, and he could not find it.

THE WINTER OF DISCONTENT

The prospect of a fight cheered him a little. He refused to train in an orthodox manner but he stole time from classes and the hospital to take long walks. The weather was fine, hard and cold, and in the mornings there was a pearly mist on the sea and hoar-frost on the links, with a veiled chilly radiance of sunlight and no wind.

Peter would walk northwards along the beach that lay between Inverdoon's two rivers, over a bridge and back to the beach, and north again between golf-links and the white-curtained sea. Slowly, as the sun climbed, the mist would rise and sea-gulls, flying under its fringes, dropped with wings aback to the sea that grew from uncoloured mistiness to shallow blue. The wet sand gleamed like weak gold, and shoreward it was nearly as white as the rime that had lately covered the grass. And in front of him the view became longer and clearer, the curving beach stretched farther, mile after mile, to little green and brown cliffs that thrust stubbornly into the sea. He wanted to walk on and on, with the careless slurring of the sea beside him, and the cold sunlight overhead, and the shining miles in front. There was a diamond-like exhilaration in the air, hard and glittering, and to turn back towards the smoky banner that overhung the town was like defeat.

Or he would walk countrywards, under trees robbed by winter of their gossiping leaves so that they stood silent and black, many-limbed, tortuous skeletons against the crystal sky. Ploughlands, scarred and heavy, slept in solid ease after the pangs of harvest. Here and there smoke climbed straightly from farm-houses. Dull yellow ricks stood about them. Dung and straw littered their yards. There was a smell of turnips and wood-smoke.

The country in its fat winter sleep was not so exciting as the sea except when sometimes, at the corner of a road, he

167

caught sight of distant hills, snow-covered, brilliant and serrated triangles on the horizon. They were remote and untouched by the dutiful, recurring fecundity of the fields. They stood unmoved by the wants of man, disdainful of his hunger, bearing in turn their purple carpets of heather and white mantles of snow, beautiful and dangerous and aloof, accepting as their right the savage wooing of storms, the roaring salute of wind and hail, and the equal companionship of the sun. They were static and changeless and far away, and it was like a renunciation when he turned his back on them.

His fight, when the day arrived, was disappointing. It was an inter-University contest but his opponent was unskilful and slow, a red-haired man with red down creeping upwards, under a white singlet, from his chest to his throat. He knitted his brows, swung sullenly, grunted when hit, and wiped a bleeding nose on the back of his fore-arm. Peter knocked him out early in the second round.

He worked for a few days afterwards, and then Joyce MacRae's pothooks and hangers of biological philosophy caught him again. He read Anatomy, and the winds of imagination blew about the dry bones before him and brought them to life; dry bones ridged for the attachments of muscles, polished for amazing articulations, made like strong levers; dry bones that were coral reefs built by dead cells; the scaffolding of a marvellous house, designed on immemorial lines. And designed for what? For the inscrutable slavery of Nature? For the beneficent, illogical service of a Hebraic, irrationally anthropomorphic God? Or had man played a trick on Nature – grown slowly and imperceptibly to con-sciousness and, in the midst of purposeless creation, evolved a purpose of his own in defiance of Nature? Shed his tail and proclaimed his independence? – and by that very proclama-

tion made possible his ultimate defeat of Nature? Had some
unknown Prometheus, benefiting from a strange conjunction
of parental characteristics, added a new trait to the chromosomes on the human chain? Would mutation succeed on
mutation, strength follow strength, till Man by his own unconscious will to dominate, actually won control of life?

It was an alluring thought. Knowledge seemed the most
desirable and exciting thing in the world; to see all things and
know all things. But the way to knowledge – and such a
petty fragmentary knowledge – was like a muddy lane
through a dead forest of books, a damnable lane, ankle-deep
in the mire of centuries; and the light of vision was narrowed
so as to creep in a microscope instead of bursting full-blaze
through a cosmic spy-glass.

The weather broke and rain fell for days on a sodden land.
Formless clouds hung miserably overhead and the earth was
full of wet clothes and black umbrellas. Peter's biological
excitement disappeared; there was nothing to be enthusiastic
about in a world like this. Time was a humid enemy whom
wise men found ways to destroy. He sat by the fire and read
detective stories.

III

THE end of term drew near, and as the necessity for conserving energy became more apparent the opportunities for dissipating it increased in number. Dances and dinners multiplied as Christmas loomed redly in the distance, and among them, like a Recording Butler, stood the Old Year scribbling on his tablets.

Again the realization of wasted time came to Peter. He had done barely a quarter of the work he had meant to do. Whole days had gone by in which he had read nothing, days that could never be recaptured, days lost in the ghostly wilderness of past time. The thought of that wilderness was like a vast grey field stretching far beyond the stars, in which were myriads of shrinking unknown spectres and the echoes of dead winds. Though all Time emptied its ghosts into the field by a million doors, and the processions were unceasing, the field was so large that no two ghosts ever met.

Waking early in the morning or lying awake at night a feeling of futility – of lonely futility – seized Peter with something like panic. The loneliness was the worst part of it. Thousands of people were futile, amiably futile in families or blatantly futile in crowds. But however futile their work and their amusements might be they had something to hold on to, something they believed in, something that gave them companionship. Loneliness was a spectre to frighten God. And Peter had found no one and nothing to which he could hold, neither work nor woman. Slowly he began to admit to himself that he hated his work, the endless routine of study, the dull time-table of books, long sitting in lecture-rooms, prosy discourse, the ceaseless laborious acquisition of minute and unrelated facts, the petty trial of examinations. He hated it, and there was nothing else he could think of to do.

THE WINTER OF DISCONTENT

He had no commercial instincts in his blood. Twenty generations of Fletts had lived on their farms or drowned in their ships, but not one had ever sold other men's goods across a counter or added other men's money in an office. There were plenty of trades and professions in the world, honourable callings and lucrative ones, but Peter could think of devil a thing to make his living by. It wasn't a case of making only his living. It was a case of making his life, and he couldn't make his life in an office. Medicine was a better profession than most, for you dealt with people, no ledgers or law-books or dusty files; but the way to it was three years long, three years of printed words, and the stimulus of completion was too far off to carry him. He should have been bound apprentice to the sea when he was sixteen, and the sea would have buffeted discontent and sickness out of him, broken him and mended him and hardened him to a service that admitted no rivals.

He had no friendly work to fill his hands and – the thought came to him like an admission of weakness – no woman to close his eyes against the wilderness of Time, the jungle and desert of life. Did men marry because they were afraid of loneliness, because they were frightened to walk solitary through the wilderness and in the jungle? Probably.

Peter thought of the women he had known. There were only two or three; far fewer than most men of his age could remember. But a certain fastidiousness had flavoured his youth and a strain of romance, never admitted but often evident, had kept him aloof from the commercial promiscuity which so often seems an adventure before it becomes a habit.

There was a girl in Norwich, in the early days of the War, one of those who raised white arms to excitement and laughed at Armageddon. She was young, full of sudden wisdom, glowing like a rainbow in the storm. She intoxicated him, stayed him with the flagons of her ardour, comforted him with apples of delight, and at the end waved him to France with the sulky complaint that men had all the luck. . . . And there was the girl he lived with during a week's leave in Paris. He didn't realize it at the time, but she mothered him, cosseted his soul, strengthened his weariness with the warmth of her body and gave him peace out of her own broken store. She was a War-widow, young enough in heart to love and hate, old enough in spirit to be gentle and comforting. She had said to him: 'After the War they will put up memorials to the men who fell, but will anyone build a monument to the women who fell? And yet you need us now more than your ghosts will need crosses in the market-place and panels in churches.' He had gone to her sullen and hungry and tired, cold from the trenches and beaten about the head with noise; she had sent him away warm and strong in heart, with a tenderness for her and her people. He had remembered the Old Alliance of France and Scotland, and she had replied: '*Les Ecossais ont toujours deux patries, la sienne et la France.*'

And then there were girls with whom he had been friendly more recently. Joyce MacRae. They talked about life, but they never considered living together. This was Scotland, a cold country, a hungry and austere land still in the gaunt shadow of John Knox. In the country districts license ran wildly at nights, more roughly than even Burns could grace in song, but in the towns decorum ruled. He thought of Norna. But Orkney was far away; it was a different existence. And somehow, irrationally, he shrank from the thought of Norna because he had revealed his weakness to her, shown his dependence, and been rebuffed.

Pat Geddes. . . . The old scar, silvered over, broke redly at the pinprick of her name. She was one of the ghosts in the hinterland of Time, a laughing ghost, the shadow of April in a dead year. There had always been something remote about her, the intangibility of youth, and now she was as far from touch in miles as she had been in spirit. Once, with a fine confident philosophy, he had said, 'This is summer love and must die.' But that was in summer, when the heart is strong and one lives for the day. In winter things are different. The dead earth is a melancholy place, dark and unfriendly, and a man needs the warmth of the hearth to keep him from despair. You cannot contemplate death and loss with indifference when all the year is dead around.

In the old days in Orkney they had shut themselves up against winter to drink the dark months under. Winter was too strong an enemy to defeat but he could be forgotten in the warmth of the bed and cheer at board. Then in the spring they got out their ships, heartened by the new green earth and the coming of the sun over shining seas, and went to seek their meat from dark-haired people with an alien god and rich abbeys. This hereditary winter lassitude reinforced his feeling of failure and loneliness, and Peter lay miserably awake, waiting for the cold dawn that came so reluctantly.

He went down to breakfast and found Mackay unpleasingly cheerful.

'I met Moncur last night,' he said, 'Some sprite of humour or forky-tailed imp of cynicism must have entered his stolid mind. He had just been sitting a term examination in Pathology. There was a question of tumours of the uterus, and Moncur wrote: "The commonest and most malignant tumour of the uterus is undoubtedly the fœtus." I wish I had said that myself.'

'You can,' Peter answered.

'Yes, but it will be some time before I feel that it's my own. I shan't be able to use it with any confidence to-night.'

'Where are you going to-night?'

'My dear fellow! The Celtic Dinner, of course.'

'The devil!' replied Peter irritably. 'I meant to work.'

Mackay laughed unfeelingly. 'But you wouldn't,' he said, and as my guest you really ought to conceal your reluctance to dine with us.'

'Would you mind if I didn't come?'

'Damn it, Peter, you must come. What does one evening at the end of term matter, anyway?'

Peter looked moodily in front of him and said nothing. Every good intention seemed to carry an obstacle with it.

In the University of Inverdoon a Celtic Society Dinner is an event notable for its melody, its historical associations, and its ultimate air of abandon. The main difficulty attendant on it is always to find an hotel willing to house it, for the scars left by one year have scarcely healed when the next dinner is due. The Celts stand a little apart from the Lowlanders. Some of them still think in Gaelic when they first go up to the University. They remember clan histories and old feuds. There was a time when the Highlanders left the Lowland students to graduate alone, while they went to fight at Culloden. They still argue about Simon Fraser, the traitor or patriot, and their arguments seem to waken again the noise of claymores in College Bounds and of dragoons galloping through the narrow streets of the Old Town.

Peter sat beside Mackay, half-way down one of the long arms of the trident-shaped table. Opposite him were a blue-eyed, black-haired man named MacRitchie, and a rat-faced MacArthur. Garry Duncan, another guest, sat near the head of the table. A Gaelic grace preceded dinner. The ritual of the haggis came soon. A piper, blowing shrilly, marched in front of the waiter who carried it round the length and breadth of the table to the Chairman. Everyone stood up. The Chairman gave a tumblerful of neat whisky to the piper,

who drank it solemnly, and blowing louder than ever marched
out again. In time the tables were cleared of everything but
glasses and decanters, and they came to the toast-list which
was long and elaborate. Loyal toasts and local toasts, patriot-
ism and personal affections, sporting toasts and desperately
serious ones all found a place on it.

Some of the speeches were in Gaelic. There were gentle
sounds in them like wind among the birches, shrill notes like
a pibroch, and the noise of waves on the shore. They excited
their hearers. Men stood up, shouting, and drank to the
speakers. Peter, who knew not a word of Gaelic, was excited
too, and drank with his heated neighbours.

They honoured the toast of His Majesty's Forces and Garry
Duncan, by virtue of a commission in the Special Reserve,
replied to it. He told a wartime story of Glasgow street
urchins miscalling each other and each other's relations.

It was a good story, Peter thought. But although there was
polite laughter and politer applause for Garry, funny stories
were not in the Celtic mood. They wanted something that
appealed to other emotions than humour. Even Mackay was
displeased.

'Can't he forget his street-corner stories for one night
in the year?' he said. 'This isn't the place for smutty
jokes.'

These Celts took themselves too seriously, both drunk and
sober. You had to be of their mood, whether tearful or
hilarious, or they quarrelled with you. Someone was singing
a wailing song of the Hebrides now. Oh, damn their Celtic
twilight, Peter thought. Thank God, I'm Norse. We knocked
the stuffing out of them pretty thoroughly in the Viking
years. They were probably boosting a Celtic renascence
then, and the Vikings, not liking their poetry, went to tell
them so.

Peter chuckled loudly.

'Hush!' whispered Mackay.

'I've just discovered that my ancestors were literary critics,' said Peter.

The song came to an end and the pianist ran almost immediately into *Charlie is my Darling*. Three or four men jumped on to the tables and began to do reel-steps among the glasses. The piper found his pipes and drowned with their defiant clamour the urbane tinkle of the piano. Soon half the men in the room were dancing with nimble high-stepping feet. Here and there a glass flew crashing off the table. At intervals a shrill cry, the high-pitched call of the dancers, rose from the medley.

The manager of the hotel came in, flustered, loud-voiced, worried and angry. The noise quietened and desperately he announced that no more drinks would be served unless peace was restored.

A lean, red-haired Macdonald from the Isles snorted with laughter and ran outside. He came back carrying his overcoat.

'When I dine at the house of a lousy Sassenach I take my own drink with me,' he said, and pulled a bottle of whisky from the pocket of his coat.

Laughing loudly a dozen other men went to the cloak-room and brought back the bottles they had secured for such an emergency.

The red-haired Macdonald leapt on to a table and told, in Gaelic, some story of Highland strategy and Lowland discomfiture. He told it well, with expressive gestures and grotesque mimicry, turning from one hand to the other, making his voice change from abject entreaty to scorn and triumph and laughter. It came to an end in a roar of general delight.

Mackay, who was drunk, started to his feet and shouted:
'Math thu fein! Sin am balach!'

He said to Peter: 'Drink to him, you dilapidated Viking.'

'I've drunk enough,' Peter answered.

'It takes a Highlander to carry his liquor as a man should,'
said the rat-faced MacArthur opposite.

Peter felt an insane desire to stand up and brag of his
prowess in drinking, in war, in anything and everything; to
brag as Charlemagne and his peers bragged over their wine;
to brag as the Jomsburg Vikings did before they went to war
and extinction at Liavaag; to brag as men used in every drink-
ing-hall from Kirkwall to Rouen. All about him men were
talking, louder and louder. Men of a different race, dark-haired
men from the West; and he was fair and out of the North.

He stifled the impulse, angry that it should have arisen. Two
men who had been arguing about some obscure question of
clan precedence came to Peter to put their case before an impartial judge. They were stupid and confused with drinking.

Peter listened to them for a moment or two and then said
roughly: 'Neither of your clans is worth a damn anyway.'

One of them grinned foolishly, but the other picked up a
half-full glass and threw the whisky in Peter's face.

He stood stupidly for a minute, blinded by the spirits. Out
of the darkness he heard Mackay's voice rise clear of the
hubbub in an angry shout, and when he rubbed open his
smarting eyes he saw his assailant bent backwards over the
table with Mackay's hands at his throat. His shirt had burst
open and between the stiff white ellipses a strip of hairy
chest showed darkly. Mackay was talking fiercely of breaches
of etiquette and breaches of hospitality; to throw a glass of
whisky in anyone's face argued a lack of manners, but to
throw whisky in the face of a guest was blasphemy.

'It's all right,' Peter said, 'it was my own fault.'

The little storm-centre had attracted a periphery of attention.

'It's not all right,' replied Mackay. 'Nobody's going to insult a guest of mine without paying for it.'

'Flett said that their clans weren't worth a damn,' interjected somebody.

'And are they?' shouted Mackay, suddenly inflamed by opposition. 'What are they? One's a bastard sept of the Campbells and the other came from behind a dyke where a tinker Stewart woman had been sleeping.'

The man on the table heaved himself convulsively to get his hands on Mackay. The table, thrust backwards, fell with a crash into a ruin of broken chairs and glasses. Uproar spread through the room. There were angry men, and men shouting with laughter, and men desperately trying to establish peace.

Then the lights went out.

Peter, who was hemmed against a wall with Mackay, felt the press of men about him loosen and grow slack as if a current had been switched off in them as well as in the lamps. The noise quietened, and then woke again in a clamorous demand for light.

'A tinker Stewart and a bastard Campbell,' Mackay hoarsely told the darkness.

'Keep your mouth shut,' said Peter.

Someone thrust his way to them and whispered to Peter, 'Get Mackay outside.' It was Garry Duncan. Together they pushed and found a way through the crowd. They reached the door as the lights went on again.

'The manager went to telephone for the police,' said Garry, 'and I thought there was a chance to get you people away under cover of night. So I put the lights out. Let's wait outside and see what happens.'

They got their coats and left the hotel.

'We ought to warn the rest of them,' suggested Peter.

Mackay snorted. 'They wouldn't move if you told them a field-battery was coming. I should rather like a brush with the police myself.'

'Don't be romantic,' Garry advised him.

Mackay shivered a little. 'I apologize,' he said. 'The cloak of civilization swung open for a minute, caught by an older wind. But look. Five of them!'

Four constables and a sergeant were tramping down the street. They turned into the hotel and from their doorway opposite Mackay and Garry Duncan and Peter waited with the complacent expectancy of a theatre audience.

They heard vague noises. In a little the noise grew clearer, and like a holiday train emerging from a tunnel the head of a procession appeared in the doorway of the hotel. The constables had each a prisoner. The captives were apparently flattered by this attention and offered no resistance. Behind them the remainder of the Celtic Society formed in a ragged column of route. The piper appeared and blew the discordant prelude to a march.

The sergeant tried to interfere, but a dozen hands held him off and a score of voices told him to be reasonable and behave like a gentleman.

The piper's face swelled like the bag under his arm, the empty street filled with the insolent echoes of his music, and its time was taken up by marching feet. Near the police station the air changed. Gleefully and tunelessly they sang:

'Oh, there's many a man in the Cameron clan
And a hell of a lot in the gaol.'

'Well, that's what I call a successful dinner,' said Garry as they walked away. 'I wonder if there's anything else we can do?'

Mackay shook his head. 'I feel cold,' he said. 'I'm going home.'

And after Garry had left them he added: 'I made a fool of myself to-night. I can't stand whisky *and* emotion.'

I V

CHRISTMAS was only a week away. Peter was undecided whether to go to Orkney for the short vacation or not. Martin had written to him, obviously hoping that he would, and commenting, as a kind of attraction, on the extraordinary mildness of the weather. 'There has been sunshine every day for a week,' she wrote, 'and one afternoon it was almost sultry. People talk vaguely about the Gulf Stream, and the old folk shake their heads and say that it can mean no good, as warm weather in December is clean contrary to nature.'

A sentence or two at the end of her letter worried him. Martin asked: 'Do you know a man called Isaac Skea? He has a bad name and a bad record – though I don't suggest this as a reason for your knowing him. He came here one day when I was out, and asked Bella (a maid) if you were coming home for Christmas. Bella says he was drunk at the time and went away swearing.'

The possibility of Skea making a nuisance of himself in this way had not occurred to Peter, and he disliked the idea of Martin being worried by him. But he could do nothing, even if he went to Orkney. And he didn't want to go. There would be questions to answer, hearty, well-meant questions from the Redland people; careless and understanding questions from Martin; questions that could not be satisfactorily answered. He had done a certain amount of work, but nothing like so much as he had intended to do. The rest had slipped past in a tangle of wasted days . . . wasted days, wasted time. The theme recurred with the monotony of a chorus. Time was a river stupidly running into a desert and disappearing. What did it matter? The source of the river wasn't likely to go dry in a hurry. There was plenty more time. But he couldn't explain that very readily to his friends in Orkney. Not that it was any concern of theirs; but they liked asking questions, and they had the manners to wait for an answer. Martin would accept his argument and laugh at the hole in his logic.

Mackay gave him a reason for staying in Inverdoon.

'How would you like a little midwifery practice over Christmas?' he asked.

Peter looked at him. 'There's not much chance of that, is there? We're not exactly ready for it, and I don't suppose there would be any vacancy even if we were.'

Mackay explained enthusiastically and with facts to support him. At this time, when the medical schools were still flooded with the backward tide of men from the Army, there were scarcely enough infants being born in the country to provide students with the necessary experience in the art and practice of obstetrics. The most vital part of the general practitioner's knowledge could only be acquired with difficulty, and opportunities to attend the practical courses in midwifery were eagerly sought. At Inverdoon two or three weeks' residence in rooms adjoining the Maternity Hospital was required; two or three weeks being generally sufficient to introduce a student to the proper number of infants. These rooms – the Howdie Digs which had entertained a midnight party on an earlier occasion – were engaged for many months, almost years, ahead. But a vacancy had suddenly occurred by the resignation of their turn by the two men next for duty.

'They're South Africans,' said Mackay. 'One of their fathers is in Paris and has invited them over for Christmas. He's probably stolen some diamonds,' he added thoughtfully. 'Anyway, it's our chance. We forgot to put our names in at the proper time, and the rooms are booked up for eighteen months ahead. Let's risk it. We can't do much damage, whatever happens.'

Peter was doubtful. Midwifery practice is intended to be done in a student's fourth year. There might be trouble with the authorities. But Morrice, the resident physician at the Maternity Hospital, was an old friend of Mackay's.

'Morrice says that all you want is twopence' worth of knowledge and a bob's worth of common sense.' Mackay had made up his mind – it was a compact, smoothly-working mind; easy indeed to make up. 'Nearly everybody has gone home for Christmas. Nobody will 'worry us, and nobody that matters will know anything about it till we've finished. And it will save time later on.'

Peter consented and wrote to Martin saying that he could not leave Inverdoon. He explained what he intended to do and said, trying to feel virtuous but finding it difficult: 'By doing this now I shall save time next year.' He added a postscript: 'If Skea worries you again put the police on to him.'

They took up their residence on Christmas Eve. The other men in the rooms were pleasant fellows, a little surprised to see Flett and Mackay. One was a quiet, hard-working man. The other played Rugby and danced in the winter, played golf and danced in the summer, and succeeded unobtrusively in filling the intervals between amusement with enough work to get him through examinations. His life appeared smooth and untroubled, and obviously contented him. He said to them: 'Look here, you fellows, if you kill anyone don't drag me into it,' and laughed heartily. His daily joke was: 'Well, done any manslaughter yet?' It never changed. But playing Rugby he could swerve either way at full speed. Peter envied him, after a fashion.

Peter and Mackay dined with Morrice, the resident, in Sandy Broun's, which was only a few hundred yards from the Hospital. The restaurant was full of Christmas Eve parties, full of a cheerful noise; decorated with great clusters of holly, chrysanthemums cinnamon-coloured, sulphur-coloured and deep-red; silver clattered and glass tinkled, and men and women laughed; warmth and a savoury smell made all minds genial. Snow was falling in the streets, lightly, in crisp flakes that blew against the windows and clung for a moment till they melted into rain-drops.

Untouched by the surrounding gaiety Morrice talked shop throughout dinner. He ate rapidly, scarcely looking at his food, and between the oysters and the fruit delivered an admirably concise and graphic lecture on the conduct of an accouchment. He was an enthusiast, and at times his voice rose a little too clearly, so that people at neighbouring tables turned in shocked amazement to hear expressions made vocal that, they thought, never escaped the privacy of a text-book. But when the coffee came Morrice could say with satisfaction: 'There now. If you remember half that you can't go wrong, and if you remember it all you'll know more than many a G.P. does.'

'I remember you talking in just such a tone to a patrol you took out once,' said Mackay. 'They came back all right, but you made a non-stop journey from the Struma to London, on a stretcher.'

'Well, that was a handsome reward. Confidence always pays, if you're confident enough.'

They talked idly for a while. Most of the diners, consciously full of the spirit of Christmas, had pulled crackers and put on paper caps. Flimsy headgear of all shapes and centuries perched on top of heavy red business faces, flopped rakishly over thin domestic faces, or sat happily on faces still young and adaptable.

Morrice looked at his watch, and as he did so a waiter came to say that he was wanted at the telephone.

'Come on,' he said. And Peter and Mackay got to their feet.

The snow was falling more heavily and already the house-tops were covered with a white mantle.

Shivering a little after the warmth they walked over to the Hospital. The theatre was hotter even than the restaurant. It was brilliantly lit and full of a heavy anæsthetic smell. On a bed, stripped to a hard mattress, a girl lay groaning. A sister stood beside her and a nurse was busy at a white enamel trolley that stood in a corner.

The girl looked up as they went in, saw Morrice in his white coat, and sobbed convulsively, 'Oh, doctor, doctor!'

'How is she getting on?' he asked.

'Splendidly,' answered the sister. 'Aren't you, Annie?'

'I wish it was you that was lying here and – O Christ! – I'd say that you were splendid,' said the girl.

'Come, come,' said Morrice, patting her shoulder, 'you mustn't talk like that. Everybody is being good to you and you'll soon be all right now.'

The girl clutched his hand feverishly. Her cheeks were red and blotchy. Normally hard-featured, young and insolent, her face was soft and relaxed with pain. Mackay looked at the card which gave particulars of the case. . . . Annie Cameron. Age 20. Mill-worker. The father of the child was stated to be J. Paterson. 'You'll find most of them like that,' whispered the nurse cheerfully.

Peter felt curiously excited and uncomfortable. He had nothing to do except watch. The room was oppressively hot and over-burdened with a sweet, sickly smell. He felt perspiration breaking on his forehead and in the palms of his hands.

Morrice said to him quietly: 'If you want something to do

hold her hands and try to keep her quiet. She's taken a dislike to the sister.'

The girl's hands were hard and hot. Peter stroked her arm,
feeling foolish, and muttered: 'There, now,' and 'Steady,
steady; it's all right.'

A long time seemed to pass before Morrice said cheerily;
'Well, that's over now, Annie, and you've got a real bonny
boy to take home with you.'

The girl lay motionless, worn-out with agony, and paid no
heed. But in a minute or two she said: 'A boy, did you say?
Where is he?'

The nurse was bathing him. A thin piping cry came from
his crumpled face.

'Give him to me,' she demanded.

Morrice took the child, wrapt round in a cloth, and held
it to the mother. 'That's a proper Christmas present for you,
isn't it?' he asked.

The girl took it with hands that seemed suddenly to have
grown tender, and looked down into the purple, grotesque
little face. Then she found something bitter in Morrice's
remark, for she turned defiant, and said in a harsh voice:
'Ay, it's a proper Christmas present. And he's my bairn and
no other body's in the world. He's the bonniest bairn in all
Scotland though he is a bastard!'

'Hush, hush,' said the sister, 'you mustn't make a noise
like that.'

'To hell!' said the girl. 'I've done more than you ever had
the guts to do, and I'll make a noise if I like.'

The sister, calm and unmoved, went about her work.

'Come to my room and have a drink,' said Morrice.

They looked out from the main door of the Hospital. The
small quadrangle in front of them was covered smoothly with
snow. None was falling now. Buildings stood black and

rectangular on a white carpet. The queer stillness that comes with snow lay about them. Suddenly it was broken by a sound of bells. A far-off lonely one pierced the silence first, and then a chorus followed it; a deep-voiced clock solemnly told the hour, booming melodiously through the clamour.

'A Happy Christmas,' said Morrice heartily. 'Come and have that drink.'

He led the way to his room, happily whistling something that he thought was a hymn; it was a kind of common denominator of all hymn tunes.

' "Unto us a child is born," ' Mackay said soberly as he lifted his glass. ' "Unto us a son is given" – poor little devil!'

'It's a cruel business, isn't it? You get used to it, of course. But the first time you see a child born makes you think. I've seen the toughest of tough fellows come in here and sit as serious as parsons after it. Then you begin to get interested in the mechanics of the thing, and once you're really interested – professionally and humanely interested – you stop philosophizing and concentrate on the case.'

Peter sat dumbly, staring into the fire. His shoulders filled the wide chair he sat in; his heavy jaw was thrust forward; and firelight or shadow threw the harsh lines of a scowl onto his face.

'They'll canonize Marie Stopes some day,' he said abruptly.

'I once wrote a song about her,' – Mackay became flippant – 'It went to the tune of "Hark, the herald angels," and the chorus was:

"Hark, the panel-doctors sing
Now our night-bells never ring!" '

For the next fortnight day and night were hopelessly tangled in each other. The child in the womb waits for no man, but as soon as the door begins to open presses to be through, impatient of confinement, unconsciously reaching to the world beyond.

'The little devils wouldn't be in such a hurry if they knew what sort of a world they were coming into,' Mackay grumbled when the telephone took him out of bed at two o'clock in the morning. They might go back in time for breakfast, tired and hungry, and assist at the birth of twins between tea-time and dinner. Their life was a procession of beds; the clean, disciplined, hygienic beds of the Hospital, and dismal, unwholesome beds in slum houses. But they grew interested in their cases, professionally interested in the management of them and humanely interested in their patients.

Here and there was a touch of comedy. One woman, stout and muscular, gave her age as twenty-nine. She looked older – and it was her first child – but her husband agreed with the age she stated. They spent a long and anxious night with her, and then in the morning, at the height of her agony, she screamed: 'O God, I was tellin' a lee, I was tellin' a lee! O God forgive me, I'm thirty-eight!'

And on one occasion Mackay went to the wrong address and woke up an old dame of seventy, who was enormously flattered and chuckled delightedly at his enquiries.

A few of the families with whom they came in contact were happy and contented, but more often the birth was illegitimate, the mother miserable or defiant, and the surroundings melancholy. Meanwhile the rough festivities of the New Year went on. Mean streets, alternately black with rain and bitterly streaked with snow, echoed to drunken songs, and the squalid rooms where frightened girls were in labour reeked with stale spirits.

Life, the great adventure, too often looked like a sordid

escapade; conceived in a rat-like intensity of primitive emotion, born in squalor, and doomed to endless repetition. The magnificent waste of Nature ran, not like a turbulent splendid river, but like a fierce black sewer.

Even Mackay became a little depressed towards the end of their residence.

'We're getting a one-sided view of life,' he said. 'I know that. But it's unpleasant to find that there is such a side. Our last five cases have included a criminal abortion, two illegitimate male children, and one female addition to a family of nine whose father is permanently unemployed. I feel a little unhappy. I feel that I don't want to work for ever in these surroundings. I want to grow orchids for a change, or spear fish from a coral reef by moonlight.'

Peter held a flaming spill of paper to his pipe and sucked hard. The bowl was over-loaded and would not draw. He hit it impatiently on the fender, and said bitterly: 'I hate the whole damned show. What's the use of it all? What's the use of these wretched children being born? What's the use of these filthy streets and dark, stinking little houses? And we're sweating our brains to get a degree that will allow us to live on these people. We've got to spend our lives patching up their bodies so that they can beget more children for us to deliver. That's our ambition: to be botchers and midwives. For some unknown reason people are determined to live, even in filthy lanes and tenements, and we're going to take advantage of that determination and profit by it.'

Mackay's pessimism had been no more than a kind of languor, but Peter spoke with a savage energy. He was physically tired and mentally excited. His eyes were red and he was carelessly shaved.

Mackay immediately reacted to his intensity, and said: 'You're talking nonsense, Peter. I don't want to be pietistic

189

but damn it, we're going to help these people as well as profit by them; there'll be little enough profit from most of them, incidentally. And they're worth helping, although they're dirty. Think of that girl last night. Have you ever seen anyone braver?'

'But it was wasted bravery. That's why I'm angry. It's all waste – or nearly all.'

'Nature's fond of wasting things. Think of salmon spawning.'

'Yes, but salmon spawn easily, on a clean river-bed; not in pain and a gutter.'

Mackay groaned. 'You're hopeless, Peter. Do you think these people would change places with a salmon, in spite of the inducements of running water and painless parturition? Can a salmon go to the pictures, or drink bottled beer, or read Sunday newspapers, or eat fish and chips, or clap its hands at a football match, or put half-a-crown on a horse? Not a bit of it. If human beings get all the pain they get plenty of rewards to make them happy. And they wouldn't thank you for your sympathy.'

'All right,' said Peter, slowly refilling his pipe. 'You can have it your own way. But I'm not cut out for a midwife, and I don't like crowded houses.'

For another day or two Peter and Evan Mackay played hide-and-seek with Time, sleeping for a few hours in full daylight, going out at midnight, and coming home for breakfast.

Their last case was a district one. They set out to look for an obscure court that burrowed like a tunnel into the side of a narrow lane. A policeman helped them and at the entrance to the court they found a little shivering man, his ragged collar-turned up, and his cold hands thrust deep into trouser pockets.

He led them up a winding stair to a room feebly lighted by a naked gas-jet. An untidy bed filled half the room. The mother lay with her face to the wall, and sitting up beside her, playing with the travesty of a doll, was a solemn child of two or three years. In a corner, on a heap of rags, an old woman lay half-asleep. She was white-haired, withered and yellow, scarcely distinguishable from the rags on which she slept. They roused her. She got up and took the un-complaining child from the bed.

There was no furniture in the room except a chair and a packing-case that served for a table. There seemed to be no dishes, no crockery, or pots and pans.

The mother turned weakly and spoke to them.

Mackay went out to look for the husband.

'Has she had anything to eat to-day?' he asked.

'Not very much,' the man answered.

He was nervous and looked half-starved. His cheeks were pinched and blue with cold. He hesitated for long before admitting that none of them had had much to eat for a week past. He was a hawker, and trade had been bad. He wasn't eligible for unemployment relief because he had never been employed by anyone. And they were almost strangers to the town. His wife didn't want to go to the hospital when they had a room of their own. She was a Highland girl, he said with a certain pride, and didn't care to go among strangers. The old woman was his mother. He was afraid that there was no food in the house for the morning. He hadn't thought what he was going to do.

Mackay sent him to the Hospital with a note asking for milk and bread.

The mother, weak with hunger, bore her pain almost in silence. She was dark-haired, pretty in a wasted way, and spoke with a soft Highland accent. A flood of tears came when they gave her baby to her, and she sobbed convulsively till the old woman rebuked her. She made an effort to control herself, and thanked them, very gratefully, for their trouble.

They gave what money they had to the husband – he took it reluctantly – and walked back to their rooms, Peter in silence, Mackay cursing softly to himself.

THE FIFTH SYMPHONY

I

THE illusion of starting a clean page is the most comforting feature of early January. The dusty backboard of the old calendar has been taken down, and a bright new one looks heartily out over its protruding pad of days, each embellished with didactic optimism, drugged with Emerson, or smoothly glossed from *In Memoriam*. A new ledger is opened. Bad debts and unfulfilled promises are alike forgotten. The future is bright and empty and waiting to be filled.

But Peter was deprived of this kindly deception by his attendance at the Maternity Hospital. His duties there lasted till well into January, and he returned to his ordinary work without enjoying the break between the old and new years which is necessary to give the semblance of completion and the illusion of inception. And he was tired. He could not forget the poverty and misery he had seen, and he could not see them in their true perspective though Mackay argued about relative values, the individual attitude, and the difference between considering an environment from outside and experiencing it, as a native, from within.

'Well, go and preach Socialism,' he said at last.

'I would,' Peter answered, 'only I don't like Socialists.'

A Christmas card and a note from Patricia Geddes had fallen lightly into the turmoil of nativity. She was in Lahore, riding, dancing, thrilled with India. She had been to Delhi and Agra. A shiny photograph of the Taj Mahal gleamed on her Christmas card.

Martin wrote from Orkney, telling of an extraordinary gale which had swept the islands in the last days of the Old Year. Peter had seen some story of it in a newspaper – a trawler had been wrecked, a roof blown in, and an old man killed by a falling tile – but in the hurry of the time he had not read it carefully. Martin's letter was more vivid than her usual style of matter-of-fact narration. She had evidently been impressed by a curiously dramatic accident of the storm.

'You remember,' she wrote, 'that I told you how mild the weather had been. Christmas Day was warm and humid. I felt as if there was going to be thunder, but when I said so at Redland they laughed at me. The idea of thunder at Christmas was absurd, they said. But I was right. It grew blacker and blacker, after a windless and almost airless morning, till the sky looked like an iron pot pressing down over the earth. And then the pot cracked. There was a huge jagged streak of lightning and a roar of thunder. It was terrible. The thunder seemed close above us, and you could see the lightning darting into the ground. Rain fell solidly, noisier rain than I have ever heard, and afterwards the wind came, as though it had been waiting for its chance behind the clouds, and swept everything like a scythe – if you can imagine a scythe swung at eighty miles an hour.

'A lot of damage was done. A horse was killed by lightning, and one flash struck the Viking Stone just above the Cross. The cross has disappeared and a grey scar runs down the Stone, looking like a wound in the soft licheny surface.'

The Viking Stone was one of a broken circle of megaliths that stood on a strip of moorland between two lochs. There had been fifty or sixty stones in the original circle but more than half had fallen to the weather, and the survivors, battered and worn by stormy centuries, stood like ragged mourners of a lost religion. Old sun-worshippers, dead and vanished before history started, had dragged these giant monuments to their places in the sacred ring and set them perilously on end; dug them in, trenched them round with a moat; and bowed between to their image the sun with no one knows what rites. A broken-down altar stood at a little distance and a mile away, over one of the lochs, there was a chambered burial-mound.

The Norsemen, raiding the islands, found this savage temple and were afraid. They had forsaken the old gods and taken in their place the white Christ. This uncouth circle of stones looked evil to them. So on the tallest of the stones, a grey top-heavy giant, some of them carved a deep cross, the symbol of Christ, to keep at bay the ghosts and restless spirits of an elder worship. Old things, impossible to understand, are full of fear. But the cross, new carved, looked bright and comforting on the worn stone and doubtless did its office of guardianship well enough. In time the cross itself weathered, its harsh edges grew smooth and round, it filled with yellow moss, and seemed part of the very stone. And now the lightning had come like a white-hot chisel and ripped it off, leaving in its place a staring scar.

It was a freakish trick for the storm to play. Peter wondered whether any superstitious fears would be wakened by the blasphemous cantrips of the lightning. He picked up the letter again.

'Old Becky Bews is very upset about the disappearance of the cross,' Martin wrote. 'It means something bad, but exactly what I can't find out. Becky says that her father told her what the old people in his young days used to prophesy would befall the islands if the cross went. But Becky's memory went before the cross, and she can't remember the tradition more precisely than that it was something eery and uncomfortable. "But maybe we'll see soon enough," she said, and sniffed indignantly when I laughed at her.'

Martin finished a long letter with news of the dogs and the pigs. There was no further mention of Isaac Skea.

Monotonous days filed past and slid mysteriously into weeks. Stormy rifts of sunshine broke the blackness of winter and grudgingly daylight began to lengthen. Peter took little exercise and smoked heavily. He was sinking into an acquiescent weariness of mind and body. When Mackay tried to rouse him he yawned and said lazily: 'What's the use?'

Mackay was worried. His own laziness – he said: 'What's the use?' as often as Peter – was a cheerful gloss on his thoughts, a protective varnish of happy-go-lucky cynicism over a body of sound, if unobtrusive, common-sense. But when Peter said 'What's the use?' it was in a tone of sullen inertia.

For a day or two he had shaken off his sloth and roused himself at the prospect of a fight – a harder fight than he had had for a long time. The only important contest for the Spring Term was in Edinburgh, and the Edinburgh heavy-weight had just distinguished himself by winning an amateur championship at the Universities, Hospitals and Services' Tournament. He had been highly praised by competent critics for his speed in attack and his masterly footwork. His punch was heavier than an amateur's usually is, and he had won both his semi-final and final bouts by a knock-out. Peter read the newspaper stories of him with interest and told Mackay that he meant to start training at once.

But he put it off for a day or two and his enthusiasm flagged.

'I don't think I'll fight after all,' he said. 'I can't be bothered training. In any case the Edinburgh fixture is too near the end of term. It would mean sitting examinations almost immediately after; probably with an eye closed and my head still ringing. It isn't worth it.'

'People will say you're frightened of him if you give up your place in the team,' Mackay objected.

'They can say what they please,' said Peter, and stood up to kick a toppling coal deeper into the fire.

They were making a desultory pretence of working, but Peter dozed over his book and Mackay's thoughts kept straying to an etching of McBey's that he had bought.

'I don't know if Ely Cathedral really looks like that,' he said, 'but I have an idea that that's the sort of thing people dreamt of when they started to build a cathedral. There was mystery and a kind of soaring darkness in their minds, and they wanted to house it nobly and hold it down to earth.'

The brittle impact of a pebble thrown against the window interrupted him. He got up and looked down into the street.

'A girl. Young, apparently well-dressed, making an imperative gesture. It must be a friend of yours, Peter. No one loves me so frowardly as this.'

Peter went down and found Joyce MacRae standing outside.

'Don't be flattered,' she said. 'I smoked my last cigarette an hour ago. The shops are shut, and I grew desperate. How many can you spare?'

'A hundred or two. Come in and help wrap them up.'

'But would that be proper, or even safe? I only came for cigarettes, you know.'

'Mackay is in, and he's a hound of decorum,' Peter answered.

Mackay met them with a cry of delight.

'My old enemy!' he greeted her. 'Get out the wine, Peter. Do you drink beer, Miss MacRae? We've nothing but beer and Eno's, I'm afraid. And look at my Ely Cathedral. Doesn't it soar into gloom? Early religious architecture is so deliciously ingenuous. The nearer it climbs to God the darker it gets, till right at the top you can see nothing at all.'

'And modern architecture?' Joyce suggested.

'Oh, futile or utile. Futile as regards art, but it hides the bathroom and keeps out the rain. Do have a cigarette.'

'That's what I came for.'

'I wish you had come for Peter. He needs someone to call for him and take him out long walks, and talk to him about foreign stamps, and birds' eggs, and things like that. Are you still doing Zoology? – you ought to know a lot about birds' eggs.'

Joyce stretched her legs to the fire and watched a smoke-ring wavering upwards.

'Do you want me to talk about eggs, Peter?' she asked.

'If you know of a good roc's egg anywhere I shouldn't mind attaching myself to it for a voyage or two.'

'That's the way he talks, Miss MacRae. And I shouldn't mind if he were optimistic enough to believe in rocs. But he isn't.'

'Do you believe in them?'

Of course I do. But then I'm not a scientist like you – I'm going to be a doctor.'

Joyce sighed. 'I shall never be a scientist either, I'm afraid. I always confuse Newton and Darwin, and no real biologist would do that.'

Mackay looked puzzled but Peter, with sudden illumination, said: 'Of course! They were both mixed up with the Fall of Man, weren't they? One with the apple and the other with apes.'

'Do you see it too?' asked Joyce happily. 'They always get tangled up in my mind, and when I think of biological Man I see a vague picture of Newton with an apple in his hand talking to Eve about gravity while Darwin examines Adam for his vestigial tail.'

'It sounds like a pre-Raphaelite nightmare,' said Mackay.

'I once dreamt of Botticelli's *Primavera* with Queen Victoria as the central figure,' Joyce remarked a little proudly.

'For heaven's sake don't tell me your dreams. That one defies analysis, I think, but I've lost more friends by listening to their dreams than I ever lost by borrowing money. If you only knew some of the things that people have told me, on tram-cars and brazenly in public places! Of course they didn't realize what their dreams meant, but I did, and I've had to shun them ever since.'

'Do you honestly believe in dream analysis? Don't you think that the popular jokes are true and that dreams are gastric as much as mental?'

'You mean that if we go to bed on beef we dream beefishly? That's like the old magical idea of a man gaining strength by drinking the blood of bulls or his enemy. And according to you the dreams of the vegetarian, living on a pure fruit diet – '

'There's only one pure fruit,' Peter interrupted, 'and that's the banana. Did you know? I found out some time ago that bananas are parthenogenetic.'

Joyce giggled and was ashamed of herself, while Mackay said: 'Are they really? I always thought they had a cold, prudish look. That explains it. And the way they hang to-gether – it's like a girls' school being enthusiastic about someone, isn't it?'

'I ought to go home,' said Joyce, 'May I have another cigarette?'

Mackay struck a match for her.

'Don't go,' he said. 'I won't let Peter say anything more to shock you, though he's aching to talk about all the illegitimate children he delivered a few weeks ago.'

Peter laughed and protested. 'In any case,' he added,

'there wasn't any difference between the legitimate ones and the others.'

'Of course there isn't,' said Joyce. 'I don't think those words, legitimate and illegitimate, should exist. If a woman can afford to look after a baby, and wants a baby, why shouldn't she have one? Four times out of five a husband is only an added nuisance and needs more looking after than the baby, without giving in return the interest of watching him grow up or the excitement of teaching him things – husbands can't be taught, can they?'

'But this is matriarchal heresy,' objected Mackay. 'You want to abolish the husband and make a serf, or a cipher. You'll ask for polyandry next.'

'And why not?' asked Joyce. 'Only instead of husbands call them lovers. Think of the different sound of those two words. One's music and the other's noise. I don't want a husband but I'd like a lover – not yet,' she added hastily as Mackay seemed about to speak.

Let me be godfather to your first child,' offered Peter.

'I'd prefer to be its father,' said Mackay unblushingly.

'And now I am going.' Joyce got to her feet. 'A poor defenceless girl – '

'Don't be offended,' Mackay begged. 'At any rate take some cigarettes with you and remember my address.'

Peter walked home with her.

Joyce said abruptly: 'I've got a new enthusiasm. I've just discovered – really discovered – that there's such a thing as music, and I've sold all my goods to buy gramophone records. I feel a little bit shy and ashamed of my discovery, like a dog that has grown up before it finds that it has a tail. But I want to wag my tail, now that I know it's there. Will you come and hear the Symphony Orchestra with me next week?'

'I'd like to, if you don't want me to make intelligent re-marks. I don't know an octave from an oboe.'

'That's why I asked you. I should be ashamed to go with anyone who was erudite and I don't want to go with someone who snores.'

Peter laughed. 'I promise not to snore,' he said, and walked back to his rooms without thinking any more about it.

THE orchestra, a half-moon frailly barricaded by music-stands, faced the long rectangle of the audience and silence succeeded the hum and multifarious plaintive responses of tuning strings on the one side, the buzz and chatter of conversation on the other. Into the silence, to break it with polite applause, came the conductor. He had a commanding air with something saturnine about him, as if he distrusted the value of a provincial welcome and was yet grimly assured that he could sharpen souls to emotion at his will, quieten them, or lift them to enthusiasm.

Silence grew again. He gathered a still, expectant attention with his bâton. Something of Purcell's opened the concert, a suite for strings that suggested a country-dance in a cathedral, birds, and an organ playing in a wood. Then something competently exquisite, strength most admirably controlled and sweetness delicately poised. . . . Peter looked at his programme and saw Mozart. He felt guiltily that he should have known. The applause was prolonged and consciously hearty. The third item was a tone-poem by Strauss. It was concerned with death – an individual death – and opening tremulously passed through successive frenzies that may have indicated hæmorrhage to a kind of distracted beauty. The applause was dubious and died gratefully into the half-way interval.

Peter was enjoying himself without knowing why, responding sensuously to rhythm and exhilarated by motifs that the whole orchestra took up and worked to their destined summit of expression. He was dimly aware that these patterns of sound were made up of interwoven threads, but he could not unravel them. The music had excited Joyce and made her restless. She talked hurriedly of inconsequent things as soon as the clapping of hands was over and then, after a little pause, said: 'Last week, when I came round to your rooms, I was serious when I talked about lovers and marriage. I did want to be married once. I was seventeen, but don't laugh; it was War time. And the boy I was going to marry was killed when they took the Hindenburg Line. It was his first battle. He was nineteen. He was older than me and now I'm older than him. I think that's why I want children and not a husband.'

She tried to laugh, with a pathetic note of apology.

'The world's full of broken things,' said Peter slowly.

'We're not really young, are we? We only have a kind of hard, make-believe youth that's lasting longer than the real thing would.'

'Or have we grown an extra skin, a defence that's waiting to be scratched?'

'It's the same thing. Youth doesn't defend itself. I read somewhere that the cadets of St. Cyr, going under fire for the first time in 1914, wore white gloves like girls going to their first Communion. No one puts on white gloves for defence.'

Peter said nothing. He could think of nothing to say. He suddenly found it difficult to remember how and why the conversation had started.

The second half of the concert began with a dancing thing by Rimsky-Korsakov. It had brazen Oriental tones in it and a whirling precision of movement. The name of Delius offered no meaning to Peter but he liked the melody and the pretty reminiscent melancholy of the piece. The last item on the programme was Beethoven's *Symphony in C Minor*.

There seemed to be a tauter expectancy in the quiet that preceded it; a silence stiller and more intense than the others waited as if for a deeper challenge to break it. An explanatory

note on the programme said something about 'Fate knocking at the door.'

The challenge came and was repeated; a sonorous imperative, a herald's trumpet sounding under enormous battle-
ments, Prometheus calling to the gods behind Caucasian
mountains. A confused succession of images passed through
Peter's mind: Laocoon, timelessly fighting the coiling snake;
the runner to Marathon; trumpets, and the walls of Jericho;
Rodin's *Thinker;* King Lear in the storm. They passed and
left nothing pictorial, nothing in words or colour, but an
excited awareness that all these things – Lear and the *Thinker*
and the Runner to Marathon, and what they thought and felt,
were happening in a new element. His brain was full of a new
knowledge, a knowledge rugged and terrible but strangely
sweet. 'Out of the strong came forth sweetness.' And it was
knowledge that either passed at once into emotion or from
the beginning was inextricably fused with emotion.

The music changed into something more peaceful. The
hills were still there but the storm had left them and they
stood serene, conscious of their climbing woods and pleasant
valleys. Strength and Beauty walked confidently, glad because of their strength and beauty. And then laughter came
to join them, whimsical as swallows, deep as the earth.
Movement and time grew sportive, changed bewilderingly,
and yet all their games seemed to be part of the one game.

The scherzo gathered itself into a crescendo and swept
triumphantly into the finale. Peter could never estimate how
long the last part took to play. It might have been a minute
or an hour; or perhaps all clocks stopped, beaten at their own
game by something which took no count of daylight or dark
but poised like an albatross, alone and independent in space.
All he could remember was a magnificent stormy triumph,
the sound of banners in a gale and the gold and crimson of

banners that dared the sunset. His heart was like the sea at Salamis, and bore with almost insupportable pride the conqueror's ships. The Persians were dead and drowned, making rich the weedy darkness of the sea's bottom. And then Triumph and Time were welded into a great hammer that struck resoundingly the brass disc of the sun. And when the shock of that clamorous vindication had passed people looked round and saw their little white-faced neighbours and remembered dully that they had homes and daughters and rheumatism and a position in the world.

Peter and Joyce, wedged silently in the crowd, slowly moved to the doors and the lamp-stippled street.

'For God's sake come and walk,' he said.

They walked rapidly over pavements crisp with a touch of frost to a road that climbed up and out of the town. They scarcely spoke. Peter was full of a mental and physical elation that drank the frosty air and was fed by memories of splendid music, isolated phrases and dominant motifs, music that was like Shakespeare's laughter, 'broad as ten thousand beeves at pasture.' Joyce was tremulous, as at the sight of too much beauty, and in her mind she heard again a lonely flute rising clear in the forest of strings.

Stars, sharp-edged, like silver prickles, shone in a deep clear sky. They stood leaning against a wooden gate and looked at the town below them, hidden in a dark haze made evident by a thousand yellow points of light.

Joyce said: 'There's no reason on earth for it – I'm as happy as anything – but I feel somehow that I want to cry.'

'Cry?' said Peter. 'This is what I want to do.'

He stooped and gripped the middle bar of the gate, strained, heaved it off its hinges, and flung it down with a thud on the frozen ground.

Then he laughed. Joyce, startled for a moment, laughed

too and they stood, moved ridiculously to mirth, chuckling, shouting, their laughter pealing under the hard bright stars.

'But you must put it up again,' said Joyce at last.

Peter with an effort lifted the gate onto its hinges.

'And now we'll go home,' he said, and took her arm through his.

III

'WELL, what did you hear last night?' asked Mackay at breakfast-time.

'Beethoven,' Peter answered. There was a letter from Martin waiting for him.

'He who sits at the left hand of God.' Mackay had a hearty manner even in the morning. 'One of my most satisfactory images of heaven is God sitting in a pleached arbour drinking tea with Shakespeare and Beethoven. Did you like him? When he was on his death-bed the doctors tapped him for dropsy and the old man, looking at the water coming away, said: "Better from my belly than from my pen." Pass the marmalade, will you?'

Martin had more to say about the damaged Viking Stone.

'People are talking arrant rubbish about the disappearance of the cross from the Viking Stone,' she wrote. 'Old women are the chief offenders, and the trouble is that they are frightening the children with their stories. Nelly Macafie, the tinker, was at Redland the other day, begging and telling the news of the countryside. The whole family gathered round her, as they always do, and Maria asked her if she had seen the Stone. "Ah, God have mercy," she answered, "it was an ill day when the lightning took the cross away. My son Andrew says that he saw the Peerie Folk[1] dancing there the last time there was a moon, and Andrew's a good lad that wouldn't tell a lee to his own mother." The children laughed at her, but Norna says the little ones were frightened afterwards.

'Half the people you meet say foolish things like, "My, an' I wouldna go past there at night, no, not for nothing." Apparently the folk at Hallbreck (a farm two or three miles

[1] Peerie Folk] Fairies.

from the Standing Stones) have been talking this kind of
nonsense, like everybody else, and poor Daft Sammy has
been frightened out of what wits he had left – you know who
I mean? The boy who fell off a rick and fractured his skull,
when he was little. He hadn't given any trouble for years,
except when children teased him, but Nelly Macafie says
that when she passed Hallbreck he came out and screamed at
her. "His hair was in a raffle," (Norna told me this, as Nelly
told her), "and his face as white as cruds, an' he grat an' he
howled an' he screekit, an' God, he fair fleggit the shalt[1] so
that I never got doon from the cart at all. I'm thinking that
Daft Sammy's maybe seen the Peerie Folk as weel as my
son Andrew." The truth, I suppose, is that he has heard his
people talking just this kind of nonsense and got properly
scared.

'Superstition is so rife that Mr. Johnson talked about it in
his sermon last Sunday, and warned us – there were seventeen
people in church including his wife and her sister – against
harbouring these evil and heathenish ideas. He wandered
vaguely into mists of symbolism and told us that the cross
itself meant nothing. It might just as well have been a circle
or a right-angled triangle. Poor Mr. Johnson, he hasn't
a very graphic mind, has he?'

She mentioned Skea casually. 'I saw your friend Skea
yesterday – is he your friend? He shouted something as I
passed, but I didn't stop the car to find out what. He isn't a
nice-looking man to talk with on a country road.'

The letter worried Peter a little. He knew his own people
well enough to realize the power that such superstitious
fancies might have over them, for although they laughed
and proclaimed their matter-of-factness, their freedom from
the old night-fears that had plagued their ancestors, Peter was

[1]fleggit the shalt] frightened the pony

was convinced that superstition was not really dead among them, however soundly it might sleep. This *coup de théâtre* of the lightning might be the sort of thing to awaken it.

He remembered Daft Sammy; a shambling fellow with a fluffy little beard that had never been shaved, and staring, vacant eyes. He could generally be distinguished half-a-mile away by the grotesque patches with which his mother prolonged the shabby life of his trousers.

But Peter, with the exultant declaration of the Fifth Symphony in his head, was not in a mood to nurse anxious speculations.

He went out to look for Sandison, the secretary of the Boxing Club.

'Look here,' he said, 'if you haven't filled my place yet I'd like to change my mind and fight at Edinburgh.'

Sandison was delighted. 'You're the only heavy-weight we have who can stand up to Matheson for more than a round,' he said. 'But you've got to start training at once and go on training till the last day. You're damned fat and flabby at present.'

For the next three weeks Peter trained in the Gymnasium, worked in the Dissecting-room, attended classes and the hospital when he could, read methodically in the evenings, and slept soundly. He sloughed his pessimism like a discarded snake-skin. The mood induced by Beethoven's triumphant music stayed with him. He would waken in the morning with jubilant recollections of it, and while he boxed with his sparring partners rhythms and phrases from it seemed interwoven with his movements. He felt confident and elated, free from care.

Mackay was puzzled by the sudden change. He could think of no reason for it, and Peter, who was conscious enough of the alteration in his feelings, was not inclined to analyse them either for his own benefit or for anybody else's. He accepted the dispensation and w.s content. Had anyone told him that the audible externalization of his own emotions and the audible fulfilment of his own inarticulate desires had purged and purified his mind, he might have agreed, but amiably and without curiosity in the process.

He met Joyce once or twice but they said nothing about the concert. They did not want to discuss it. The music had affected them to an extent that neither would have considered possible, and they were reluctant to disinter an emotion which dissection might make embarrassing.

When the day came on which he was to go to Edinburgh Peter was fitter than he had been for months. He joined the other members of the team at the station, and as the train pulled out he looked round the carriage, from face to face, and felt full of laughing satisfaction. A casual but alert observer, he thought, would be puzzled by this little company, utterly unlike each other in many ways, and yet owning as a common feature the aptitude for combat. They looked like fighters. Mitchell, the welter-weight, had eyes – light blue, contentious eyes – almost completely protected by the bony protuberance of cheek-bone and frontal ridge. Anderson and MacIver were red-haired, one dark and the other sandy, one square-faced and bold, the other narrow and hard. Stewart, the middle-weight, had a chin that stood out like a ram, a flat, aggressive nose, and enormous ungainly hands; he was a Divinity student, quick-tempered and proud. The fly-weight, Richardson, was the only one who looked out of place in a ring. He had delicate features, a quick, mantling colour, and long eyelashes. They called him Little Lord Fauntleroy, for lace and velvet seemed the proper things to dress him in. Sandison, a light-weight, was the *beau sabreur* type, reckless and accomplished.

Peter felt none of the nervousness which usually attacked him before a fight. The Edinburgh men, when he met them, seemed pleasant fellows and he liked the look of Matheson, the successful heavy-weight.

The audience was large and inclined to be noisy. Richardson started well for Inverdoon, winning his fight by a decisive majority of points. Peter watched him darting lightly in and out, hitting lightly but hitting often, showing marvellous foot-work. Graceful accuracy and an almost bird-like rapidity of movement made Richardson delightful to watch and his victory was greeted enthusiastically.

'Do you think my left eye is going to be black?' he asked anxiously as he came out of the ring. 'I'm dancing to-morrow night.'

The initial success flattered Inverdoon, for after Richardson's win fight after fight went to Edinburgh. Anderson and Stewart were knocked out, Sandison broke a bone in his hand and had to retire, Mitchell and MacIver lost on points after hard-fought contests.

Peter heard the news of these successive defeats without much emotion. They hardly seemed to concern him. He was conscious of a growing excitement. His heart was beating a little quicker than normally. He felt eager and alert, like a runner waiting for the pistol. Matheson's reputation was only an incentive to additional effort. It could not overawe his mood of elated anticipation.

He entered the ring before Matheson. The audience, made happy by the succession of Edinburgh victories, greeted him with enjoyment rather than with critical regard. When Matheson followed he was acclaimed exuberantly. They considered his victory assured. He was already a champion and Edinburgh was in a winning vein.

Gradually the clamour grew less and settled into a dim belt

of silence round the brightly-lit ring. But there was a quality in the silence that made it living. It was different from the dead stillness of night or the empty calm of a windless day at sea. It was a nervous, expectant silence, waiting for the release of drama as the silence preceding the Fifth Symphony had waited.

And Peter thought: I'm an actor this time, not a spectator. . . . The echo of that opening challenge sounded in his memory like Roland's Horn in the mountains. . . . But Roland's Horn cried for help, didn't it? The trumpets of Jericho are better. Or Fate knocking at the door. Knocking at Matheson's ribs. His seated ribs; no, his seated heart. Knocking against the use of Nature. Like the two-handed engine at the door. Where the devil did that quotation come from? . . . It didn't matter. The music was going on.

Matheson sat in his chair looking easy and assured as a champion should. He was handsome in a heavy, aquiline way, and his hair looked heavy. It was glossy and black. A little upward rush of hair came over the edge of his singlet, growing from his finely-developed chest. The muscles that give a man strength to hit swelled under his shoulders as he gripped the ropes. His legs were long and powerful.

A gong sounded and the seconds lifted the chairs out of the ring. Matheson and Peter met in the centre, shook hands, all four gloves together, and stepped back. Matheson moved rather languidly, as if too sure of himself. Lazily he stepped in and like a yard-measure flicked his left glove to Peter's head. Peter avoided it. Then, with the rush of flood-waters leaping a broken bank, he sprang in attacking. Those behind him saw the muscles of his back rippling under the thin white vest as he hit or feinted, first with his left, then with his right. They saw his right arm, hooked and massive as the muscles flexed, jolt fiercely upwards and they heard the thud as his glove met Matheson's jaw. Matheson fell with a crash.

There was a yell of excitement and amazed delight from the half-dozen Inverdoon men about the ring; the rest of the spectators looked with dismay and heard in silence the referee impassively counting.

Matheson struggled to his feet and fell into a clinch.

They broke away and Matheson covered himself as best he could. Peter forced him round the ring. The advantage for the moment was his, and he must make use of it. Matheson, though weak, was clever in defence and his strength was coming back. But Peter drove him continuously and without rest. He was fighting to win, exultantly intent on winning, master of himself and triumphantly master of his opponent. A phrase or two from somewhere in the middle of the dominant Symphony woke in his brain . . . a fragment of the scherzo, jocular and fierce and amazingly alive. Something that seemed to sing with hilarious pugnacity: 'Hit him again, hit him again, hit him again, *Hit* him again; HIT – HARD, hit him again. . . .

Peter hit him, once, twice to the body – his seated ribs – and then poising, lifting on his toes, he hit straight with his left, swooping in like a sea-bird on its prey. Matheson's head went back, his arms dropped, his knees sagged, he fell helplessly to the floor. The referee had counted seven when the gong sounded and his seconds pulled him to his chair.

The minute interval passed slowly for Peter, but it was brief enough for Matheson, painfully and doggedly fighting for strength. 'Go easy; hold him this round; you'll get him the next one,' his seconds whispered, and Matheson nodded obediently. He rose gallantly to the gong and used all his skill to guard himself against Peter's immediate attack. He succeeded in hitting Peter flush on the teeth. Peter threw back his head, laughed, and forced his man into a corner. Matheson's dark head and Peter's fair one were close together as they drove short-arm punches into each other's ribs. The tune had changed in Peter's mind. It had swept into the ineluctable triumph of the finale. His memory was full of imperiously insurgent echoes, and the knowledge of imminent victory was instinct in their splendid harmony. His eyes were shining. He swayed backwards, out of the towsy scuffle, and swung suddenly in again with a stiff, half-hooked punch that took Matheson under the right eye and knocked him on to the ropes. The taut ropes were like the string of a bow and, half of his own will, half of the strength of their recoil, Matheson lurched forward. As he came Peter hit. His right arm straightened like a piston, with the strength of his shoulders and the balanced weight of his body behind it. His fist landed on Matheson's jaw with a crash. Matheson dropped, sitting, and fell backwards. His legs twitched and relaxed, and he lay still. The referee's 'Eight – Nine – Out!' was like the concluding hammer-strokes of the Symphony.

MACKAY had a small pile of newspapers at his side. 'For two years,' he said, 'I have been living with greatness, all unaware of it. Like Philemon and Baucis I have drunk and supped and jested rudely, after my fashion, with divinity in disguise, and now the sporting reporters have flung aside the veil and spoken in the loud and lordly tones of unmistakable revelation. One calls your style tempestuous. Another writes of your "hurricane attack." And the *Edinburgh Evening Mail* says that you smashed through Matheson's weakened defence like a tornado. Stormy Peter! None of them compares you to a cyclone, however, which I think is a pity.'

'A cyclone goes in circles, doesn't it?' suggested Peter.

'I am relatively ignorant of meteorology,' Mackay answered calmly. 'All I am concerned with is your abrupt and inconsiderate manifestation of superiority. Here am I, like Baucis – and I have always thought of Baucis as the Hellenic ancestor of the lady whose photograph advertises an empirical cure for bad legs in the weekly press – like Baucis I have croaked good-morning to you in your dressing-gown, liverish, miscalling the good breakfast before you, and never recognized in your surly reply the god-like note of tempest which must have been there.'

He picked up a newspaper and read the blunt, diminutive type of the sporting page.

'"Flett put Matheson down with a terrific half-arm jolt. Matheson struggled to his feet looking sick, and Flett followed up his initial success like a tiger." Then you change from a tiger into a storm, Peter. "He drove him round the ring with hurricane tactics." The "he" is you and the "him" t'other fellow, I suppose. We need more pronouns. You also have a lightning left and a tearing right hand, and are in conclusion "one of the most promising amateur heavy-weights we have seen for many a long day." But are you one of our most promising anatomists and physiologists? In forty-eight hours – or forty-seven and a half hours, to be exact, – we shall be sitting in that confounded examination hall again. Does that shake your complacent attitude?'

'Not very much,' said Peter. 'I've done a lot of work in the last month and I feel pretty safe. We're both going to get through this time, I think.'

Mackay looked at him questioningly.

'If I don't get through now I never shall,' Peter continued. 'I thought that things were hopeless a couple of months ago, but those ideas have gone. I feel confident. My luck's changed, I think. Anyway, winter's past, or nearly past. March is a good month, don't you think?'

'It came in as a lamb and it's still lamb-like.' Mackay thought for a minute and went on: 'I feel pretty confident myself. I think we ought to celebrate our emancipation, or our prospective emancipation. I want to go over to Belgium for a week or two to see Ghent and Bruges – not battlefields – and then have a look at windmills and tulips and so on in Holland. Will you come, if we both get through?'

'Yes, I'd like to. What about passports? I haven't been out of the country since the War.'

'We'll go and get our photographs taken now. Cook's will do the rest.'

On successive days they sat the examinations in Anatomy and Physiology. With a feeling of immense relief Peter scored double lines under the last question, handed the book to an attendant, and walked out into the windy quadrangle. The granite walls were white and sparkling in clear sunshine, and woolly clouds like round-bellied coracles swam down the wide blue river of the sky. Immaculate white pinnacles – granite mysteriously carved to a semblance of airy grace – soared upwards till their slender girth dwindled and abruptly disappeared. A gull, blowing in from the sea, tried to settle on the tip of one. Its wings flapped for balance and its webby feet slid and scrambled for a hold, but it could find no footing and sailed indifferently away to look for a broader perch.

Mackay came out a few minutes after Peter.

'Thank God that's over,' he said. 'Come and have some beer and we'll talk about Belgium.'

Both of them felt that they had written satisfactory papers and they waited with only a minor impatience for the oral examination that would follow in a few days. The weather was fine, with bright blustery mornings and calmer afternoons. The confidence which had inspired Peter for the last month seemed justified. He snuffed the March winds and rejoiced in a great sense of freedom. He and the earth had come out of winter durance and were glad.

Lists of names for oral examinations were posted. Mackay was somewhere in the middle. Peter had to wait another day – he mildly damned the order – as his name was in the last batch of all.

Idly he awaited the last phase, the ten or fifteen minutes during which the examiners would patiently and pessimistically question his knowledge, like a dentist thrusting his probe into the interstices of a doubtful tooth, seeking the rotten parts, reassuringly tapping the sound. Nothing happened to disturb him. Mackay came out happy after a brief interview, convinced that he had persuaded the examiners his knowledge equalled theirs.

'They're both in a blissful good humour,' he told Peter, 'and we parted like brothers – happy to have met and not

sorry to go. Banish care, cast out fear. Luck's with us this
time.'

On the following morning Peter went into town, bought
tobacco, and decided to go to the beach and walk northwards
for a few miles along the sands. Lunch at half-past one.
Time for a pipe or two and an hour's reflexion; or a nap; say
reflective napping. And then the oral examination at half-
past three.

He came out of the tobacconist's and stood for a moment
on the pavement looking up and down.

A small dusty car passed on the other side of the street.
The driver looked curiously familiar. She turned her head,
glanced at him, and threw out her right hand either in greet-
ing or as a signal that she was going to turn. Peter felt his
heart pounding in sudden excitement and a pulse throbbed
in his neck. The dusty car wheeled dangerously through the
traffic and halted abruptly beside him. A girl in a little close-
fitting hat and a brown leather coat slid along the seat and
held out both her hands to him.

'Peter!' she said. 'I just saw you out of the corner of my eye.
A second earlier and I should have missed you!'

'Pat. . . . Where have you come from? I thought you
were in India.'

'We sailed early because Margaret's graduating now, and
mother wanted to see her. We got home a week ago. I
thought you might have seen Meg and heard.'

'I haven't met her for weeks; not since before Christmas, I
think. But where have you come from now?'

'York. Mother's there, with my uncle – oh, I can't be
bothered explaining. Mother wouldn't come by road, so I
did it alone. It's been perfect. I left Edinburgh this morning
just after sunrise and I've had a glorious run. And now meeting you. Isn't it fun?'

Patricia, coming like this out of nowhere, on a blue March morning; out of the skies in a dusty car with a suitcase strapped on behind. Pat, laughing, her eyes excited and her lips parted in laughter. Little brown tangles of hair pushing their way into the sun out of her close-fitting hat. Pat, driving like unexpected April into windy March.

'Well, don't stare at me like that,' she laughed. 'Can't you say you're glad to see me?'

'Of course I'm glad.'

She had changed a little, subtly, but perceptibly. The soft remnant of childishness had gone.

'Come and talk somewhere,' said Peter. 'There's a hundred things I want to hear from you.'

'I ought to go and look for Meg. But perhaps she's out. I didn't tell her when I was coming.'

'Put your car in a garage.'

'No. Get in and we'll go out somewhere and have lunch.'

Peter hesitated. 'I must be back at half-past three,' he said.

'I'll bring you back at any old time you like. Where shall we go?'

For another moment Peter doubted, and then got in beside her.

'We can't go too far,' he said, 'I've an inquisition to face at three-thirty.'

'Poor Peter!' Pat swerved recklessly in front of a tram-car and looked round at him, laughing. 'What sort of an inquisition?' she asked.

Peter explained and she said idly: 'I thought you had finished all that last year.'

They left the streets behind them. There were trees on either hand, their thin black branches dusted with bursting green, and a river ran beside them. Sunlight chequered the

road, here a broad belt untouched by shadow, there a motley
of light and shade that flickered and disappeared under the
wheels. A patch of spiky gorse was just touched with yellow.
Fields rose greenly on their left. . . .

Pat, home from India, radiant and unexpected as an Indian
dawn. Pat, driving on country roads with the wind in her
hair, talking in sudden falls and freshets of Agra and the Red
Sea, tennis and dancing and punkahs and the Taj Mahal,
and turning to laugh at him with open lips and lovely, excited
eyes. Pat, and slim white birches on a dark hill-side. She had
changed; a subtle but discernible change. She was no longer
frightened of youth; she had taken hold of it and made what
was shy and ingenuous a vivid eager thing, conscious of its
beauties and its opportunities. It was as if she had caught
a bird on the wing and said to it: 'Stay with me!' and put it
on her finger to keep till one or the other should grow weary.
A year ago she had been a creature of wilful moods, and now
the moods were her creatures, like slaves and dancing girls
and lithe, smiling acrobats.

'And there are women just like Mrs. What's-her-name in
Kipling,' she said. 'Greedy and hard, or greedy like cats.
All of them greedy in some way. They make love as if they
were playing bridge, counting the tricks and cheating about
honours.'

Her face in profile against a rushing background of trees
and brown hill was like a young moon carved to beauty and
flushed with speed of racing round the earth. A madcap
moon, shining out of season, truanting with earth instead of
the sullen deep sea.

'Stop the car,' said Peter.

Pat drew up by the roadside. 'Why?' she asked.

'For safety,' he answered, and put his arm round her
shoulders.

'Coward!' she mocked. 'Or do you want to kiss me because you can't think of anything to say?'

'That's one of the reasons. My brain's like seaweed thrown up by a storm, and I want action. Action is such a relief from thinking. That's why most men of action are men of action.'

'And because deeds speak louder than words. But they shouldn't in this case. Peter, do you think that people who eat their soup noisily are loud kissers? I always have a suspicion about them.'

'It depends on the passive agent. Bortsch and a negress give one effect, a maiden aunt and Julienne another.'

'How beastly. And what am I in the menu?'

'Oysters, coupe Jacques, asparagus tips, young salmon, vanilla ice done up in rose-leaves, and a new liqueur that no one can find a name for.'

'Are you hungry?'

'Starving.'

A car raced past them in a flurry of dust. It disappeared with a derisive, plebeian hoot, and the dust behind it looked like a fluffy wedge under its back wheels.

Patricia frowned after it. 'Where shall we go?' she said.

'It's ten minutes to twelve,' said Peter. 'I must get back by half-past three.'

They drove on through trees as naked as flag-staffs below but capped with foamy, dancing green, and over a bridge that echoed with the roar of the tumbling, white-and-tawny river. The road wound back, as if blindly, between a wood and a hanging hill and came suddenly to an open valley, a long, oval meadow of ploughland and pasture, walled in by hills and full of the sun. A small inn, whitewashed and unpretentious, stood at the roadside.

'This looks nice,' Patricia said, stopping abruptly.

'Cold mutton and tinned pineapple,' said Peter. 'I'll go and see.'

He returned in a minute or two. 'In half-an-hour they can give us cold mutton and a choice – I underestimated their resources – of tinned pineapple or tinned pears.'

'I love pears. Look out, I'm going to back.'

Later, in the dark, narrow dining-room – a hastily-lit fire smoked badly – she pushed aside her plate and with bare elbows on the coarse white tablecloth said: 'Peter, isn't this fun? I always have fun with you. Why did you never write?'

'I would probably have made a fool of myself. Ink tempts you to. It's more intoxicating than any other liquor. And a letter is so unsatisfactory. It's a thing of a moment and a mood, and the mood in which I write may be utterly foreign to the mood in which you read.'

'But I like fools – happy fools, at any rate. Have you read *Le Jongleur de Notre Dame?* I think we all ought to cut capers, and be glad fools, and laugh and love ourselves and still laugh. Why don't bishops turn somersaults to God instead of looking dignified and browbeating Him?'

'If every Plymouth Brother turned Catherine wheels – '

'And Methodists did the splits – '

'The world would be a better place. Come and shout things at the sun. It's only a quarter-past one.'

Woods filled the lower end of the valley like the stopper in a flask, and through them a shallow stream ran noisily among smooth white boulders. They found a grassy bank, open to the stream, sheltered and warm with sunlight, cut off from the road by trees and a tangle of undergrowth. A wagtail skipped jerkily in front of them, suspicious and daring.

Pat threw herself full-length on the grass, kicking up a slender, tawny-silk leg, cupping her chin on her hands, staring into the running water.

'Peter,' she said over her shoulder, 'I'm going to get married; at least, I think so.'

It might be the noise of the stream, twisting her words, mocking him. . . .

Peter said slowly, 'Get what?'

'Married. M-a-r-r-i-e-d. Go to church and then go to, oh, all sorts of places.'

'But – '

'Lots of people do it. I don't see why I shouldn't.' She still looked into the flowing green water and spoke too loudly, as if to overcome its clamour.

'But Pat, you're – How old are you?'

She turned and sat up, crossing her legs with a rapid, scissor-like movement.

'It's better to get used to it when you're young. Oh, Peter, sit down and don't look like that.'

He sat down, clumsily, and she put a propitiatory hand on his knee.

'Peter, listen to me. I want to get married. And he's a dear. He's as big as you and he laughs like you. It was in the Red Sea, coming home. There was a moon, and we had been dancing, and we laughed at everything, and I was in love with everything.'

Peter sat and said nothing.

'Aren't you going to speak any more?'

'Pat, it's so sudden.'

Patricia giggled. 'That's what I should have said. But I didn't. Peter! Oh, if you're going to sulk I'm going to paddle.'

Swiftly she took off her shoes and pulled down her stockings.

'I'm not sulking. It's got nothing to do with me.'

'If it hasn't got anything to do with you why do you think I told you?'

She swung her legs into the eddying pool that undercut the bank. The green, glass-clear water went over her knees and her feet stood on bright, grey and yellow gravel.

'Ooh! it's cold,' she cried.

What did she mean: 'If it hasn't got anything to do with you why do you think I told you?'

'I'm coming out,' she said. 'It's like a melting ice-berg.'

She sat on the bank again, looking at her toes pink from the icy stream.

Suddenly Peter stooped and kissed her wet white leg a little above the knee. She put her hand on the back of his neck, bent, and kissed his head.

'Peter. I love you. But you're not going to be a likely husband for years and years, are you?'

'No. Oh, damnation, no! Pat, I'm a fool, and not a happy fool this time.'

'Don't be unhappy. You wouldn't love me long.'

'I would. For ever. For ever and a day, if you like. Let me dry your feet.'

'Don't say for ever; it's unlucky. Just say a day. Days are too good to lose in a misty sort of thing like "ever." Oh, you're tickling!'

She jerked her foot away, and Peter laughed with her. To the devil with gloom. She kicked it away, laughed it away. It ran like a shadow from the dancing light of her gaiety.

Her toes were straight and smooth, with little pink nails.

He gripped her foot again and asked: 'What shall I say to them? – "This little pig went to market, this little pig stayed at home?" '

'No. Say "this day, next day, some day, never" . . . and see what they answer.'

The stream chattered and laughed to the solemn smooth

boulders, whose blanched and ponderous gravity seemed moved to a rumble of answering mirth. The wagtail stepped jerkily along the bank, suspicious and inquisitive, and was joined by another wagtail. Together they dipped and lifted their feathery sterns like staccato signs of interrogation.

The sun, portentous, golden and remote, slid with infinite solemnity down the wide blue arch of the sky, and the trees in answer to its westward march threw longer and ever longer shadows. Presently a shadow reached Peter and Patricia where they lay in the shelter of the bushes.

Peter sat up, as if waking in the morning, and looked at his watch. He stared dumbly at its white face, remembering.

'What's the time?' Pat asked him idly.

'A quarter to four.'

'It's getting late, and – Peter! You said you had to be back at half-past three!'

'I know.'

'Does it matter? Oh, it does, doesn't it? Dreadfully.'

'No, I don't mind.'

The winter's work gone to waste again. Success thrown away at the last moment. The pass-lists would be published in an hour's time. The last two or three men would be waiting for their orals now; at this moment, sitting anxiously in an ante-room while one of their number was answering, fending off, or stuttering foolishly at the examiner's questions. It didn't matter. The house of cards had collapsed again, under the weight of a tree-shadow. It had been no stronger than that.

Pat was sitting up, crying. 'It's my fault,' she sobbed.

'There's no fault in it,' he said, and kissed her.

Her arms were round him and he felt her lips warm on his neck.

'I love you,' she whispered, 'and we only have to-day.'

He kissed her again, on eyes and lips, on her soft throat and on the round white shoulder that had slipped like a flower into sight. There was no flower of the March earth so beautiful. She came to him passionately. And in his memory, echoing like a tune lost in the mountains, was a refrain that mocked him and sang; something from the middle of the Beethoven Symphony; something that sang itself into words like: 'Youth is a fool, youth is a fool, youth is a fool, *Youth* is a fool, SWEET – FOOL, Youth is a fool. . . .'

He heard it again, that and other wandering phrases, in the hum of the car, the rush of wind, the scattering of gravel under-wheel, as he drove back to Inverdoon. Patricia sat very close, quiet and trying to comfort him. Not that he needed comfort in that hour. He had thrown away the winter for a day and the taste of the day was sweet in his mouth. There would be time enough to balance and bemoan his bargain later on. He held Pat to him, driving with one hand.

'But you've got to pay for what I meant as a gift,' she said.

'When you grudge paying for a thing it's time to die,' he said.

GREEN EARTH

I

'CHRIST!' said a thin, white-coated figure shuffling along the deck. 'Christ, it's cold!'

The islands lay ahead and to one side of them, dead black shapes in the lingering darkness. The sea was sombre and muttering, and the sky was full of whining wind. The steamer nosed its way through the black archipelago that lay so close to the restless, unpredictable sea.

Peter had stepped aside, holding the rail, as the steward staggered past. The crest of a wave leapt up and lightly whipped his face. An Orkney welcome: the stinging slap of a wave and the sight of the black islands, secret to the last darkness of night, low on the waters, cold rock and strong earth between the night and the sea.

He had sent a telegram to Martin saying that he was coming. There was no use staying in Inverdoon. Pat's mother had arrived on the morning after their day together, a charming woman who was not particularly pleased to meet Peter. The mother and her two daughters were, by the momentarily dominant will of the mother, a self-sufficient social unit, a family complete and guarded. He had seen Pat alone for a minute or two, in a hotel sitting-room.

'Are you angry with me?' she asked.

'No. And I never shall be. But I'm going away, almost at once.'

He was standing looking down at her, and she got up to go to him, before her fingers touched him, they heard a step outside and the door opened. He said good-bye and did not see her again.

It had been difficult to face Mackay. Peter had found him waiting in their rooms when he returned.

'Where the hell have you been?' he demanded. 'What in God's name have you been doing? I thought you had been killed, run over, drowned, heaven knows what. I went to the police, to the hospital, to every pub in the bloody town to look for you or your corpse. Where have you been?'

'Oh, I don't know. Everywhere. Nowhere. It doesn't matter.'

'It doesn't matter! But damn it, you've thrown away – '

'I know. Don't rub it in, Evan old man. There's no need for you to be upset. It's my funeral and I'm not wearing black. Not yet, at any rate.'

'But what have you been doing?'

'I can't tell you. Ask me again in ten years and perhaps I'll explain, but I can't now. I don't know that I can explain everything to myself yet. . . . Have you passed?'

'Yes.'

'Good man. I'm glad.'

'And our holiday in Belgium?'

'That's off, I'm afraid. I'm sorry. I'm going to Orkney.'

'But you'll come back?'

'I suppose so.'

He had fled northwards, to the dark islands, like a sick dog to its corner or a child, suddenly lonely at a Christmas party, to the familiar comfort of home. There was Martin to face, Martin to whom he would have to tell some kind of a lie. Or he could say simply that he had failed again.

The islands were closer now, black shapes on either side. A cold white gash of sky, a dismal wedge of light, was sluggishly forcing in its way from the east. Dawn was tardy, still shivering in bed.

Peter's mind fled from the cold and turning inwards held

out vain hands to a picture of a green river-bank in the sun
and Pat lying white and slender, laughing between her kisses
under the whispering screen of the trees. He thought: It's
time to die when you grudge paying for a thing. That's true
enough, and I believed it when I said it. I don't grudge
paying. I think the whole thing was inevitable; but then we
always claim that the past was inevitable. God knows.
Pat. . . . I've had her. She was mine for a day, and a day's
better than misty ever. I thought I should never see her
again. I said last summer that she was summer love, and I
tried to put her out of my mind. But I only buried her;
buried her alive. And she came out of the sepulchre, out of
winter, out of India in the flesh, and gave herself like April
to the earth, knowing that she couldn't be spoiled. April
isn't touched. It comes and goes, and the world gets old, but
April's always the same. . . . Though it's March, of course.
April in March. And last summer it was June. They're
lovely names. She must have lost them in India; they don't
mean anything there. And there was a moon in the Red
Sea. Perhaps it was my moon as much as the other fellow's.
Sown in June, moon-ripened, reaped in March. That's
my calendar and Pat's, and now the year's over. I thought
it had died in bud last summer. But it's over now. I've
picked the flower and that's all my harvest. O God. And
here it's winter still, black and wet and cold. A different
country and a different year, and the Lord knows what's to
come of it all.

The cold crept with a shiver down the upturned collar of
his coat, and he walked about the deck briskly. A naked grey
light was creeping over the sky to show low cliffs and fields,
the straight line of dykes, and little stone houses. Kirkwall,
a cluster of tiny buildings in the shelter of the great Cathedral,
lay before them.

Martin met him. Peter could see her on the quay, stamping her feet to keep warm. The dogs clustered together, a black patch in the lee of a shed.

'Hullo, White-maa!' she said. 'Feeling cold?'

'Not very. How are you? Everybody fit? – dogs and pigs flourishing?'

'Like green bay trees. I'm going to pull down my barns and build greater. Hurry up and let's get home.'

In the car she asked: 'Have you failed again?'

'Yes,' said Peter.

'I thought so, when I got your wire. White-maa, you *are* a damned fool.'

Martin said no more on the matter nor asked another question, and Peter, though he tried for several days to think of an explanation which would to some extent rehabilitate his credit, could think of nothing. The subject died. The Redland people, when he met them, asked no questions either. They knew from Martin that he had failed, somehow or other, and the shy grace and tact of their kind kept their curiosity dumb.

'But you won your fight in Edinburgh?' Martin said. 'Well, if you will fight I prefer you to win.'

They reached Ottergill and Martin told him: 'You've time to shave and get a bath before breakfast. Do you want beer or tea?'

The living-room at Ottergill was warm and cheerful, the glow of a peat-fire at either end heartening the bleak light let in by the tall windows, and the long, loosely-packed bookcase offering its assorted cargo with a genial air of easy, catholic hospitality.

Peter and Martin sat with their feet to the blazing turf and talked of the countryside.

'Are people still excited about the Viking Stone,' Peter

asked, 'or have the elders carved another cross on it and laid the ghost?'

Martin moved uneasily.

'A dreadful thing happened last week,' she said. 'At least it seems dreadful. I don't know. People are frightened.'

She stared into the fire, biting her lip as if unwilling to speak.

'What was it? What happened ?' Peter asked.

'It sounds so utterly ridiculous that I hardly like to tell you. But it's true. Twice last week – on Tuesday morning and on Friday – a lamb, with its throat cut, was found lying in front of the Stone. They were little things and their throats seemed almost to have been torn open, so they say.'

'A dog may have done it.'

Martin shook her head. 'There isn't a dog on the island that would worry lambs. Our sheep-dogs are respectable even though their masters aren't. And why should a dog take its kill to the Viking Stone and leave it there?'

Rain suddenly lashed the windows and the wind rose to a howl, hung on its wild note of meaningless anger, and sank again to dismal moaning. A downward curve of smoke blew out of the fire-place and then the flames roared bravely upwards. Peter felt a tinge of awe, a kind of inward goose-flesh, at the thought of that broken ring of Stone, that ragged temple on the strip of moor between two lochs, ageless and unperturbed in ruin, with a bleeding lamb at the foot of the tallest stone; the stone that had a new scar where the Vikings' Cross had been.

'What do people say about it?' he asked.

'They don't say anything. They're frightened – I know they're frightened – and they keep silent. That's what makes it so horrible. I keep telling myself that it's all unreal and impossible, and the conspiracy of silence is only something to preserve the illusion, to keep it intact by preventing inquiry. And yet it is real – it *is* real. And I don't understand.'

'Who found the lambs? Surely there aren't many people who go to look at the Standing Stones except summer visitors.'

'A stonebreaker working on the road a little farther along. He heard seagulls fighting and screaming over something and went to see what it was. That was on Tuesday morning. He went to Hallbreck – it's the nearest farm – and told Tom Corrigall. Tom said at once: "That's my lamb, then, and here's the yowe it was taken from." They went back together and Andrew Nowland, the stonebreaker, says that Tom "gaed as white as a cloot and the swat stood on his broo' like rain" when he saw the lamb. And then on Friday morning the same thing happened, the noise of the seagulls, Andrew Nowland getting up from his heap of stones. . . . But this time he didn't dare go alone. He ran to Wasbister, so that he wouldn't have to pass the Circle, and got a man from there to come with him. And they found another lamb with its throat torn open in the same way.'

'And where had this one been taken from?'

'A croft not far from Hallbreck.'

Martin threw more peat on the fire and its hot glare was dimmed.

'It's all nonsense, of course,' Peter said. 'Some damned fool having a joke.'

'Country people don't kill lambs for a joke.'

'Then what is it? You don't seriously believe that somebody, or something, is making sacrifices to the powers of darkness, do you?'

'No, no. Again and again, no. And yet, if you had only been here and seen the beginning of it. The queer sultry

weather at Christmas, with a yellow sun in a damp misty
sky; and then the storm, thunder like an earthquake and
flaming lightning; and two days after Norna coming over to
say, with an unsuccessful laugh, that the Viking Stone had
been hit and the Cross burnt off. After that the head-shaking,
the silly stories, the vague idea of something boding, and the
children beginning to be afraid. The winter is still dark here,
White-maa. We haven't got electric light yet.'

There was a sound of scratching at the door. Peter got up
and opened it and the three spaniels raced in, a tumbling,
excited flurry of silky black hair and flapping ears. One
jumped on Peter's chair and the other two threw themselves
on Martin. The interruption was welcome and they said
nothing more about the Standing Stones.

'How are the people at Redland?' said Peter.

'Well enough. Norna is very excited about her journey.
She sails in four or five weeks.'

'Sails? Where is she going?'

'I thought I told you in my last letter. She's going to
Vancouver to visit Uncle James. He invited everybody –
all the Redland people, you remember, and us as well, didn't
he? – and Norna has decided to go. Jean thought of going
too, but she's changed her mind, or had it changed for her.
She's going to get married instead.'

'A sudden decision?'

'The usual thing. But she's chosen wisely and everybody
is quite pleased. It's young Jock Sinclair of Eastabist.'

And Norna was going to Canada. Peter felt unreasoningly
dismayed. Though Jean or any of the rest should marry it
would not sensibly alter the Redland scheme of life, but if
Norna left the pattern would break. To think of Redland
without her was to think of the Willow Pattern dinner-plates
without the figures on the bridge.

Martin went out to see that her pigs were being attended and Peter sat alone considering the fire, the black peats glowing red on the under side, the white flaky ash, the serpent flames. He had scarcely thought of Norna in Inverdoon. When Martin's letters came, when he thought of Orkney, she was there as a necessary part of it, but he had never lifted her out of her own landscape. She was in Orkney, in it and of it, a more vivid feature than her surroundings, but still dependent on them. And now she was going away.

I'm living two lives, Peter thought. I'm like a penny that sits on its head, tails up in Inverdoon, and then I'm tossed over the Firth and come down heads up in Orkney. A week ago it was tails: the fight, examinations, and Pat. To-day there's sheep-stealing and old wives' tales, a wedding, and saying good-bye to Norna. I'm getting a lot of practice in saying good-bye.

He winced, remembering too clearly the river-bank, Pat, the tears caught in her eye-lashes. . . . He stood up and said aloud to the empty room: 'I'll go and help Martin,' as if to shout down the chiding of garrulous memory.

THE kitchen at Redland was as noisy as ever. There was another dog about the place, one of last year's puppies grown up. There were more puppies in a shed. The oldest cat of all, a benign, inscrutable, yellow beast, came in with two new tabby kittens at its tail. Maria herself had had another baby at the New Year. It lay in a battered wooden cradle and cried unnoticed.

'I thought she was past bearing, but God, I was wrong,' said John Sabiston, and his wife laughed delightedly. She clapped her hands on her hips and stood in the middle of the floor laughing with the honestest merriment in the world.

'I gave him a surprise,' she said, and wiped her eyes with the back of her hand, still laughing. Then, as one of the children started the gramophone: 'Dareen on't,' she cried, 'stop that noise when I'm talking!'

A high-pitched screaming whirr came from the cream-separator that Jean was turning in the adjacent milk-house. 'There's something wrong with that separator,' John said. 'It'll burst one of these days.'

Peter talked of this and that, but even a guest was seldom more than one of the chorus at Redland. They had heard of his fight at Edinburgh. A Sunday newspaper that dealt intimately with sport of all kinds had found its way round the parish and the description of Peter's victory had been read and magnified. Maria asked what the fight was about, and Peter found it difficult to answer. A minute later he explained that they fought with padded gloves.

'Oh!' she said, 'just in fun.'

'Man,' said John, 'I mind the time old Tam of Eastabist tell't o' the hammering you gave Peerie John that was herding here. "In he went," said Tam, "peck, peckin' awa' like a

white-maa, and his mou' a' white wi' cruds like a white-maa."
Ay, and Tam's dead this many a day, but you've still got the
by-name, White-maa.'

Norna had met him with a fine carelessness, turning from a
joke she shared with Elsie to greet him with outstretched
hand, still laughing. No memory flushed her face or betrayed
itself in her voice. She was at ease, as if the mere prospect
of her holiday in Canada had given her poise and freedom.

'So you're going to visit Uncle James?' Peter said to her.

'Yes, won't it be fun? See what I've been reading and
gloating over for the last week.' And she showed him
opulent-looking publications of the Canadian Pacific Rail-
way, broad leaves of glowing description, impressive photographs of forest and river, snow-capped mountains, and
prairies that carried miles of wheat on the thick glossy
pages.

Nobody said much about Jean's approaching marriage.
She herself moved about cheerfully, apparently unexcited,
fair-haired and fat, cream and roses in her complexion,
blissfully at ease with life. Elsie had grown much prettier,
with a wicked vixen-look about her, and her blue-black hair
growing to its widow's peak on her white forehead. There
was a boy springing up, fair and square, at sixteen as tall as
his father, with the wrists and shoulders of a young giant.
The youngsters, dark as gipsies or fair as wheat, quarrelled
and played, stole sugar and tormented the dogs under the
table.

Every now and then someone would remember the gramophone and Harry Lauder, *Onward Christian Soldiers*, or the
Macgregors' Gathering would add to the tumult.

In the momentary backwater of quietness Peter said:
'Martin told me about the Viking Stone and the lambs that
were stolen. It's a queer story.'

The silence that had fallen so casually grew heavy and settled. Maria turned as if to say something, thought better of it, and stared at the table. The children sat still and the gramophone, its record finished, scraped idly round without anyone rising to stop it. John Sabiston roused himself and grunted.

'Old wives' talk,' he said, and spat into the fire.

Maria looked up and said shrilly: 'Best[1] forgie us, will none o' you stop that gramophone?'

Three of the children ran together. The enormous green trumpet that projected from it fell with a crash as they collided in their efforts to put the brake on.

'That's not the one Uncle James bought, is it?'

'No, it's the old one,' Norna answered. 'Uncle James's gramophone was too good for Redland and died young.'

Conversation started on a new track and Peter was left with the impression that in talking of the Viking Stone he had lifted a sleeve and shown a sore not meant to be seen. But when he stood up to go home John Sabiston went with him, and half-way to Ottergill broke the silence to say: 'It's an ill business, White-maa.'

Peter had forgotten the topic more than an hour old and thought for a moment that John was referring to his daughter's marriage. He tried to think of something to say.

But John continued: 'Hundreds of years ago – thousands, maybe, for nobody kens their age – those muckle Stones were lying where the ice had left them, ten miles from where they are now. And the folk o' that time – and they were peerie men, they say – hauled them to the loch when it was frozen, and over the loch, and set them up in a ring where you see them still. The Stones are there, but where are the peerie men. Dead, you say. Ay, dead as herring. They were a'

[1] Best] God.

dead before the Viking came, ten hundred years ago. But nobody saw them die just as nobody saw them live. None kens where they came from – maybe they grew here like the heather – and none kens how and why they died.'

He turned suddenly to Peter and asked: 'Why did the Norsemen cut that cross on the Viking Stone?'

'Superstition,' Peter said.

'Ay, superstition.' And John Sabiston looked at the ragged black and white cloak of the sky. 'Weel, I've come far enough,' he said. 'Good-night to you.' And turned homewards.

Peter had left Inverdoon in the mask of a false spring but winter lay darkly on Orkney till the beginning of April. Then blue skies and mild weather came north, and the islands quickened under the daffodil caress of the sun and the fingers of the south wind. Sullen black hills and barren meadows shook themselves, opening their veins to the warmth, preening themselves all day. The earth awoke and found that it was full of a sweet new vigour and hurried to put on its green livery of grass and pied finery of primroses and quaint ragged flowers that grew in ditches and under dykes, on the lip of a burn and the edge of the loch, in grass and heather, hill and field. The black islands flamed with colour, a mad hilarity of green disguised them, and every field was radiantly enamelled with white and pink and yellow flowers.

The peewits came and flung themselves into their wild abandon of courtship. Swooping and swerving, somersaulting in the blue sky, diving headlong to earth, flattening out within an inch of the heather and turning again to mount the quivering air, the peewits danced to their mates. The pattern of their dances was a whirling intersection of feathery arcs and winged circles, a tireless multiplication of intricate designs, an infinite repetition of movement in three dimensions on a medium that took no trace of their drawing. The peewits danced, and their fleeting shadows startled the small blue flowers that thrust astounded heads through the grass.

Everything awoke and began to build and sing. Redshanks whistled at the water's edge and paddled daintily among the little green stones. Ivory-white terns paired and flew together with inimitable grace. Larks climbed their invisible ladders of song and starlings chattered round broken gables and empty houses. Lambs frisked ungainly on their doubtful legs. Mares were heavy with foal. The earth was full of sap and the song of generation rose in a tumult of melody from the exultant procession of spring.

Once again Peter threw overboard useless regret, jettisoned the shabby winter-gear of unease and thwarted hopes, and sailed lightly before the winds of spring. A day at a time was enough when dawn came white and windless in a gossamer veil of mist, and mornings were green and gold, and blue afternoon went laughing to the haphazard carnival of sunset. A day was enough when day got up in opals, and emerald fields vied with the wet sapphire of the sea. A day alone was worth living for, and no life was wasted that knew such days as these.

Mackay wrote from Brussels with unexpected news in his letter. 'The first people I met here,' he said, 'were Joyce MacRae and Mary Innes, also on holiday. I refrained from exhibiting surprise – surprise is so vulgar, especially abroad – and remarked affably: "Dr. Livingstone, I presume?" Why have you never told me how charming Joyce is? Or are you so obtuse that you failed to see it yourself? We are getting very friendly. She listened to me for half-an-hour this morning and only contradicted me twice. I like her more and more. And we all play at tourists with the greatest ease, saying naturally at lunch: "Ugh! What's this?" and giggling lewdly when we look at the acres of Rubens. There's nothing like travel for broadening the mind.'

Peter felt a momentary pang as he read, a rueful twinge of impatience with himself; but they passed. Pat had not written, nor did he write to her. There was nothing to gain by writing.

He walked one morning to the Standing Stones. They looked benign and harmless, like old men in the fields. A couple of black-headed gulls flew lazily about them and on either side a shallow loch lay placidly in the sun. The grey circle had the ancient insignificance of outworn history. It was nothing, a ring of meaningless stones put up by dead children, and the fallen altar half-a-mile away was a toy house, forgotten. The Stone Men stood mildly in a ring, patiently waiting till some day winter should blow them over. Only on one of them was there a mark that did not look like impotent benignity: the discoloured scar on the Viking Stone.

III

THE day of Jean's wedding approached and irrational waves of activity swept over Redland as now one, now another realized that some preparation had to be made. They brewed ale for a start, enough ale to keep sweet and malleable the clay of a hundred guests over a night's dancing. Jean and her man – a good-humoured, good-looking fellow who worked hard and said little – went to Kirkwall to buy her wedding clothes, and within an hour of their return new garments were scattered through Redland as Maria and all her daughters over the age of five paraded in some bit of them before every looking-glass in the house. The hired man coming in from the byre found Elsie in his room, standing on a chair to see how Jean's bridal knickers looked in a square of shaving-mirror; and when he went into the kitchen Maria had just pulled off her blouse and was examining intently a frilly shift of some kind before essaying its entry. The hired man went back to his byre muttering: 'God! there's mair naked women in the hoose than a married man sees in a' his days.'

Alec, the eldest boy, saddled a pony one afternoon and set out like a postman with a sackful of invitations to distribute through the parish. At every house where he left one he was offered a drink, and Alec's head was not as hard as his hands. Peter, walking over the hill, saw a familiar pony grazing where he had no right to graze, and going to investigate found Alec sleeping soundly under a dyke. Peter roused him, but Alec could neither stand nor sit upright, not even on the broad ground.

'Tak' you the letters and let me sleep,' he muttered, and lay down again with a heavy sigh.

Peter took the sack, caught the pony, and rode cheerfully

on his round. His cheer increased the farther he went and by sunset he had asked a dozen guests of his own, honest passers-by who answered a jest with a jest and got an invitation as reward. He rode up narrow hill-paths to lonely cottages and galloped heartily over empty fields. Half-a-dozen envelopes were lost as he wildly jumped a ditch.

'It's time thoo were gettin' merrit theesel', boy,' said an old fat woman to him.

'There's not a girl in the country will have me,' Peter answered.

'I'd walk a mile in my bare feet over broken bottles to see the man who couldna get a wife if he wanted one,' said the fat woman, and they laughed together while her lean, grey husband slowly pulled the cork out of a bottle.

It was dark before Peter got back to Redland. His face was as red as burning peat and the pony was lathered white with foam.

'It's going to be a grand wedding,' he said. 'The whole country's coming to it, men, women and children.'

'But where's Alec?' Maria asked.

Peter looked blankly at her and then roared with laughter. 'I forgot all about him,' he said. 'He's under the dyke between Northbigging and the road.'

'I tell't thee the boy would get fou',' said Maria to her husband.

'It'll teach him to keep sober at the wedding,' John replied, and went to find his son.

Peter sat and told his day's journeying through the parish with enormous gusto, the jokes he had heard, the gossip, the ripe comments on bride and bridegroom. Jean, fat and laughing, listened to everything and laughed more. Norna joined the circle and was merry too. She did not like Jean and had refused to be her bridesmaid, but she felt petty dislikes and resentment melting in the strong solvent of laughter, and gave a cheerful voice to the chorus.

By-and-by she said: 'We ought to taste the ale to see if it's good,' and brought in great blue and white mugs creaming over with the sweet new ale.

A timid knock at the door was heard.

'Wha' can that be?' said Maria. And for a minute no one thought of going to see.

The knock was repeated and Norna, opening the door, found an apologetic, oldish little woman with a big cardboard box.

'It's your dress, Jean,' she called, and the little dressmaker explained diffidently that she had knocked several times – for about five minutes, indeed – before being heard.

'And why did thoo no' walk right in instead o' chap, chappin' at the door?' Maria demanded.

The dressmaker explained that she thought perhaps they had company, and glanced shyly at Peter.

'I'm one of the family,' he said. 'Go and try your dress on, Jean.'

'She can't; it's bad luck,' Norna said. 'I'll go and put it away.'

The dressmaker would not stay, though heartily pressed, but sipped a little ale, admitted it was good, and timidly disappeared.

Elsie, too, slipped quietly away, and no one noticed her absence till she reappeared, giggling, in Jean's wedding-dress.

'Am I no right bonny?' she asked. 'But it's too big for me round the waist.'

Jean leapt up with a cry of anger. A heavy table-spoon half-full of jam – one of the children had been stealing – lay on the dresser and Jean, snatching it, hit Elsie savagely in the face. The jam spattered over her cheeks and a red blob fell on the dress. Elsie, howling with pain and temper, clutched at Jean, but Jean's anger had spent itself in the blow and she caught Elsie's wrists and held her.

Between them they wiped the jam off Elsie's face, quieted her cries, carefully scraped the trickle on the dress – it left a dull pink stain – and pulled off the wedding-gown there and then. Elsie retired glumly, disgusted at the way in which her joke had been received. She was going to be Jean's bridesmaid.

For a week there were cheerful evenings at Redland. People would drop in to see the bride and stay to talk with the family and other neighbours who had dropped in. Only Jock Sinclair, the bridegroom, never came; he worked hard and had to be early to bed. Three days before the marriage it was found that the wedding ale was nearly gone and instantly all other preparations were abandoned to make more. A few gallons were borrowed from Ottergill, and John Sabiston bought bottled beer in case the new ale should not be good.

The smell of brewing still hung over Redland when the wedding guests began to arrive. It was a fine afternoon though all the morning the rain had fallen heavily, and the ways about the farm were deep in mud. The first arrivals found confusion in the house. The ben-room and an adjacent ground-floor bedroom had been cleared for the guests; tables set in them and chairs of all description placed around. But a chest of drawers and a wardrobe or two had been left in their own place, and half-clad members of the family kept darting in, pulling out drawers, fumbling for wanted garments, and talking excitedly over their shoulders to anyone who would listen. The men stood about outside and smoked, while a servant-girl frenziedly finished washing the kitchen floor.

The minister arrived, but there was no one except guests

to welcome him. He talked to Peter and Martin, amiably, now and then looking at his watch. People were coming from all directions, and there was still no sign of John Sabiston and Maria, the bride or bridegroom, except the muffled sound of agitated voices in a room above.

Martin began to look anxious and whispered to Peter: 'I think I ought to go and see if I can help them in any way.'

She found Maria at the top of the stairs with a shirt in her hand, and Norna sitting on the edge of a bed helpless with laughter.

'Jock's lost his shirt,' she said weakly, 'and he's got to wear father's. Oh, Martin, I can't stop laughing. Jean's sulking and Elsie's making fun of Jock through a keyhole, and mother isn't a bit worried.'

Jock Sinclair, being unwilling to show himself in his wedding garments before the ceremony, had taken them to Redland on the previous evening, so that he could dress there. But his clothes had somehow got entangled and muddled with everybody else's clothes in the confusion of shifted furniture and lost wardrobes, and his shirt had disappeared. The only other white shirt in the house was on John Sabiston and John, having no important part in the ceremony, had been compelled to undress, give his shirt to the bridegroom, and put on a flannel one himself.

They were ready at last and everyone walked over to the barn which had been emptied and swept clean for the wedding. Maria was absent-minded, her thoughts doing mental arithmetic among the tea-cups, and the minister spoke twice to her before she realized that he was suggesting as a suitable paraphrase to sing, *O God of Bethel*.

'Dareen on't,' she said wildly, 'I've clean forgot about the Bibles.'

She caught desperately at Norna and whispered loudly:

'For God's sake, lass, go an' see if thoo can a find a Bible or a hymn-book in the hoose, for there's nane o' them will ken it else.'

The groom and his groomsman stood waiting, their red faces perspiring a little over the unaccustomed stiffness of their collars. Jean came in on her father's arm and Elsie stood beside her. A slight pink stain on the bride's dress and a pale bruise under the bridesmaid's left eye were the evidence of a joke that had failed. The congregation waited patiently for their Bibles, the minister coughed and looked at his watch, and Martin, sitting at the piano which had been carried into the barn, played softly as much Sunday music as she could remember.

Norna brought in at length two small Bibles and three hymn-books which were distributed among the front ranks of the multitude, and the service began. Jean, softly veiled in white, had the placid, full-lidded look of a bovine Madonna. This was her hour, and she took it with the serene air of one taking her right and calmly promising fruitfulness. The bridegroom stood straight-backed and square, intent and hot, sweating a little. The minister took the ring and gave it to him. Jean, still ceremoniously gloved, held out her left hand to Elsie, and Elsie tugged in an embarrassed way at the white fingers. The glove was tight and Jean's hand was red and warm. The glove stuck till Elsie put down her bouquet and took both hands to her task. There was a sharp tearing sound, the glove came off, and Jock slowly fitted the ring on Jean's moist finger.

Martin played an energetic impression of the Wedding March as the bridal couple turned to the door, and when they stepped outside a gun was fired, in obedience to old custom Arm-in-arm Jean and her man led the Bride's Walk, a muddy half-a-mile pilgrimage, loud with hearty jests and constant

246

scrambling for a place of honour near the leaders, round a field and back to the house. The Bride's Cog was ready for them when they returned, a wide three-handled wooden bowl out of which rose the heady steam of a mixture of hot ale, whisky, cream, beaten eggs, sugar and spices of different kinds. From lip to lip it passed among the five or six score guests, and then those first in degree were beckoned and led, nudged and whispered, to the tea-tables.

For two hours Maria and her helpers – neighbour-wives of experience in handling tea-pots and crockery – fed the wedding guests. They came in batches and went as they were filled. Hens without number were dismembered, rounds of beef sliced liberally, towering plates of brown bannocks and white bannocks, of oat bread and flour bread, were carried through to the tables. Out of cavernous pots came gigantic plum-puddings that Maria ruthlessly broke into with an iron spoon. Buns and cakes, big brown cakes and little pink and white cakes, and cakes with cherries on them were assembled and set on the unemptying board. Tea flowed in dark gallons, butter vanished in portentous wedges, and the storm of condiments fell unceasingly. Outside whoever tarried or passed was given ale.

Everywhere people talked and laughed in knots and clusters; here they argued of crops and soils, there of a funeral, a scandal, or a brood mare; now one made a joke and now another belched and begged pardon.

'Be God,' said a big cheerful man, speaking of a year-old wedding, 'Geordie was fairly had when he tried to tak' a rise oot o' the minister. "Meenister," he said – they'd been waiting twa-three minutes – "Meenister, thoo're late." "Ay," said the minister, taking just one look at the bride, "Ay, I'm late. Near seven months late, I'm thinking." And Geordie never said another word the hale night.'

Three fiddlers arrived, ate and drank, and went to the barn. The dance began.

Stable-lanterns hung from the rafters and before the fiddlers two smaller lamps burned brightly. Their music was sweet and quick, beating an imperative time, urging the dancers to disciplined agility, lifting their heels and ordering their swift movements. Highland Schottische, Eightsome Reels, a waltz, the Lancers, a polka, Quadrilles; the fiddlers' eyes were impassive and their faces grave, but their wrists jigged with incredible life and their bows flew briskly over the strings like unwearied shuttles in the web of the dance. At regular intervals the players halted, looked about them, and drank solemnly out of the ale-mugs at their side.

The Cog, hot with a new cargo, was handed round. A thirsty soul followed it eagerly as it neared the end. 'Is thee coo still milking, boy?' he said hoarsely to Alec who carried it.

At midnight the tables were loaded again and supper was served. Norna sat next to Peter, Martin was on his other side, Jean and her husband opposite. Suddenly Peter felt Norna's hand on his arm, gripping it convulsively.

'Look !' she said, and pointed to the window.

A face was pressed against the glass; a face with mad, glowering eyes and a snarling mouth. The nose was flattened whitely on the window and a thin, soft-looking beard covered the chin. The room grew still as everyone turned in startled obedience to Norna's finger and saw for a moment the yellowish mask. The mad face vanished and all they looked at was the smooth blackness of the window.

Peter thrust back his chair and sprang to the door. Martin said quickly: 'It was Daft Sammy from Hallbreck.' And everyone with relief flooding redly in their cheeks, smiled foolishly and spoke to neighbours: 'Of course, and who else could it be but Daft Sammy? Goodsakes, who ever saw the like o' that?'

Jean had gone very white and started to sob noisily. She was given whisky and appeared to recover. In a little time Peter came back and said: 'It's Sammy Corrigall from Hall-breck. I found him hiding under the wall and took him into the kitchen. He's perfectly quiet.'

'Come through and talk to him,' Martin said. 'He was probably more frightened than we were.'

'He's been wilder than he used to be, since the storm,' Norna whispered.

Daft Sammy sat in a corner gnawing busily at the drum-stick of a fowl. He was a lumpish fellow, uncouthly made, and the lower part of his face was covered with a fluffy beard. An irregular scar ran down one temple and there was a de-pression in his skull above the left ear. His speech was thick and mumbling, and as he spoke his eyes moved restlessly about the room, sullen, suspicious, or frightened. Norna made him happy with a mug of ale. There was a huge yellow patch on one of his trouser-knees and as he turned to set down his beer they saw a vaster patch on his haunch.

'Poor Sammy,' said Martin as they went back to the barn.

She played a couple of waltzes to give the fiddlers time to sup. They were three brothers. By two o'clock in the morn-ing they were too drunk to stand but they sat and played as deftly as ever, with as swinging a measure and as clear a beat. The barn was full of a misty warmth, the smell of humanity and of corn-sheaves piled in one corner, the odour of home-brewed ale, the tang of clean night-air blowing in through the open door. Two boys, overcome with a little drink and a lot of excitement, slept on the sheaves, deaf to the rhythmic crying of the violins, the ceaseless beating of feet, the shrill

yell of the dancers as they trod nimbly alone in the middle of
an Eightsome Reel.

Warm and a little breathless, Norna turned to Peter, her
eyes laughing, and said: 'You're the best dancer here, White-
maa.'

'I'm the hottest,' he answered. 'Come out and see if there's
a cold wind blowing anywhere. I've danced with everybody
from chits of fourteen to Maggie of Mossetter, who's heavier
than a load of hay.'

They stood at the end of the barn looking over a long downward slope to the grey sea dimly luminous with starlight.
The moon, that had come up like a shaving of lemon-peel,
had disappeared, but the sky was sprinkled with stars and a
belt of clouds like enormous smoky silk bolsters rolled slowly
through indigo deeps.

'I'm in love,' Peter said abruptly. 'With you and all these
people and your mother and the bride and the Bride's
Cog and the fiddlers and the wind; the taste of everything
and the smell of everything. With Orkney. By God,
I am.'

He clipped Norna in his arms and kissed her with a hale,
unspecific enthusiasm.

'With me because I am me, or because I'm part of Orkney?'
Norna asked.

He looked at her. Pale in the starlight under her shining
black hair; her face oval and white as ivory, with dark eyes and
lips that looked dark in the starlight. The noise of the fiddles
came softly to them, the smell of the island in its sleep, the
briny smell of the ebbing tide.

'I don't know,' said Peter. 'Both, I suppose. Because you
are you and because you're Orkney. Because – '

'I'm going away in ten days.'

'As soon as that? Oh, damn it, Norna – '

Norna laughed. 'But you'll have mother, and the bride, and the Bride's Cog, and the fiddlers.'

'You devil. You black and pearly devil.'

'And I'll send you postcards.'

'I've more than half a mind to go with you.'

Norna stopped laughing. 'Oh, do!' she whispered. 'Do come, White-maa. But Martin would never forgive you, or me. Would she?'

'I'm sick of Inverdoon. I don't know what I want to do. I want to stay here, and yet I'm restless. I want to get on a ship and go to – oh, Rio de Janeiro, San Francisco, Yokahama, Dar-es-Salaam, any place that's got a good name.'

'Like Vancouver?'

A clumsy figure, singing low and tunelessly, passed them. It was Daft Sammy.

'Where are you going, Sammy?' Norna asked him.

He peered at them, waved his arm in an uncouth gesture, and said thickly: 'Hame, hame. Gaun hame noo.' And shambled away.

'Vancouver,' said Peter thoughtfully. 'Lumber camps and salmon rivers. I don't know. I never do know. Come and dance again.'

Norna went silently in with him. The barn overflowed with a yellow steam in which the lanterns shone richly. The fiddlers played with unabated vigour the jigging tune of a polka. It was a variation on the ordinary, unimaginative polka, and partners were changed repeatedly in the course of the dance. A man would wink at a girl and if she winked back he left his own partner and danced with her. There were tentative, incompetent winks that got a man nowhere; brazen winks and lewd, unspeakable winks; calmly assured winks and winks that were only a mechanical flicker. An old man with red eyes and a cap pulled to the side of his head danced energetically with a girl of fifteen. His eyes were glassy – he was a little drunk – and the lower lids sagged, showing their bright red inner surfaces. He passed Jean dancing with her husband and winked fantastically. Jean, looking like a blowsy Madonna, fat and fair and laughing, winked back and they jigged away briskly.

'Jean's enjoying herself,' said Peter.

'Why not?' Norna asked, and calmly left him to dance with Jean's husband.

Morning drew coolly near and its whiteness struggled unevenly with the yellow lamplight. The fiddlers, who were dark men, looked bristly and unclean. Girls' faces were patchily flushed and their dresses hung creased and soiled. In odd corners about the farm a few men, beaten by drink, slept heavily. Norna and Jean and Elsie danced to the end. Martin had gone home a little before it.

The guests were summoned to breakfast, and ate heartily in their damp dresses and suits that looked oddly shabby in the morning. Maria was spruce and brisk as ever, laughing clearly, and delighted that her daughter's wedding had gone so well. There was still some ale left, half a bottle of whisky, and an apparently untouched abundance of food.

THE STONE KNIFE

I

PETER was awakened at mid-day by Martin bringing him a cup of tea. He sat up and drank it while Martin stood at the window, her hair blown by the breeze, looking out at the windy blue stretch of the Flow. She made little or no reply to Peter's casual remarks.

'Is anything wrong?' he asked.

She turned and sat down on the side of his bed.

'Another dead lamb was found under the Viking Stone this morning,' she said.

'Another!'

Martin stood up again and walked restlessly to the window.

'There's a madman on the island,' said Peter. The morning wind felt suddenly cold, as if the soft, blue sky had turned into a glazed vault.

'And what has made him mad? Why should he kill lambs? White-maa, I've been here all winter alone, and I'm – I'm beginning to get frightened.'

Peter moved uneasily. 'Nonsense,' he said. 'Come and sit down. Who told you about – '

'Manson, the postman. He heard it from someone on the road; from Nelly Macafie the tinker. She was drunk, so early in the morning, and weeping. Her people had been fighting – her sons, and their wives, and the old man – and her own face was cut and bruised. She was standing in the middle of the road, and Manson got off his bicycle. She screamed to him: "Another lamb, another lamb, an' there'll be mair yet!" Manson was still frightened and I gave him a drink.'

'What had they been fighting about?'

'I don't know. She told Manson that they had got whisky

253

from somewhere, and a terrible fight started. Manson thinks that it was some of them who killed the lamb.'

'But why? The tinkers never do any harm to anyone. They never have done, and they've been here as long as anyone remembers.'

Martin said quietly: 'Longer than that, perhaps. We don't know much about them though we see them often enough. They're secret people.'

'Martin, you're being silly. If you talk like this what can other people be saying, people without a quarter of your sense?'

'They say nothing,' Martin answered. 'I'm all right. I admit that I'm frightened – or nearly frightened. They don't. And God knows what they're thinking.'

'Anyway, this superstitious terror is nonsense. Absolute nonsense.'

'Can you explain why these things have happened?'

'No. Yes. It's a madman's work.'

'What madman? A tinker? And why is he mad?'

'Oh, I don't know. I'm going to dress.'

Peter dressed himself irritably, ate, and went to look at his boat. He had taken it out of winter quarters a few days before, let it soak to swell the seams, and smoothly re-varnished it. The varnish was dry and glossy in the sunlight. There was a fresh, steady breeze.

He busied himself with sails and tackle and in twenty minutes was heading for Stromness, listening to the water chuckling merrily under the lee gun'le, looking at the taut, white sail smoothly rounded by the wind, glancing at the narrow fan-tailed wake.

Peter was unreasonably angry at the recurrence of the lamb-and-Viking Stone mystery. He felt that he ought to solve it and he could not think how to start. No one had ever suggested calling in the police. The two or three constables on the island probably knew as much about the matter as anyone else, but they had done nothing. They would do nothing. Somebody should watch the Standing Stones, night after night, till revelation came, with a glint of moonlight perhaps, or some shadow was seen in the moving cloud-darkness. Peter thought: I ought to watch. Things are getting serious, and no one else will sit all night under the Stones. I ought to do it. But nothing might happen. And it seems damned silly to sit out all night waiting for nothing.

Slowly, like a creeping thing, he admitted the confession that he did not want to sit alone, at night, all night, with that silent circle of Stones, between the two lochs, on the cold black heather, under a sky of black, shifting clouds. There was nothing in the prospect to disturb a rational being; nothing except a little discomfort. But rationalism did not abide with the Standing Stones and had no habitation on a narrow moor at night.

And slowly, like a lifting cloud, the feeling of irritation – the prickle on his conscience – disappeared as Peter watched that taut, white sail and listened to the waves that cheerfully slapped the weather-bow, flinging inwards a spatter of diamond-bright spray. He sailed into Stromness harbour and picked up Billy Scarth's familiar moorings. A small boy rowed him ashore.

Peter walked up the steep hillside to Billy's home. He had not seen Mrs. Scarth since the previous summer.

The old lady was sitting in a high, straw-backed Orkney chair. Her fingers held a letter and she looked unseeingly at the window which framed a shining picture of the Flow and its green islands. Graciousness brought her to life when Peter came into the room. The placid ivory of her features under gleaming silver hair softened as she greeted him. The room was gently warm, as if a fire burned for amenity only, and not to comfort an occupant who felt or feared the cold. Sunlight shone in polished furniture and foreign brass, and there was a green glint of plants.

'Where is Billy?' Peter asked.

'In Glasgow,' Mrs. Scarth replied. 'His ship arrived two days ago.'

'Is he coming here?'

'Only for a few days. He sails again for St. John's in a week or two.' She sighed, almost imperceptibly, and looked unseeingly at the window again. Her fore-finger tapped steadily on the letter she held.

'I didn't know he was in home waters. It's luck, seeing him again so soon.'

'A sailor is at the beck and call of the world. But tell me about yourself and Martin. And Jean's wedding. I wanted to go to it, but I scarcely leave Stromness nowadays. Did she make a pretty bride?'

They talked for an hour or so, and when Peter left he had again that feeling of leaving something remote, something desperately disciplined to quietude; a harbour of tragic peace.

He sailed home in a rising wind.

Billy arrived in Stromness at the end of the week and Peter motored to see him and take him back to Ottergill.

As they drove carefully down the narrow, winding street Billy said: 'There's a familiar figure ahead. Are you going to run him over?'

Peter squeezed the bulb of his horn and the man stepped aside. The street was barely broad enough for the passage of a car, two pavements so close together that the road had been left out. The man stood in a doorway while they passed. It was Isaac Skea.

His face darkened to a scowl as he recognized them, and

he shouted something that was lost in their echoing progress between confining walls.

'How has he been behaving?' Billy asked.

'I've heard nothing about him. He went to Ottergill once, when Martin was out, and once he shouted at her – he seems to be fond of shouting – when she passed him on the road. I haven't seen him till to-day and I don't want to see him again.'

Billy Scarth was as red, as square-faced and square-shouldered as ever; happy to be ashore, his energy salted to last by Western Ocean brine; but there seemed to be an under-tone of grimness in his geniality, and his eyes were brooding even when he laughed.

'Got on well at Inverdoon?' he asked.

'No,' said Peter.

Billy said nothing, but glanced quickly at Peter, whistled a bar or two of *Bonny Dundee*, looked at the road white in front, the ploughed fields on one side, and the hill on the other.

'Are you coming for a voyage with me, then?' he suggested. 'It's nearly your last chance, if the tinker-wife spoke truth last year.'

'Last chance? How?'

'Don't you remember the tinker who told our fortunes? You had death in your hand and I had three more voyages and then nothing.'

Peter laughed. 'I had forgotten. But I can't go with you, Billy. I should like to, but I must carry on at Inverdoon. I had bad luck this time!'

'Well, just as you please. I'm leaving for St. John's, Newfoundland, in a week or so, and there's a berth for you if you want it. There's nothing like the sea for settling your mind and telling you what to do.'

'I know well enough what I ought to do.'

'Books!' Billy grunted scornfully, and leaned forward to light his pipe in the shelter of the windscreen.

They spoke of different things. Martin met them at the gate when they reached Ottergill. Norna was with her.

Their talk, as they sat, reached over sea and across a continent. Norna, on the edge of her journey, was full of an excited impatience. Billy, home from the sea, was warm with the comfort of home, stretched his legs, and looked back contentedly as if from a bridge on the twenty years' Amazon of seafaring that brought him, every minute, memories on its flood.

'We'll go out of the Clyde together perhaps,' he told Norna. 'But we won't see each other after that. You'll leave me behind and I'll still be at sea when you're in the train with prairie all round you. You'll see more than I've ever seen. I only know the fringes of the world. Ports. Nearly every port on earth and nothing of what lies behind them. You're going through a country. I go round them.'

Norna's mind was like a school atlas, open at maps of Canada and the Atlantic. Billy for a moment thought of the world as an unending coast-line, charted for sailors, lighted for sailors, pierced with noisy ports for sailors; but for sailors like a Chinese Wall closing within it a mysterious and delectable land.

Martin heard idly and without discomfort their talk of voyaging. Her farm prospered She had plans to improve it, to breed more and better pigs, to grow more food for them, to sell them more wisely. She had thrust the roots of her being into the soil and daily the roots were spreading and multiplying. As for travel, her mind made secret and lonely excursions enough among books, and journeyed farther than Billy Scarth; to a seaboard Bohemia, Miranda's island, the tempestuous oceans and wide palaces of the Elizabethan stage. She was not unhappy, though she was only a little older than Peter.

But Peter listened moodily. Both Billy and Norna had tempted him, and both temptations he had withstood because of an unwilling, angry determination to continue a study that he hated; because, confusedly, he wanted to please Martin.

Norna's excitement was like a glow within her. Her lips moved deliciously when she spoke. She wore a red dress, soft and wine-coloured. Sometimes when she moved there was a glint of deep, incredible blue in her black hair, and her eyes were gleaming darkness. She was strong and slender, her legs shapely, her arms white and smooth.

No one mentioned the Viking Stone. Billy had heard nothing of all that madness. Norna would as soon have spoken of the indelicacies of her toilet as talked of that. Both Peter and Martin found the topic in their minds and both suppressed it. To speak of it meant laborious discussion of something unpalatable to them both, something that seemed sour and incongruous in the presence of Billy home from sea.

It was late when Peter took Billy back to Stromness, and as he drove home alone the roads were like desert paths, meaningless ways in vacancy, as if the island had been left untenanted. Its people had fled to the refuge of sleep, bolting behind them the gates of consciousness; the island was empty except for the droning car, a rabbit that scuttled blindly in front of it, a peewit that rose with a mournful cry.

Two days later Peter took Martin's car and went again to Stromness. He found Mrs. Scarth alone. Billy had gone out, she did not know where.

It was a flauntingly fine afternoon. Little white clouds tumbled gaily on the sapphire floor of the sky and their shadows ran helter-skelter on earth, breathlessly racing the wind. Peter drove slowly northwards, towards the black cliffs of Marwick that confront the Atlantic like an unhewn corner-stone. One of the dogs had begged to go with him and sat by his side, snuffing the changing air.

The road became a cart-track and the cart-track lost itself in grass. Peter left the car and climbed a steep green slope. The hill seemed to fling itself forward like a wave, a surging green imperious wave; and then it broke abruptly, cut short by the inward-cleaving lofty cliff. Wind battled vainly against this huge rampart and far below waves broke leisurely on half-seen rocks, sliding back in foam like a mermaid's hair. Gulls and shags and puffins made populous every ledge. West and north the sea stretched, green and glimmering into cloud; the Atlantic ditch between the Old World and the New. It was here, under this cliff, that the *Hampshire* sunk; here that Kitchener drowned in a Viking's grave. On the edge of the cliff a stumpy pillar of earth rose irrelevantly, like a grass throne or a stalagmite of turf. It was said that the King came here to see where Kitchener died and sat on this throne for a long time, alone, looking seawards.

Peter lay and stared downwards at the tide creaming so gently over flat rock-shelves. A wave would fall and break apart, and the sloping rock was covered with a slow cascade like mermaid's hair blowing in the wind. Gulls and guillemots stood mutely, wing to wing, on their precipitous ledges, quarrelled briefly, and threw themselves indifferently into the air. The spaniel nestled to Peter's side, timid at the height, puzzled and excited by salt foreign smells that its brain could not translate into a familiar image. The sun came slowly down, growing rounder as it neared the horizon. The light changed and lost its warmth. The noise of the sea became louder.

The spaniel whimpered and Peter, almost hypnotized by the ceaseless rhythm of the waves, got reluctantly to his feet. He walked back to the car, the dog racing ahead.

Something had gone wrong with the engine. It would not start. Peter damned it heartily, sounded the petrol tank, examined plugs and carburettor. He swung the handle till he was tired and no life beat responsive in the engine. The magneto was at fault, and Peter's attitude to a magneto was a generous inclination to leave it to experts. He swore again, roundly at first and then with resignation. There was a farm close-by, and at the moment a man leading his horse to stable.

The man chuckled gravely, found a rope, hitched his horse to the car, and helped push it into a vacant shed.

'You'll be hungry,' he said. 'Come in and have your tea. There's an old hen in the pot, or should be.'

Peter accepted the invitation gratefully but without surprise, and paid for it by telling as far as he could the gossip of his part of the country. It was quite dark when he stood up to go.

'It's a long walk you have,' said the woman of the house.

'Fourteen or fifteen miles,' he answered. 'I'll send someone out for the car to-morrow.'

The man walked with him for half-a-mile or so.

'What road are you taking?' he asked.

'Between the lochs,' Peter answered. 'That's the nearest way.'

The man looked at him in the darkness and said: 'I wouldn't go that road at night, no, not for nothing.'

'Why not?'

'Past the Standing Stanes; through the very shadow o' them?'

'They're only Stones.'

'Maybe. But there's queer things going on at the foot o' them, I'm thinking.'

The man spoke no more till they came to a turn in the road and then said gruffly: 'Weel, good-night to you. You'll send for the car?'

'Yes,' Peter answered. 'Good-night, and many thanks.'

'You're welcome.'

He stood for a moment as Peter walked on and then turned heavily homewards.

There should have been a moon – full or nearly full – but the wind had veered to the south and brought up heavy black clouds. The road was dark and the sky was moving darkness broken by patches of grey. Huddled in night, the countryside had lost its shape. It looked as though tarpaulins, black canvas or blankets of camel-hair, had been thrown over it. Because the road was hard the road retained its individuality, but on either side was amorphous darkness. The spaniel kept close to Peter's heels.

He walked on, thinking not of the Standing Stones – their name and the man's voice as he spoke it had made a momentary prickle like gooseflesh on his mind – but of Norna. This was Tuesday. Norna was leaving on Thursday; Thursday morning, by the mail-boat. Billy would be going to-morrow. The house was emptying. Billy was a bird of passage. You thought of the door banging behind him as soon as you saw him. But Norna was different. She was part of the Orkney pattern, a leaf, a whorl in the design; lines radiated from her,

twisted and curled and cut their proper angles, and returned
to her as if to a key. And when she left the pattern would
break.

The earth was quiet, though a sound of wind echoed restlessly in the sky, and Peter heard with a growing distaste the
reiterated tramp, tramp of his feet on the metalled road. A
sudden twanging of wire startled him. A sheep had run into a
fence. He had walked two or three miles. Another twelve lay
between him and Ottergill.

Four miles an hour. Three hours. One o'clock before I'm
home, he thought. And it looks like rain. It will rain unless
the moon breaks through. I wish my feet wouldn't make so
much noise. Fearfully and wonderfully made. Yes, but
clumsy. Only our minds are agile. I can think to Ottergill
and back while I take one step; but my body stays here. I can
think backwards and forwards, through space and time, but
my body's a grudgingly mobile vegetable. Backwards and
sideways. Arras, the Somme, Sandy Broun's, Pat. . . .

'Quiet, Pickles!'

The spaniel had yelped sharply at another twanging of
wire.

. . . . Why did I say that? It doesn't matter if Pickles
yaps all the way home. Because it's quiet and dark I feel that
we ought to be quiet; and hide ourselves. Why? Nervousness
of some kind. Primitive inhibitions. Fearfully and wonderfully made. Our bodies are safe-deposit vaults, full of secret
things locked up by our hairy ancestors. The immortal
chromosomes. Bits of me lived in the bodies of the Vikings
who stole a ship in Norway and sailed westwards to the
deserted islands they had heard of. The Vikings who were
frightened at the Standing Stones and cut a cross on them.
Odin hadn't a cross. Odin was old. Christ was new and had a
cross that anybody could draw. So Christ was better. I can

think back to Christ, back to Thorfinn Skull-splitter, Eric
Bloody-axe, Torf Einar. Back to the Menin Road and Ypres
and Peronne. To Inverdoon and Pat. Pat and Torf Einar.
They're history and I make them live as I please. I breathe
and they breathe; I stop thinking and they die.

Peter walked uphill at a steady pace; up the darkness and
down darkness on the other side. The sky was changing. The
black cloak was slowly dividing into huge black fragments. A
star or two shone mistily between the masses, and a veiled
suffusion of light showed where the moon was hidden. The
road disclosed itself for a few yards ahead, and on one side a
different kind of darkness, a darkness with grey in it, told
him that he was nearing a loch.

The chorus of a song repeated itself, over and over again,
in his brain. He hummed a dance tune, but it wouldn't fit
itself to walking time. Another fragment, unrecognizable at
first, took its place, repeated, was lost, and came back. He
remembered it then with something like a shock. It was a bit
of the Fifth Symphony, a morsel from the first movement that
stuck undigested in his memory.

He lit a match and looked at his watch. Twenty-five
minutes to twelve. There was greyness on either side now.
The moor was narrowing down for its passage between the
two lochs. The dark mass of the sky had split into round,
black clouds, moving slowly northwards. One of them had a
silver edge. The moon was coming.

Light grew, though the moon itself was still hidden, and as
the silver radiance gathered strength the grey darkness of
the water changed to hard, shining black. The country rose
through its dull tarpaulin, and showed the round outline
of a hill, the straight-edge of road, the margin of the loch.

Peter walked down hill now, and as he came nearer to the
level of the lochs a mound rose in front of him. A mound that

bore dimly visible, towering Stones. The broken circle seemed to gather a menace from the moonlight that showed its ragged structure. The Stones grew insistent, dominant. And as though the moon clarified sounds as well as things seen Peter heard the gentle metallic lapping of water on smooth stones, and a little breeze rustled through the grass.

He felt his heart beating too loudly, and a shiver crept down his back; as if his body were frightened while his mind was still at ease. He laughed at himself, looked at the Stones, and thought with perfect honesty: I'm not afraid; there's nothing to make me afraid. . . . But fear of that kind strikes inward, like cold. . . . My skin's quicker to catch it than my mind, he thought. To keep fear at bay he tried to think of distant things as the Stones came nearer at every pace, clustering round him. He tried to think of stories, funny stories . . . and what he thought of was Thrawn Janet, and Tod Lapraik, the 'muckle fat white hash of a man like creish.'

He was almost beside the Circle. The spaniel had come close to his heels, so close that he kicked it and tripped, and as he recovered from the stumble he realized that unconsciously he had been holding the middle and index fingers of his left hand firmly crossed. Children call it 'crosses on.' He laughed, with a quickening pulse, at the discovery.

And as he laughed the moon came out in a white blaze of silence and a figure showed itself in the centre of the stone circle. For an instant Peter saw it as something monstrous, with legs and a huge mis-shapen head. Then panic took him suddenly, blanching panic, and he leapt to the ditch at the roadside. The dog snuggled, whimpering, to his side.

The contact with earth, cold soil and the wiry roots of heather, sobered him, and the white rush of fear gave way to an excited curiosity. With infinite precaution he wormed out

265

of the ditch and into the flattened dry moat that ran round the circle. The dog, quiet now, kept pace with him. Slowly Peter crawled on into the backward shadow of one of the Stones. Carefully he looked up.

The figure stood in the centre of the Circle, still and horrible. It had two legs, like a man, but its shoulders seemed to support a great curving head, broader than the shoulders and faintly shining in the moonlight. It stooped to the ground, crouching for a minute, and then stood straight again. An ordinary head had replaced the curving monstrosity.

It was a man. He had been carrying a lamb round his neck like a scarf, and now the lamb, unseen, lay on the ground. He stood utterly still. Then his arms were raised and hesitantly, with jerky movements, he began to walk in narrow circles. The circles widened and his movements became freer. His paces quickened into an ungainly run. His arms were flung up and flung apart, and the run became a shambling dance. He tossed his arms, flung back his head, and pranced with ungainly steps on an ever-widening circumference.

The moon shone brightly in a clear gulf between the clouds, and at every circle the dancer came nearer to the wide circle of stones. Peter lay still, not afraid, but cold with horror. He recognized the man, and under his cold hands he felt the cold stalks of heather and the chill soil. The dancer ran widdershins, arms and head flung back, leaping uncouthly, making no noise. As he passed Peter saw the staring patches on his knees and rump. They looked like a necessary part of the ugly pattern he was weaving; and not long ago Peter had laughed at them. For it was Daft Sammy, the farmer of Hallbreck's son, gone mad in earnest now. He came near again, leaping high; his teeth showed whitely in the midst of a dark fluff of beard; and as he passed the spaniel, barking shrilly, charged at him.

Without thinking Peter jumped up and shouted, 'Come here, Pickles!'

Daft Sammy's dance stopped abruptly. He turned and looked for a moment at Peter standing beside a tall Stone, and at the furious little dog in front of him. He held, like a grotesque statue, his last broken movement. Then his arms dropped and a wild cry broke from him, the plangent bellow of a wounded Caliban. With head down he ran desperately out of the Circle, fell in the moat, picked himself up, and galloped down the moonlit road in the direction of Hallbreck.

Slowly Peter walked to the centre of the Circle, where the spaniel was sniffing at a dead lamb. It was still warm and its throat was cut deeply and raggedly. A stone knife lay beside it.

Peter picked up the knife. A flint blade, four or five inches long, had been let into a wooden handle and the haft bound tightly with string. Arrow heads were common enough but Peter had never seen so long and finely shaped a flint as this. Sammy must have found it, cunningly fashioned a haft, and kept secret the knife for some mysterious unknown use. Perhaps he had had it for years, never knowing what to do with it, frightened to show it, keeping it to gloat over in hidden places like a savage curio, till madness became imperative and specific and occasion dictated a proper use for it.

The moon shone blandly on Peter, the slaughtered lamb, and the perplexed spaniel. Round them like brooding giants the tall Stones waited; petrified spectators stilly watching for the circus to start again. They were clear-cut and black in the moonlight. Some of them leaned a little to the side, as if watching the more intently; some leaned forward, pondering. On either side was the tarnished silver of a loch.

Peter felt that they were coming closer to him, that the ring was narrowing, the moonlight growing brighter. And he could not think what to do. What he had seen, he thought, should not be told. It was an evil interlude played to an audience of the night, and its traces should be hidden; the stage properties, the lamb and the knife, must not be left for daylight.

He put the knife in his pocket and felt a coil of string; ten or twelve yards of thick twine. He picked up the lamb. The Stones seemed to fade backwards to their proper places and he walked steadily to the road. A few hundred yards away the lochs ran together under a bridge, and there the water was deep and the bottom dark. Peter found a rough, heavy stone. He tied the lamb's four feet together and lashed them to the stone. Stone and lamb fell with a sombre splash into deep water and disappeared. A few eddies ran out, met the moonlight, glinted in it, and darkened to nothing.

Peter stood watching the black and silver loch. His mind was lighted like it with a lunar patchwork of luminous and inky squares.

This was bright and clear: that although Sammy had been discovered he had not necessarily been cured. His madness might rouse again to the demand for sacrifice. And this was dark: would the discovery of his madness, the description of its manner and the consequent discussion of its matter, do more harm than good? Would the people be more frightened at finding in their midst an idiot priest of evil than they had been at a mystery which they only suspected as evil? A familiar, harmless idiot spilling blood to forgotten gods. There was a horror in the thought that might be ruinously contagious.

Moonlight stippled the black water. Reluctance to tell anyone of what he had seen strengthened in Peter's mind to prohibition. He could not and would not publish that haggard moon-calf's dancing. But something must be done to stop its recurrence and scotch the secret fear that was spreading like a weed in the countryside.

An idea, like a flicker of moonlight, came to him. Superstition had given birth to madness and fear; superstition might kill them. The Vikings' symbol that had quietened the Vikings' fear was easy to draw. He felt the knife in his pocket and turned back to the Stone Circle.

He halted once, hesitatingly, and the spaniel pleaded with him to come home. But he went on again, crossed the moat, and found the Stone that had been struck by lightning. The discoloured scar was half in shadow. Peter took out his flint knife and scraped the moss away on a vertical stripe a foot long and an inch broad. Then he cut a transverse stripe, a quarter-length from the top of his upright. He looked over his shoulder. The other Stones were remote and unsignificant. His cross stood starkly on its grey background.

The moss and the crumbly layer immediately under it were easy to cut, but the body of the stone was hard. The flint was no use for it. But he had a jack-knife with a stout leaf-shaped blade meant for cutting tins or some such purpose. He took off a shoe, held his knife like a chisel, and used the shoe as if it were a hammer. Slowly he scored the upright and the bar more deeply. The cross ate into the pagan stone, slashed diagonally by moonlight.

When it was finished Peter's hands were tired and one of them was bloody. His brain felt numb and he gave no thought to the significance, or insignificance, of what he had done. He walked home in a sort of mindless weariness. It was nearly morning when he reached Ottergill.

A n old-fashioned gig, brown painted, sun-blistered and shabby, was hauled out of a shed and a fat pony harnessed to it. Martin climbed in and drove round to the front of the house.

Peter came out half-dressed, a jersey and a tweed jacket on his arm. He blinked at the shallow brightness of the morning sun. His eyes were heavy with sleep and a minute golden stubble of beard gleamed on his chin.

'You might have brushed your hair,' said Martin, laughing. 'It's like a hayfield in a storm.'

'No time,' he answered. 'You drive and I'll dress.'

The pony was whipped to an uncertain trot while Peter struggled into his jersey and coat. Martin and he had promised to say good-bye to Billy Scarth, and the mail-boat left Scapa Pier at nine o'clock. The fat pony was slow on the road but with Martin's car lifeless and miles away it was their only chance of reaching Scapa in time.

Peter had wakened with difficulty from his two hours sleep. He fought his way out of it as if from a bog that clung to him with cushioned, irresistible fingers, holding him back with its oozy weight and promise of soundless oblivion. A fifteen mile walk in the middle of the night was enough to explain his fatigue to Martin, but sitting astride his physical weariness was mental exhaustion. He had wrestled with a giant wonder and a malignant dwarf of fear, and he had beaten them. In his own way, and perhaps with only moonlight logic, he had floored them both. He was tired and incurious of the final decision.

The vivid water-colour hues of the country in the bright air of morning seemed as intangible as reflexions. Hill, field and sea glittered like images caught by a whimsically facetted crystal. And Martin's voice sounded remote, clear and isolated, detached from reality.

'We're going to be late,' said Martin, and whipped her pony.

The bay stretched in front of them, a blue dent in the green and chocolate land. The mail-boat lay, smoke streaming from her funnel, at the end of a stumpy pier, and the pony, infected with excitement, broke into a gallop. But the gangway fell with a thud as Martin drove half-way up the pier and they had to shout their good-byes over the rapidly widening ditch between ship and shore. Billy Scarth laughed loudly at the ancient gig, the steaming pony, and their appearance of belated hurry.

'Why don't you sell your little farm and see life?' he shouted.

The last expression they could see on his face was mirth, and then the clean lines of laughter faded into a reddish blur in the distance.

'Like a Cheshire bull-dog,' said Martin thoughtfully. 'Well, we shan't see him for another year or so.'

'I suppose not,' Peter said.

'And to-morrow we'll be here again saying good-bye to Norna.'

The mail-boat grew smaller and smaller until it was only a black smudge with a feather of smoke above it.

They drove home more slowly.

'What are you going to do to-day?' Martin asked.

'I said I would take Norna sailing this afternoon – farewell to Orkney; that sort of thing – if the weather was fine.'

Peter felt fully awake and almost alert by the time they reached Ottergill. The picture of Daft Sammy dancing in the Stone Circle was still in his mind. He could not blind it. But it was like a familiar though garish picture on a wall,

271

not like the sight of present horror. He shaved, and swam in the sea though it was too cold for pleasure, and as he dressed again he found a curious sense of comfort in his clothes; the open-collared flannel shirt, flannel trousers, old shoes, the brown, white-patterned Fair Isle jersey, and old tweed jacket. They fitted him by use as much as by intention. They were good friendly clothes to put on top of a clean body, braced and tingling from the cold green bath of the sea.

He pulled open a drawer to look for a handkerchief and saw the stone knife that he had dropped there earlier in the morning. It was a beautiful flint, mottled, polished smooth at the point and quaintly flaked above, shaped for a handle. Sammy had contrived a haft that did not look amiss. It was bound in perfect regularity, like a cricket-bat, with green oiled fishing-line. Peter had a dim memory of giving such a line to Sammy one day when he had met him wandering on the loch-shore. It was probably his own line come back to him.

He had a belt somewhere, a sailor's belt with a leather sheath attached to it. He found it in a box full of oddments – a cap-badge, a clip of German bullets, a grey German cap, a bundle of photographs, a fishing-reel, a pseudo-silver cup and the like. The sheath fitted the stone knife as if made for it, and Peter, with the idle motive that slips a signet-ring onto a bare finger, strapped the belt round his waist. His coat concealed it.

The feeling of sensuous appreciation that he had experienced in dressing exhilarated him at lunch, and he ate with an appetite that took eager new delight in old fare. It seemed as if he had never tasted cold roast beef so succulent, so sound and cleanly satisfying in flavour, or drunk beer so sparkling bright and relishingly bitter. And apple-tart had rarely been as freshly sweet as this, the pastry so crumbling-good and the fruit as crisp and piquant. Biscuits and cheese were crunching pleasure and champing delight.

Martin laughed at him as he praised the redness of the beef and the sunburnt delicacy of the pastry, passed his plate for more, and lauded the savour and smell of good food.

'You're a picture of lean gluttony,' she said.

'It isn't greed, it's zest,' he answered. 'I'm not piggish, I'm – oh, what's the word? *Alacer*, I think.'

'But why to-day? Are you glad that Billy's gone?'

'I'm glad about everything. We can't explain a mood. Can I have some more beer?'

Norna came an hour or two later, and the man who had been sent for Martin's car arrived with her, contemptuous about the trifling disorder he had found in the magneto.

Martin said: 'I think I'll go into Stromness and see Mrs. Scarth. She'll be feeling lonely. When will you be back?'

'Early evening,' said Peter.

There was a light, singing breeze and they sailed carelessly, less heedful of where they went than of the pleasure of going. They spoke little. Norna, on the edge of leaving Orkney, felt her eager anticipation halted by a sudden reluctance to go. Her eyes searched the familiar landscape, looking for new details to cram her memory against the hunger of exile. The steep hills of Hoy that rose with a leap from the sea, the low islands creeping so casually out of the waves, the green wind-tufted transparent water, a house that jumped abruptly to a bare sky-line, a dyke that lay like a ruler between shining fields and dull fields, the nestling brown cluster of Stromness, the white spire of a light-house, the wing-tip silver of a gull; all these she tried to impress on the film of her mind.

'I want to go,' she said, 'but I don't want to leave Orkney.'

'You're greedy.'

'I'm not as greedy as you. What do *you* want?'

'Nothing, for the moment. Yes, I do. I want the moment to stretch into hours and days, and always be such that I shan't want anything else.'

Norna did not reply. For a long time – too long for comfort – the one thing that she had wanted was Peter. She had been silent about him by day and her dreams had been clamorous of him at night. She had guarded her desire in a white castle. Once or twice it had shown itself despairingly at a window; once, she remembered, in this boat. Once she had been rudely called on to surrender and had stood fiercely with a white shoulder to the ivory door. She had wanted him miserably under a front of pride and dumbly behind a mask of talk. And then a score of rebels, like impatience and reaction and scorn and common-sense, had risen to fight desire and had succeeded in forcing it to the dungeons of the white tower. The castle was free but for a far away prisoner and quiet except for the soft occasional jingle of chains. Lately her mind had been busy with holiday thoughts of Canada, and new excitement had comforted what was still showing of the old hunger.

She thought: It isn't Orkney I want to keep, it's White-maa.

'My heavy luggage went two days ago,' she said inconsequently.

'That's good.'

Peter yawned widely and stretched his legs more comfortably. The breeze was so light that he had grown careless. His head nodded.

Norna looked at him and said with a hint of exasperation: 'You're nearly asleep.'

'Am I? I'm sorry.' Peter sat up straighter. 'I had a long walk last night and not much sleep.'

The drowsy iteration of the sea and the gentle breeze were

like a drug, and his earlier exhilaration had changed to a yawning acquiescence in simple being, a lazy contentment with immediate surroundings. But he roused himself, and looking at the sail and the sky said with some concern: 'The wind's falling. Hang it, there's going to be a flat calm in half-an-hour. And it's getting late.'

They were close to Hoy shore, several miles from home. The sea was streaked by glassy patches of calm, like mirror-islands with quietly ruffled streams about them. The calm patches were spreading, and a few minutes after Peter spoke the sail flapped idly once or twice, and then hung in slack folds.

'If you row out a little way we may catch the wind,' Norna suggested.

Peter took the oars and pulled steadily for five minutes.

'It's no use,' he said. 'The tide's turned. It's taking us inshore. Anyway, the wind's gone altogether now.'

The whole expanse of the Flow was a shimmering, un-flawed mirror. Islands seemed to be lifted above it, clear of its glassy surface, and reflexion made hills stand on their heads and gave everything prominent a heels-up fore-shortened water-twin.

'Let's go ashore and wait, then. The wind will rise again. Row in to that burn-mouth.'

Peter pulled the head of the boat round.

'That's Pegal Burn,' he said.

He rowed ashore and together they hauled the light boat almost up to high-water mark on the pebbly beach. Peter opened a locker and pulled out a tin.

'Cake, apples, and chocolate,' he said. 'We'll picnic here.'

He carried the tin and a rug to a sandy hollow under a hanging crest of turf and heather, and recognized the place

as he set them down. It was the nook where Billy Scarth and
Dick Heddle and he had lain the previous summer, waiting
to tramp the burn for trout.

The sun had disappeared behind the hill and the shore lay
in quiet blue shadow. But it was still warm.

Norna sat leaning against the sandy bank and Peter lay
with his head in her lap. His eyes felt heavy again and would
scarcely keep open in the quietness of the evening that seemed
a conspirator with slumber. It was easier to talk – a gentle
word now and then – with his eyes shut. By-and-by he fell
asleep.

Almost imperceptibly the darkness grew. The hill shadows
crept farther out to sea as the invisible sun went down, and
pale greys and umber on the level water changed to purple
and blue. Everywhere colours deepened, slowly and mysteriously, as they were drawn into the monotone of night.
While sunlight still lingered on a high feather of cloud a star
appeared, shyly twinkling. No wind came, and the whisper
of the tide was like a cradle song.

Norna's thoughts were timeless. She felt her lap warm
under Peter's head and softly she thrust her fingers into his
thick fair hair. His face was younger in sleep than she had
seen it for a long time. He looked as he had looked on his
first leave from France, when a new firmness about the jaw
and a clearer outline of cheek and brow were beginning to
dominate the softness of boyhood. His mouth was gentler.
A flood of tenderness took her, and bending her head she
whispered his name, soundlessly, over and over again. She
thought: He's mine now, mine while he's asleep. She yearned
over him with the fierce hard yearning of youth made gentle
by this brief possession of her desire. His shirt was open at
the throat. She slipped her hand inside it, downwards till
she felt the calm, unhurried measure of his heart. Half-

dreaming, she thought of it as his life beating, strong and peaceful, in the cage of her fingers.

Norna sat for a long time like that, heedless of the stars that multiplied and shone brighter, crowding the sky like glittering sight-seers rushing for a vantage point. No noise disturbed her, for the only sounds between earth and sky were the crooning of the nearer tide and a ghostly bass of seas that rumbled on far-away cliffs.

She slid, without noting the doorway between sleep and waking, into a dream in which she and Peter were crossing a turbulent stream by a narrow bridge. The river ran boisterously, leaping and tumbling between round white boulders, and the bridge they were on was only a single tree-trunk poised between bank and bank. They moved slowly, because they were face to face, with their hands on each other's shoulders, and so Peter had to walk backwards. They laughed to each other merrily, with gay eyes and teeth glinting. Suddenly Norna was frightened. There was a noise, like the rattle of stones behind them, as if someone had fallen off the bridge. And she dared not look round. Her fingers, in their dream, tightened convulsively on Peter's shoulder.

Peter wakened. 'What's the matter?' he said.

Her other hand still lay on his bare chest. She pulled it away, confused a little.

'I don't know. I think I was dreaming. Or else I heard something move.'

Peter sat up with a jerk. 'How long have I been sleeping?' he demanded. 'It looks like the middle of the night.'

Norna whispered, 'Hush! Did you hear anything?'

Peter listened for a moment. 'No,' he said. 'I must go and see if the boat's all right.'

He got up and walked noisily down the shingle beach. The moon was rising over a white wall of cloud. The boat

lay fifty or sixty yards away, round a little point. The tide
was just lipping the sternmost inches of her keel. Peter
hauled her up another yard. As he did so he heard Norna's
voice, terrified, crying 'White-maa!'

It rose to a scream that was broken by silence.

Peter ran desperately back to her, his feet slipping clumsily
on the loose pebbles.

The moonlight showed him a man kneeling in front of the
nook where he had left Norna. He heard Peter and tried to
get up, but Norna held him. He shook himself free of her
hold, savagely, and seized a gun that lay on the jutting edge
of the bank.

He turned, with the gun to his shoulder, when Peter was
three yards from him. It was Isaac Skea, his dark face
grinning in the moonlight.

He shouted 'Stop!'

Peter, not pausing, ducked and threw himself at Skea's
legs and Skea fired in the same instant. As he pitched across
Peter's shoulder the second barrel went off. The second shot
banged through the tumultuous echoes of the first, a shatter-
ing explosion that broke into a clamouring host of reverbera-
tions and wakened a hundred wailing sea-birds.

Peter hit his elbow on a stone as he fell and Skea broke
loose from the flying tackle.

They scrambled to their feet and faced each other. Skea,
with his back to the moon, towered darkly, a huge man,
broad as a barn-door. He held the gun in one hand and
fumbled in a pocket for more cartridges.

'You bastard!' he shouted. 'You bastard of hell, I've got
you this time!'

Peter jumped forward and Skea, using the gun like a cut-
lass, swung wildly at him. Peter checked himself, swayed out
of reach, and as the gun swept past he leapt in fiercely like a

darting gull and hit Skea on the face. All his weight was behind his long straight left arm and Skea, taken off his balance,
fell sprawling on the beach.

A weaker man would have been knocked out, but Skea,
almost at once, heaved himself up, cursing and swearing.
Peter flung at him and they rolled together on the shingle,
hitting and wrestling, fighting for a master hold or a decisive
blow. Skea, lying underneath, got his leg up and thrust his
knee shrewdly into Peter's belly. Peter fell back, gasping.

They were on their feet. Skea backed cunningly towards
his gun, where it had fallen against a rock, and Peter, still
breathless, attacked again desperately.

He tried to keep out of Skea's grasp, to hit and evade, for
Skea was clumsy with his fists. But he slipped on a stone and
before he could recover Skea's arms were round him, his
great shoulders pressing down, and his dark face grinning
with rage. They stumbled among the loose stones, a grotesque writhing mass in the moonlight; a focus of black energy
in the milky radiance of the moon.

Norna watched them with an excitement so fierce that it
had lost its terror.

'White-maa, White-maa!' she whispered, her hands
clenched and her eyes gleaming darkly.

The stones grumbled and rattled under their feet. Warily
shifting his balance Peter stiffened his left hip and threw
Skea over it, falling on top of him. Peter felt for his throat,
but heavy muscles and a thick jaw guarded it. Skea's arms
were round him, trying to crush him. He felt Skea's grip
shifting, his hands moving. They were under his coat
fumbling at his belt.

With a sudden terror Peter remembered the stone knife
that he had strapped on that morning. Skea had felt the
sheath and something hard in it. He was trying to get the

knife. He would stab with it, in the soft parts under the ribs, in his back, anywhere he could reach. The thought of the rough flint tearing his flesh was like madness – wounds gaping like the red throat of that lamb – and Peter spoke for the first time, muttering hoarsely, 'Damn you, oh, damn you!'

Skea grunted and snarled, 'I've got you, you bloody swine.'

His left hand was twisted under Peter's belt and the other felt for the knife.

Fiercely Peter clutched with both hands at his shock of thick greasy hair and jerked Skea's head upwards. He banged it down on the stones. The heavy neck muscles resisted, but again and again Peter hammered a flat sunk boulder with Skea's head. He felt the head grow heavy in his hands. Skea's grip had relaxed. He let go the greasy hair and the head fell with a thud.

He stood up, and Skea lay still, broken and sprawling.

Norna came towards them, tremulous. 'White-maa!' she said.

Peter bent down and ripped open Skea's shirt. He felt for his heart, looked at his eyes, lifted an arm, and let it fall heavily.

'I've killed him,' he answered, and laughed.

His chest rose and fell with the tumult of his breathing and sweat gleamed on his face.

Norna, wild-eyed, held out her hands to him.

Peter looked at his own. 'Just a minute,' he said, and went down to the sea. His hands were dirty with the grease of Skea's hair and a little blood streaked them. He washed in the cold salt water, sluicing his face and neck. Then he went back to Norna and took her in his arms and kissed her. His face was still wet and she tasted the salt on his cheeks. The moonlight poured down, making the beach whiter, and the hill-shadows blacker than ebony, and the sea a glittering floor of ebony and silver.

'He might have killed you,' Norna whispered.

'But he didn't!' Peter laughed again. 'By God, he didn't. I felt the heat of that first shot. It scorched my neck. I thought my elbow was broken when we fell the first time. I knocked him down. I thought he would break my back when we wrestled. But he didn't. I beat him at his own game, Norna. By God, I beat him!'

He looked again at the sprawling corpse, the massive limbs gone shapeless and awry, and the dark evil face gaping to death.

'There's your kill for you, Norna,' he said, and touched it with his foot. 'Come, we're going to sea.'

Norna stared at him, wondering.

He walked to the sandy nook where he had slept and picked up the rug and the tin that still held some cake and a couple of apples.

'What are you going to do with – ' Norna looked at the body of Skea.

'Leave it to the gulls. Nobody comes here. Nobody has business at Pegal Burn except poachers, and poaching doesn't start for months yet. And nobody will bother to look for Skea. The gulls will have him all to themselves.'

He threw the rug into the boat and pushed it down to the sea. Norna still lingered, wondering. He picked her up and carried her through the shallow water to the dinghy.

The tide was ebbing and he rowed out easily for a quarter of a mile. There was still no breath of wind, but the tide carried them slowly.

'Tell me what happened when I left you,' Peter said.

'I heard a voice behind me and I tried to get up. But I couldn't, because I was cramped with sitting so long – you

slept a long time, White-maa. And Skea pushed his head over
the little cliff. He must have crawled up behind us. He said –
oh, horrible things. He had been drinking. He stank of
whisky. I couldn't shout to you because I was so frightened,
and I couldn't get up to run away. Then he jumped down
and took hold of me, and I called to you, once. He put his
hand over my mouth. I tried to hold him when I heard you
coming, but he was too strong.'

The boat drifted in a white bath of moonlight. The sail
lay tumbled in the bottom like a crumpled, pearly sheet, full
of soft hollows.

Peter knelt on it and drew Norna down to him.

'You're mine,' he said huskily. 'I want you. I've fought for
you; killed for you. Norna, you're mine.'

Norna put her arms about his neck.

'I said that too,' she whispered. 'When you were sleeping
with your head in my lap I said: "You're mine, White-maa." '

Her eyes were soft pools of gleaming darkness and her hair
was like a raven's wing or lustrous jet. Her lips were dark in
the moonlight, like a red rose at night.

The moon was a perfect sphere, floating in silver majesty
on the deep calm of the sky. Her white radiance filled the
drifting boat, making the crumpled sail like pearly silk, and
losing itself in the ivory pallor of Norna's face. It threw deep
shadows on her neck and showed her bare, lithe arms. It
made her naked breast like alabaster.

They roused themselves to talk.

'White-maa, what are you going to do?'

Peter drew her into his arms again, kissed foolishly the top
of her head, and said solemnly: 'Run away and desert you.'

Her hand slipped round his neck and she looked up at
him.

'Haven't you guessed?' he said. 'I'm going with you to-morrow. Everything's simple and straightforward now. We're not going to say good-bye. I'm not going to wander like a fool and a lost thing any more. We're going together.'

Norna clung to him, crying and laughing.

'Listen,' he said. 'Put this rug round you. That' – he pointed to the shore – 'will be found some day. But I'm not going to wait for it to be found. I'm not a murderer. It was a fight, and he lost. He had a gun and I hadn't. Nor am I going to give myself up and plead Not Guilty. I'm not going to plead anything. I don't like pleading. And I'm not going to be cross-examined as to what I was doing with you on a lonely shore at midnight. That's our business and no one else's.'

'You were only sleeping,' said Norna.

Peter laughed. 'Do you think Uncle James will give me a job in a lumber camp? I've got some money. He can put me in the way of getting experience. Norna, we're going to start all over again. There's nothing like a new thing.'

'And you're coming with me to-morrow?'

'Not to-morrow; this morning. But I can't go with you all the way. I couldn't get a passage in your ship at two days' notice. I must go to Inverdoon to arrange about money and then – '

'You'll sail with Billy Scarth?'

'That's my idea. I can pack in ten minutes. I've got a passport all ready. I meant to go to Belgium last month . . . but I didn't. The passport will do for a longer journey.'

'I wish we were going on the same ship.'

'We'll meet on the other side.'

Passionately she pressed to him, holding him with arms that were as hard and white as ivory and giving back his kisses with lips redder and softer than a rose.

Twin thoughts, like arrows of doubt, struck them.

Peter said: 'Your people, Norna. Won't they be worried by your being out all night like this?'

Norna laughed softly and deliciously. 'We never worry about anything at Redland. They went to bed at their ordinary time. Father said: "Norna's late," and mother replied: "She'll be in some time." I know them.'

Then she said slowly: 'There's Martin.'

And Peter answered as slowly: 'Martin's all gold. She'll ring true, and she won't hurt by this. She may understand.'

The moonlight, dimmer now, shivered under a breath of wind, and little ripples on the water made a tinkling noise on the side of the boat. Peter hauled on a rope and the sail jerked up the mast, filling as it lifted and bellying gently over the side. He made the rope fast, set the jib, went aft, and took the tiller.

Slowly the boat gathered way, the sail leaning out in a gentle curve, and a rippling sing-song of broken water gathering at the bow. The wake stretched broad, white arms behind them. The moon was low, almost touching the hills, and the stars were little and pale.

In the east a great wedge of light drove into the darkness, a wedge of oyster-grey streaked with gleams like mother-of-pearl. The wind came through it and the glimmer of dawn rose over the black rim of the islands.

They were sailing faster now.